Unconscious Impulses

By Kevin L. Bouyer

Chapter 1

Jayden's eyes shot open, startled by the sound disrupting his sleep. He instinctively reached across the bed, expecting to feel Desiree's warm body, but instead, his hands were met with cold, crumpled sheets. He immediately lifted his head off the pillow, surveying the dark room as he squinted to focus his vision. There was just enough moonlight coming in through the blinds for him to make out a few shapes in the bedroom. The dresser, bookcase, and rocking chair came into view, all in their expected places, nothing out of the ordinary. He glanced over to the bathroom door, expecting to see it closed, indicating Desiree might be making a middle-of-the-night visit to empty her bladder. But the door stood open, and the bathroom was pitch-black.

He diverted his attention to the bedroom entrance as the wood flooring creaked, revealing the silhouette of a shape in the doorframe. He rubbed his eyes, trying to remove any possibility that he might be seeing things in his semi-conscious state. However, the shape remained, rocking from side to side as the floor creaked in unison with the back-and-forth rhythm. Common sense told him this was Desiree roaming around the apartment, maybe unable to sleep. But there would be no reason for her to be standing in one spot, aimlessly rocking from side to side. And if this wasn't Desiree, where was she, and who was this stranger by the door?

With his head completely clear and senses heightened, Jayden's adrenaline skyrocketed, thinking about Desiree's daughter, Maya, in the bedroom down the hall. He shuddered at the thought of not knowing whether this person might have threatened or hurt her in any way while he slept.

He pushed up on his elbows, supporting his upper body to get a better look at the unconfirmed shape. This person appeared to be of similar size and shape to Desiree, allowing Jayden's mind to relax somewhat from the stratospheric levels of stress consuming him.

"Desiree? Are you okay?" he asked, hoping his assumption was correct.

Nothing but silence followed.

"Desiree? Do you hear me?"

The figure continued to sway without acknowledging his question.

He rotated his feet off the bed and stood. He kneeled, grabbing a baseball bat from under the bed, while also focusing on his peripheral vision to confirm there were no unexpected movements from this figure. He picked up his phone from the nightstand and activated the flashlight, pointing the beam toward the door. His assumption had been spot-on, as he could clearly see Desiree with her head tilted down.

He placed the bat on the floor and took a few steps in her direction. As he neared, he stretched his arm out, putting his hand close to her face. He waved to try to get her attention. She continued to stand with her eyes open, but did not acknowledge him.

He tapped her on the shoulder. "Desiree? You're starting to freak me out. What's wrong?"

Although she remained quiet, Jayden spotted a slight twitch in her body, as if she'd been hit with a sudden chill. He took a step back with his fight or flight response kicking in, wondering if this zoned-out version of Desiree could be a threat to him.

He aimed his phone toward Desiree's head as the flashlight bounced directly across her face. After a few seconds, she blinked a few times, as if coming out of a trance, and her legs buckled. Instinctively, Jayden lunged to grab her arm to prevent her from crashing to the floor. With his assistance, she landed softly on the wood floor and sat, shaking her head.

She gazed up at him with scrunched eyebrows. "What are you doing out of bed?"

Jayden hesitated before responding, still confused as to what had transpired. "I was trying to help *you* get back *in* bed."

She peered around the room, trying to clear her head. "What happened? Did I pass out?"

"I don't know what happened. I woke up and saw you standing by the door. We need to get you back in bed. Are you able to walk?"

Desiree shrugged.

"Let me help you." Jayden reached under her armpits and gently assisted her back to her feet. He put his left arm around her waist. "Let me know when you're ready to take a step."

She acknowledged with a slight nod, and they took a few steps, nearing the bed.

"Is Maya okay?" she asked.

"I don't know. I'll check on her after we get you back in bed."

A few steps later, they made it to the bed, and Desiree gently lay down, pulling the covers up to her shoulders.

"I'll be back," Jayden said.

He walked out of the bedroom and down the short corridor to Maya's room. As usual, her door was closed and all seemed quiet. He twisted the knob, and the door did not initially open. He let go of the knob and turned again, pushing with more force, which prompted the door to open. He peeked his head inside, struggling to see clearly in the dimly lit room. Maya had never fully overcome her fear of the dark, a lingering effect of the night terrors she'd experienced as a younger child. Although those episodes had become less frequent, she still encountered occasional night terrors, which had led to her reliance on a nightlight.

He stepped closer to her bed. The dull yellow light penetrating the darkness allowed Jayden enough visual confirmation to see Maya comfortably tucked under the covers. She remained on her back and did not react to him in the room. He tiptoed out of her room and closed the door.

He made his way into the bedroom, unsure if Desiree had fallen back to sleep.

"Well … is she okay?" Desiree asked in a whispered tone.

"Yeah, she's fine. Sleeping like a baby." He sat on the edge of the bed. "Just so you know, you scared the shit out of me."

"What do you mean?"

"You were standing by the door and swaying with your head down."

"Really? Sorry I scared you."

"Has this ever happened to you before?"

She didn't immediately answer and stared up at the ceiling before responding, "I remember one other time sleepwalking, but that was years ago."

"So, is that what happened? You were sleepwalking?"

"I … I don't know. I guess so," she said, and then yawned.

Jayden did not respond and stared at her as she eventually closed her eyes. He hesitated to make his way under the covers and attempt to fall back to sleep. For a split-second, he thought about grabbing his pillow and venturing out to the couch in the living room.

He glared at Desiree as her breathing grew louder, realizing she'd fallen back to sleep. He eventually rested his head on the pillow, though he refused to go under the sheets. He grabbed his phone and scrolled through his social media feeds with the intent of staying up longer. He wanted to make sure she didn't get out of bed again and put on an encore sleepwalking performance.

*****

The next morning, Jayden awoke and was immediately hit with a surge of adrenaline after seeing the other side of the bed empty. He promptly rose and scanned the room, relieved to see the bathroom door closed and to hear the sound of running water. He reached for his phone, making note of the time, which read *8:30*. If this were a weekday, he would have been halfway through his commute to work, but Saturday mornings allowed him the opportunity to sleep in.

He rubbed his eyes, still somewhat groggy from the broken sleep caused by Desiree's sleepwalking adventure. This reinforced his opinion that you never truly knew someone until you'd either lived with them or at least spent a few nights together. In the two years he'd been dating Desiree, she'd never mentioned anything about sleepwalking. He was also caught off guard since he'd spent many nights at Desiree's previous apartment, and sleepwalking had never been an issue. She'd also stayed overnight at his condo on a handful of occasions and had slept like a baby.

He understood sleepwalking wasn't a subject that normally came up in conversation, but he would have been less confused as to what had been going on last night. Although even if he'd known this ahead of time, he wasn't sure if it would have eased the creep factor much from what he had experienced.

His thoughts were interrupted by Maya appearing in the hallway. He smiled, amazed she had hit her growth spurt at nearly twelve years old and was almost even with Desiree's five-foot-six height. He nearly laughed at the cotton pink pajamas she wore, now struggling to cover her lanky frame, especially around her ankles, which were completely exposed. She waved from a distance and went straight into the guest bathroom down the hall.

"Good morning," Desiree said.

Jayden shifted his attention to Desiree, leaving the bathroom and coming toward the bed. "Good morning. How are you feeling?" he asked.

She straddled the edge of the bed with a slight grimace on her face. "Outside of still being a little sleepy, I woke up with a stomachache. I think those tacos we had last night didn't agree with me."

Jayden's normal instinct would have been to approach Desiree and comfort her as she dealt with the discomfort; however, after seeing her walking around during the night in a possessed state, he stayed put and continued communicating from a distance. "I'm sorry. You can blame me for suggesting to order from that place."

She let out a long exhale. "Don't blame yourself. It's all part of the process of moving somewhere new and trying to find places to eat." Desiree sighed and shook her head. "I can't believe you found me sleepwalking last night."

"Yeah. That was definitely an interesting experience. I'm thankful you didn't hurt yourself with all of these moving boxes on the floor."

"I was having the craziest dreams, but I don't remember exactly what they were." She balled her right hand into a fist and winced. "Not sure what happened, but my knuckles are red and sore."

"Maybe you hit your hand on the floor when I tried to catch you from falling."

"I'll be okay," she said. "Enough about me. We need to get breakfast going for you and Maya."

"What about you? Do you feel well enough to eat?"

"We'll see. I'll have some toast and hope it doesn't bother my stomach." She looked into the hallway. "Is Maya up?"

"Yeah. She's in the bathroom." Jayden grinned. "And if I were you, I would buy her another set of pajamas. The ones she has on now don't even cover her ankles."

"I swear she's going to need to get a job to start buying her own clothes. Every time I turn around, she's outgrowing something."

"What are you going to do? Can't stop her from growing."

"Speaking of Maya, can you please do me a favor and don't tell her what happened last night?" Desiree asked.

"No problem if that's what you want me to do."

"Thanks. I don't want her to worry about me."

"I'm guessing she's never seen you sleepwalk before?"

"She never mentioned anything to me if she did."

Maya interrupted after exiting the hallway bathroom.

"Good mo—" She stopped in the middle of speaking and stared at the wall outside the bedroom door. "Is there any reason why the wall is dented?"

Desiree walked toward the bedroom entrance with Jayden following behind. Just beyond the doorframe, the wall had a softball-sized indentation with several cracks sprouting outward, away from the center.

"Does anyone remember seeing this here when we moved in?" Desiree asked.

Jayden shook his head. "No. Maybe the movers damaged the walls trying to move in the bedroom furniture?"

Maya studied the indentation closer. "I hope there are no bugs behind the wall trying to get out. I wouldn't want them coming into my room."

Desiree's lips curled, struggling to produce a half-smile. "I'm sure there's nothing behind it." She knocked gently. "Besides, it's not like there's a complete hole for something to crawl through. The wall is only a little smashed in. I'm sure we can call maintenance and have them come repair the wall."

Jayden gently pressed his hand against the wall. "I guess so. But I don't know how quickly they can come out. Especially since it's Saturday."

"Well, if this can't be fixed today, I'm sleeping with a towel pushed against the bottom of my bedroom door tonight," Maya said.

Jayden patted Maya on the shoulder. "Don't worry; there's nothing on the other side of the wall that's going to come out and get you."

Maya cocked her head sideways. "Famous last words. Now I'm going to have nightmares about spiders crawling around on my bed during the night."

"We definitely don't want you to worry about it, so I have an idea," Jayden said. "If this can't be fixed today, I can cover the area with tape before we go to sleep tonight. And if everything goes according to plan, any bugs trying to come through will get stuck on the tape."

"Would that work?" Maya asked.

"In theory … yes," Jayden said.

*****

A short time later, Jayden maneuvered his way around a pile of moving boxes and entered the kitchen, pulling up a chair. "I can't wait to do some unpacking so we can have more room."

"At least the worst part is over. All the boxes are in the apartment. Now the fun begins—trying to sort through them and figure out where to put everything," Desiree said.

Jayden took a swig of orange juice. "Hopefully, it shouldn't be too bad, especially since this apartment is bigger than your last one."

Desiree gazed out the kitchen window, taking in the view of the assortment of city buildings in her field of vision. "I think it's going to take me a while to get used to the city landscape. This is the first time I've lived in an apartment that was ten floors up."

Maya leaned over her bowl of Honey Nut Cheerios to scoop up a spoonful, prompting a few of her mocha brown corkscrew curls to fall in front of her face. She tucked the renegade strands behind her ear to avoid stuffing her mouth with a mix of hair and cereal. "I think it's cool being so high up. I get to look and see what's happening down on the street."

"And why is this so important to you?" Jayden asked.

Maya shrugged. "I like the view."

Jayden folded his arms. "Don't get any bright ideas about water balloons. Your mother told me all about you making water balloons at your last apartment and throwing them off the balcony when you were younger. And you were only two floors up."

"I don't think we need to worry about it. She learned her lesson after splashing our neighbor with one of those balloons. I'll never forget the neighbor banging on our door with some choice words for both me and Maya," Desiree said.

Maya kept her head down, making no attempt to acknowledge what Desiree had said.

"I think Maya has a little PTSD from that moment."

Maya finally provided Desiree eye contact and offered a smirk, but didn't say a word.

Desiree grabbed her coffee mug and winced.

Maya caught a glimpse of Desiree's reaction. "What's the matter, Mom? Is the coffee too hot?"

"Yeah, a little bit."

Maya's eyes followed Desiree's hand as she placed the mug back on the table. She parted her lips as if ready to say something, but remained quiet.

"So, are you ready for your first day of school on Monday?" Jayden asked.

Maya frowned. "Not really. I got used to sleeping in late during the summer, and now I need to get up early again."

"It's not so bad to get your day started early. You get to go to school, exercise those brain cells, and meet new friends. Sounds exciting to me."

Maya frowned. "Not to me."

"I know it's not easy going back to school, but you'll get used to it," Desiree said.

Maya displayed a thumb-down gesture. "Can we change the subject? I want to enjoy my last weekend of freedom."

"At least after you get through your first week of school, you'll have a long weekend to look forward to with Labor Day coming up," Jayden said.

Maya put her fist in the air. "Woo-hoo. Can't wait."

"Sorry to burst your bubble for this weekend, but in case you didn't know, we'll need your help with unpacking, which means you can't sit in your room all day reading your fantasy books," Desiree said.

"I guess I'd rather unpack instead of going to school."

Jayden swallowed his last bit of orange juice and wiped his mouth. "We should probably get started. Especially since I'm only here for the weekend."

"I thought you were planning to stay for at least a few more nights to help unpack?" Desiree asked.

"That was my original plan, but I have an early meeting on Monday, and driving from your apartment adds another half-hour to my commute." Jayden grabbed his plate and stepped away from the table. "It'll be easier for me to go home tomorrow and drive into work from there. Not to mention, I'll be back during the week to continue helping you unpack. These boxes aren't going anywhere."

"We'll join you shortly to help unpack," Desiree said.

*****

Jayden entered the bedroom to start the unpacking process. He figured it would be easy to start with the stack of garment bags holding Desiree's clothes and hang them in the bedroom closet. But, knowing Desiree, he needed to be careful and hang her clothes in the same groups she had packed them, starting with her dressy attire and ending with weekend wear. He unstacked the boxes piled in the corner while focusing on the labels written on each box.

"Bathroom … bedroom … Maya's bedroom … miscellaneous," he whispered.

He grabbed the box labeled, *"Maya's bedroom."* "This is in the wrong place." He walked into Maya's bedroom.

He squatted in the middle of her room and, using a box cutter, slid his fingers along the top to sever the tape. In the process of sliding his finger across, he felt a quick jolt of pain and snatched his hand back. He studied his fingertip and realized he'd suffered a cut after seeing a droplet of blood shimmering on the tip of his index finger.

He entered the bathroom and turned on the faucet to wash the small cut with warm water. Grabbing a sheet of toilet tissue, he put pressure on the cut to prevent it from bleeding any further. Since they were still early on in the unpacking process, he assumed it would be a long shot to find any Band-Aids in the bathroom.

Jayden hadn't been paying attention initially, but the constant pressure on the tip of his finger caused it to fall asleep. He released the grip from his finger and saw that a bloodstain had formed a perfect circle on the tissue surface. He squinted at the minuscule slice on his finger, which had stopped bleeding. He tossed the tissue in the garbage and headed toward the bedroom.

"Any idea where the Band-Aids might be in these stacks of boxes?" he asked Desiree.

"Why? What did you do?"

"Got a paper cut on my finger from opening a box in Maya's room."

Desiree reached into a box, marked with a bathroom label, and searched through the contents before pulling out a box of Band-Aids. "Here you go."

"Thanks," Jayden said as he opened the box, peeled off a wrapper, and applied a Band-Aid to his finger.

He left and entered Maya's bedroom once again, hovering over the box to continue his task of unpacking. He reached into the box, clutching a stuffed teddy bear that had seen better days. One of the beaded eyes was missing, and the brown fur had lost its fluffy texture, becoming matted down. He speculated the bear must have had some type of sentimental value and put it on the floor beside him. Beneath the bear was a wooden box, emitting a strong scent of cedar mixed with a hint of citrus. The box measured roughly a foot long and was relatively flat, standing about four inches in height. At the top, a sliding door fit into grooves running along the sides. With his curiosity in full bloom, he pushed down on the top, attempting to slide the cover along the grooves to open the box and take a peek at the contents, but the top did not budge. He put more force into his attempt as the cover bent, but still did not move.

"Having fun unpacking," Desiree blurted out from behind.

Jayden turned, somewhat startled. He held the box out in front of him. "Interesting-looking box."

Desiree's eyes widened. "Where did you get this from?"

"It was sitting under a teddy bear in the moving box."

She reached out and grabbed it. "I've been looking all over for this keepsake box. I thought I'd lost it."

"Well, someone packed it up. If it wasn't you, then it had to be Maya."

"She knew I was looking for it. She would have told me if she found it." Desiree stepped into the hallway. "Maya, can you come here for a minute?"

Seconds later, Maya appeared at the door.

"How come you never told me you found this keepsake box?"

"I never did find it."

"So how did it get in this moving box?"

"I don't know. I never packed it in there."

"Don't play games with me now, because I know I didn't pack it away."

"I'm not playing, Mom. I would have told you if I found it."

"Maybe you were going so fast trying to get everything ready for the move that you didn't realize you packed it away," Jayden said.

"I guess anything is possible, but I swear this would have stopped me in my tracks if I saw it."

Jayden studied the box. "May I ask what's so intriguing about this keepsake box?"

"It's just some baby stuff I kept of Maya's. I was afraid I'd lost it."

"Do you want me to continue going through her box or leave it for you?"

"If you don't mind, I think I'd better finish unpacking it in case there are any more surprises I need to know about."

Chapter 2

After a couple of hours unpacking, Jayden took a seat on the living room sofa for a quick break while Desiree and Maya remained in the main bedroom, sorting through boxes. He observed the living room, feeling discouraged at the number of untouched boxes remaining, and his mind drifted to how they had arrived at this moment.

He had never liked the idea of Desiree and Maya moving into this apartment in the heart of Uptown Charlotte. Not only was the rent higher, but this was the second time they had moved in the past two years.

He understood there had been a few challenges at the last apartment with a neighbor; however, the living arrangements had checked all the other important boxes, and he felt Desiree should have renewed her lease. In his mind, giving up an affordable and well-maintained apartment to avoid sporadic instances of her next-door neighbor making too much noise didn't make sense. He'd had a few arguments in the past with Desiree, trying to make her understand that no apartment complex is perfect and there would always be something she didn't like. But she continued to play musical apartments until she could find that picture-perfect place with no flaws in her mind.

Desiree's nomadic lifestyle stood in sharp contrast to Jayden's living situation. He'd inherited his father's condo after his passing five years ago. Although it was a compact one-bedroom on the outskirts of Charlotte's city limits, there was no mortgage to be paid, which helped Jayden immensely from a financial standpoint. The tight living space didn't bother him much since he'd been a single man at the time he'd inherited the condo. He imagined he could sell the place if he ever tied the knot again and needed room for a family.

Now that his relationship status had changed as he welcomed Desiree and Maya into his life, he had debated on countless occasions if selling the condo would be the right move. Although they weren't married, he could have offered for Desiree and Maya to live at his place if it was large enough, which would have solved the issue with Desiree moving around from place to place while throwing money out the window on rent. He'd had a few brief discussions with Desiree regarding the idea of selling the condo for a larger place where they all could live, but she had completely shut that down as an option. She didn't want him to start paying on a mortgage for her and Maya's sake. Also, even though she didn't outright say it, Jayden could sense she felt threatened that her independence would be compromised, and she didn't want to be a burden while living under someone else's roof. She was more than content with taking care of Maya on her own and without anyone else's help.

He wiped his mind of any further thoughts and made his way back into the bedroom to check in on Desiree and Maya.

"How are things going in here?" he asked.

"It's going. As you can see, the bedroom is a mess," Desiree said.

Jayden glanced over at Maya, who showed a less-than-enthusiastic look on her face. He smiled. "Do you think this is still better than being at school?"

"The longer it takes for us to unpack, the more I'm thinking I'd rather be at school." She paused, rubbing her chin. "Or maybe I need to wait until after my first day of school ends before I decide what's worse."

"I like the way you think," Jayden said.

He turned his attention to Desiree, kneeling by the rocking chair in the corner.

"You gotta be kidding me," she said.

She scanned the chair, eyeing one of the wooden rockers at the bottom. "I told those movers to be extremely careful with this chair, and they still managed to chip off a piece of the rocker."

Jayden analyzed the damage. "You sure the chip wasn't here before the move?"

"Definitely not. I wipe down the chair almost every weekend and would have noticed this before."

He kneeled on one knee to get a closer look, rubbing the area around the chip. "I'm sure we can sand it down to help smooth it out."

"It wouldn't be necessary if those damn movers had been more careful."

"It's okay, Desiree. Just relax."

"I can't help but be upset. This chair has been in my family for at least two generations, and I promised my mom I would take care of it before she passed."

Jayden remained on one knee and reached over to Desiree, gently rubbing her back. "Maybe we can see about getting a wood repair kit to fill in the chip."

Desiree shook her head in disgust. "I don't even want to think about it now. Let's continue unpacking, and I'll deal with this later."

*****

Later in the afternoon, Jayden folded up a few empty moving boxes and placed them in the corner of the living room. He surveyed the room, feeling like progress had been made since he could see a larger portion of the floor.

Although he grumbled about Desiree moving, he couldn't deny that the apartment had some impressive visual appeal. A sizable glass door led to the balcony off the living room, which offered a great view of the uptown area, especially in the evening with the city lights glowing. The dark walnut hardwood floors complemented Desiree's off-white sectional and her white lacquer TV stand. The artificial palm plant standing tall in the corner of the living room injected a tropical feel to the space. He'd been eager to finish unpacking and clear the remaining boxes from the area to truly understand how much space the apartment offered.

He walked back into the main bedroom to see Desiree and Maya sorting through folded clothes on the bed.

"It's almost five and we haven't heard back from maintenance yet regarding the wall repair," Desiree said.

"I'm not surprised. They probably have limited hours on the weekend, and since this is not an emergency, I don't think anything will happen until Monday."

Maya tapped Jayden on the shoulder. "Do we have any tape?"

"For what?"

"For the dent in the wall. You promised you would tape it up if no one comes to fix it today."

"Oh, I didn't think you were serious, but I can tape it up if you want."

"Yes … please," Maya said.

Desiree reached into a box in the corner and grabbed a roll of masking tape. "Here you go."

Jayden grabbed the tape and stepped into the hallway with Maya trailing close behind. "Do you need to watch me put the tape on the wall?"

"Yes. I want to make sure you're putting enough on."

"I don't think we need any more than a few strips. I don't know of too many bugs that would be strong enough to bust through this tape."

"You never know."

He cut a few strips of tape and placed them across the small indentation. "There you go. Does this work for you?"

"Can you put a few more strips on it?"

Without saying a word, he cut two strips and added them on top of the others. "How about this?"

Maya stayed quiet and gave a thumbs-up.

Jayden carefully pressed the tape to ensure it stayed secured. "We should be good to go. Nothing is going to get through this tape."

Chapter 3

The next morning, Jayden sat on the floor with his legs spread, reaching for his toes as he completed his morning stretching ritual. It approached nine in the morning, and he was surprised to see Desiree still asleep, as she usually woke up early. He figured she needed extra sleep after their busy day of unpacking.

He ended his stretching routine with a few push-ups to get his blood flowing. He'd recently been more conscious about keeping his body in shape ever since he'd noticed an extra layer of fat developing around his midsection. He'd always been somewhere in the middle when it came to his body frame—not too bulky or slim. But now that he had hit the four-decade mark, he could tell any extra calories he consumed didn't burn off as fast as they used to when he was younger.

His slower metabolism wasn't the only thing reminding him he could now be classified as middle-aged. His scalp had begun sprouting gray hairs like an invasive weed, mixing in with a lush green lawn. He tried systematically cutting them out of his hair, but the more he cut, the faster they multiplied. This led to more frequent visits to his barber to keep his hair trimmed low, which helped conceal the invading gray hairs. He had also begun shaving every other day to prevent the gray hairs from showing in his beard.

He put on his robe to warm his body from the chill filling the room. Desiree had turned up the air conditioner to help cool her body down as she slept. Both Jayden and Maya had to make the best of sleeping with the cooler air circulating in the apartment. He shuffled his feet into the slippers on the floor beside the bed and had a bowl of oatmeal in mind to help quiet his growling stomach.

He opened the bedroom door and stepped into the hallway before immediately stopping. His mind struggled to comprehend what he initially saw.

To the left of the indentation, the number one had been drawn, and to the right was the number eight. In the middle, a circle surrounded the tape covering the indentation. He observed the rest of the hallway for any additional markings but found none.

"What the hell is going on?" he whispered.

He swiveled his head toward Maya's room to see the door closed. He marched over, opened the door, and spotted Maya still sleeping in bed. He didn't think she had anything to do with this surprised nighttime graffiti drawing, but he wanted to be sure.

He scanned the room, trying to locate a marker that might have been used to draw on the wall. He struggled to find one in the dimly lit space, with her blinds closed. He neared the nightstand, scanning the area closer. He didn't see any evidence of a marker or anything else that could have been used to draw on the wall, so he slowly backed out of the room before closing the door and eventually arriving on the side of Desiree's bed.

Although Desiree appeared to be sleeping peacefully, he couldn't wait for her to wake up on her own. He nudged her on the shoulder. "Sorry to disturb you, but we need to talk."

Her eyes flickered, followed by a slow shake of her head as she attempted to transport herself back to the world of the living.

"Did I oversleep for work?" she asked, still groggy.

"No, it's Sunday."

"So why are you waking me up now?"

"Hold on." Jayden reached for his phone off the nightstand and made his way into the hallway before snapping a picture. He returned to Desiree and showed her the picture.

"Wh-what am I looking at?"

"What does it look like to you?"

He showed her the picture again, and she squinted to interpret what she was seeing.

"Does that say 108? I don't get it. Why are you showing me these numbers?" She strained to look at the photo again. "Wait—are you saying these numbers were drawn on the hallway wall?"

"Yes."

Desiree propped herself up on her elbows. "Did Maya do this?"

"I checked her room, but she's still asleep. We can ask her about it when she wakes up."

Desiree rose in bed, now completely awake. "Oh, no. We're not going to wait until she wakes up on her own. I'm going to be her alarm clock this morning so she can tell us why she thought drawing on the wall was a good idea."

"Before you go barging into her room, I do have another theory you might not want to hear."

"Okay … let's hear it."

"I'll start by asking you a question. How did you sleep last night?"

Desiree stared at Jayden with narrowed eyes. "Oh, I see where you're going. Well, did you hear me get up during the night?"

"No, but I don't always wake up if you get out of bed. So, it's possible you did, and I didn't know it."

Several wrinkled lines developed on Desiree's forehead. "I'm almost certain I wasn't sleepwalking last night. And even if I did, what sense would it make for me to draw those numbers on the wall?"

"I have no idea."

Desiree folded her arms. "I'm sure what you're saying makes sense based on what happened the other night, but I'm not convinced I did this."

Jayden remained quiet, darting his eyes around the bed.

"What are you looking for?" Desiree asked.

"Nothing."

Desiree viewed along top of the crumpled blanket. She pulled back the blanket and scanned the area on top of the sheets.

"Since you don't want to admit to it, I don't see a marker or anything else I could have used to draw on the wall. Do you?"

Before he could say anything, she put her index finger up and studied her nightstand, making sure it was clear of any markers. She opened her nightstand drawers and pushed aside her undergarments and T-shirts. "Do you want to look for yourself?"

Jayden couldn't help but smirk, seeing how quickly she figured out what he was thinking. "You got me. You proved your point." He sat on the bed. "Look, I'm totally confused about the situation and don't know what to think. I hope you can understand where I'm coming from."

Desiree's face softened. "I do. But it's also confusing for me."

"If I'm being totally honest, I'm still uneasy from seeing you sleepwalk the other night. You seemed to be in this crazy trance and so far away from reality. Also, we never talked about it, but I'm almost certain the dent in the wall was caused by you punching it."

Desiree closed her fingers, analyzing her fist. "I was trying to believe I didn't do it, because it makes absolutely no sense why I would, but I can't think of any other explanation for how the dent got there."

"Do I need to sleep with the bat by my side the next time I stay over?" he asked, attempting to lighten the mood.

"May not be a bad idea." She perched herself on the bed, an arm's length away from Jayden. "I don't want to get too close because I still need to brush my teeth."

Jayden stretched his arm over and rested his hand on top of Desiree's. "Have you ever talked to any medical professionals?"

"About what? Sleepwalking?"

"Yes."

"No, because I only remember one other time when it happened, and that was long ago."

"How long?"

"Could have been ten or fifteen years."

"How did you find out you were sleepwalking then?"

"I woke up in a different room while I was living at my mother's house."

"Do you remember if you caused any damage to the house?"

"I don't think so," Desiree said before abruptly standing.

"I know we got distracted, but let me go brush my teeth, and then we can pay Maya a visit and have a nice chat with our nighttime graffiti artist to find out what the hell she was thinking."

"Might I suggest you relax and not go so hard on her?"

"Well, if we confirmed I wasn't the one who drew on the wall, then it had to be Maya, unless you have a confession to make?"

"No, it wasn't me, but ..."

"But, what? You still don't believe I didn't do it?"

"No, I didn't say that."

"You might not have said it, but I have a funny feeling you're thinking it."

Chapter 4

Desiree exited the bathroom and waved Jayden along to follow. She entered the hallway and stopped to get a closer look at the puzzling numbers on the wall. "I still can't believe she would do something like this."

She continued her march toward Maya's door and opened it. Without any hesitation, she switched on the light and entered the room, approaching Maya's bed as Jayden remained by the door, not wanting to startle Maya by having both of them hanging over her bed.

With Maya totally oblivious to what was about to happen, Desiree grabbed the covers and pulled them completely off her body. Maya immediately jerked awake from the cool air and the bright light beaming down from the ceiling.

She let out a loud moan and blindly reached, attempting to find the blanket to cover her body again. Desiree gripped the blanket so she couldn't pull it back up over her body.

"No more sleeping for you, Picasso. It's time for you to start talking."

Maya grimaced and let out an even louder moan while curling up into the fetal position, attempting to ward off the cold air from hitting her skin.

"And before you ask, this isn't your first day of school."

Maya cleared her throat. "So, why are you waking me up?"

"Maybe you wouldn't be so tired if you weren't up in the middle of the night, drawing on the wall."

"What are you talking about?" Maya asked as she squinted, adjusting her eyes to the bright light.

"Oh, so now you have amnesia and don't remember?"

"But … I wasn't up last night."

Desiree asked Jayden to unlock his phone so she could show Maya the picture.

"Does this look familiar?"

Maya tilted her head toward the phone, attempting to understand what she was seeing on the small screen. "Why are you showing me this?"

Desiree gave the phone back to Jayden and folded her arms. "I think the better question is: why on earth would you draw these numbers on the wall?"

Maya remained silent, rubbing her hands over her arms to generate some heat. Desiree released her grip on the blanket, allowing Maya to pull the covers back over her to warm up.

"I didn't draw on the wall. I didn't get up at all last night."

"It would make no sense for me or Mr. Jayden to do this, and that leaves only one other person in this apartment."

Maya rolled her eyes. "Well, I guess we have another person in our apartment we don't know about."

Desiree gritted her teeth. "Don't get smart with me, young lady. I can tell you right now, this conversation will not end well for you if you keep this up."

"Sorry. I … I'm just tired and confused right now."

Jayden observed in the background, intrigued with how this mother-daughter stand-off would end.

"Apology accepted."

A few seconds of silence followed.

Maya gave Desiree a brief bit of eye contact before putting her head down. "Can I say something?" she asked.

"Go ahead."

"And before I say this, please don't think I'm trying to be smart."

"Okay, go ahead."

"You saw yesterday how scared I was about going near the wall and having bugs come out, right?"

"Yes," Desiree responded.

"So, why would I get up in the middle of the night, in the dark, to touch the wall and draw on it?"

Desiree thought for a second. "You bring up a good point, but there's no other explanation."

Maya remained quiet.

Desiree looked over her shoulder at Jayden by the door before turning back to Maya. "Okay. You bought yourself some time. We'll talk about it later."

Jayden almost wanted to laugh at how quickly Maya had shut down Desiree's attempt to blame her for the drawings on the wall. This solidified his belief that Maya would one day grow up to be a high-profile attorney.

Jayden and Desiree left Maya and returned to the bedroom.

Desiree chuckled. "That's what I get for raising such a smart girl. What she said made complete sense, but I'm not convinced she's telling the truth."

"I honestly don't know what to think. But it doesn't change the fact that the hallway looks a mess, and it's probably a good idea to scrub those numbers off the wall before maintenance gets here to fix it. Definitely not a good look for us if they saw the wall in this state."

"Makes sense to me. I'll grab a sponge and some cleaner," Desiree said.

"I'll take care of scrubbing it off the wall," Jayden said.

*****

Jayden arrived at the damaged wall with a sponge and lemon-scented cleaner. He studied it, trying his best to interpret what the numbers meant. He dabbed the sponge in the cleaner, and then gently scrubbed the wall in a circular motion, focusing on the first number. After a few scrubs, the number one faded until it completely disappeared.

He immediately stopped upon hearing a sound behind him. He rotated his head and spotted Maya peeking out of her bedroom door. She glanced at the wall before setting her sights on Jayden. A sudden rush of sympathy consumed him after thinking about Desiree waking her up and subjecting her to a full-blown interrogation while still half-asleep.

He offered a smile to help ease any concerns she might be thinking. "Are you good?"

Maya continued to stand with her head peeking out of the door. "Yes."

Jayden scrubbed until the numbers completely disappeared. "If it makes you feel any better, I believe you didn't do this."

Her lips pulled up into a slight grin. "Thanks. But if I didn't do it, who did?"

"That's the million-dollar question."

Maya edged her way out farther from the doorframe while making sure to keep one foot in her room. "Is anyone coming today to fix the wall?"

"I don't know if anyone's going to come out on a Sunday if it's not an emergency. It will probably be tomorrow."

"Oh, okay. Are you still planning to leave today and go back home?"

"Yes. But I'll be back in a couple of days after work to help you and your mom continue to unpack and put together your dresser when it's delivered. Sound good to you?"

Maya nodded. "Do you think you can stay over for at least one more night?"

"I'm happy to know you want me to stay longer, but as I said before, it's easier for me to get to work from my house. Besides, you'll be getting up early to get ready for your first day of school and won't even be thinking about me."

Maya frowned. "Can't say I'm looking forward to it."

Jayden reached out for a fist-bump. "You and your mom will be fine while I'm gone."

"Hopefully," Maya said while staring at the floor.

Jayden proceeded with a prolonged stare. "What's that supposed to mean?"

Maya paused before responding. "Nothing. It's nothing. You're right; we'll be okay."

Chapter 5

Jayden approached his 2022 midnight blue Honda Accord and placed his duffel bag in the trunk. It was close to seven in the evening as he set his GPS to make his way back home.

After driving for a few blocks and getting caught at a light, he peered around at the high-rise buildings surrounding him, trying to get used to Desiree and Maya now being a part of this new city life environment.

He heard the brief honk of a horn behind him, not realizing the light had turned green. He pressed the accelerator and continued his journey home. The GPS estimated a drive time of thirty-five minutes, which included a brief period of traffic showing up on the map.

Prior to Desiree moving uptown, he had avoided driving here at all costs to escape any traffic hassles. After growing up in Elizabeth City, North Carolina, he only felt comfortable navigating around small to mid-sized towns, dealing with isolated pockets of traffic. But after inheriting his father's condo and landing his project management job outside of Charlotte, he had to adapt to the hustle and bustle of a larger city, which meant more traffic.

Jayden sometimes contemplated if he'd rather spend an hour in a dentist's chair than in traffic. He truly wasn't sure if he believed it, but it clearly showed how much he despised traffic for him to even consider that a difficult decision.

He merged onto I-485 as the sun descended beyond the horizon. He had successfully warded off the *Sunday Scaries* for most of the day with his mind occupied by the strange events that had occurred over the weekend. He tried his best not to dwell on Desiree's unconscious stroll out of bed in the middle of the night. He'd only read about this condition in medical journals but had never seen anyone sleepwalk until now. Based on witnessing it for the first time and seeing the aftermath of Desiree's violent tendencies while sleepwalking, his concerns were only heightened. And if that wasn't bad enough, the weird drawing of the number combination on the wall, which no one had taken responsibility for, added to the mystery.

Jayden switched to the left lane and accelerated around a truck. He eyed the GPS, which showed twenty minutes until he arrived home. He took a deep breath, attempting to control his anxiety, which threatened to suffocate all his rational thoughts and prompt him to question his relationship with Desiree, due to this one uncomfortable weekend experience. But Jayden knew better than to doubt his relationship at this point, especially after spending the last two years accepting both Desiree and Maya into his life, which, in his mind, qualified as a significant amount of time invested in a relationship.

He blinked in succession, clearing his mind. As much as he didn't want to think about it, he had to begin focusing on the looming workday. With almost four years into his project management career, burnout had become a real threat. He was unsure if it was due to the company he worked for or simply the responsibilities of being a project manager.

He peeked down at his phone in the cup holder after a chime sounded, indicating he'd received a text. While traveling on the highway at a high rate of speed, he lifted his right hand off the steering wheel and grabbed his phone to look at the text. In what seemed like an instant, a blaring horn to his right reverberated in his ear. He quickly realized he'd drifted in front of a box truck. He dropped the phone and snatched the steering wheel to the left, almost losing control of the car. The truck veered onto the shoulder of the road to avoid hitting him before straightening back out into the lane. Jayden put his arm up, acknowledging his mistake, and continued driving with both hands on the steering wheel.

This wasn't the first time he'd been distracted by the urge to look at a text while driving. Desiree had previously warned him about it, but he continued not to listen and rolled the dice when it came to his chances of getting into an accident.

*****

He pulled into his driveway and pressed the automatic garage door opener. He eased the car into the garage, wedging it between the metal shelving on the right and the bike rack positioned on the left. He'd made plenty of promises to clean up the garage to make it easier for him to drive the car in and out, but his laziness got the better of him once the weekends came around. He'd always made it a point to close the garage as soon as he entered to avoid any neighbors from getting a peek inside the overcrowded space.

He carefully opened the door and squeezed his way out of the car. This gave him another reason to stay in shape and avoid gaining weight, which would only complicate his great car escape in the garage. He shuffled toward the back of the car, popped the trunk, and grabbed his bag. He punched in the code to open the door leading into his condo and entered.

He let out a sigh upon realizing he'd forgotten to turn off the kitchen light when he'd left a few days ago. Even though he had the privilege of not paying a mortgage, money was still tight due to his expenses. He wasn't looking forward to his next utility bill.

He dropped his duffel bag and finally read the text that had come across on his phone while driving.

I heard from maintenance. They're planning to come tomorrow morning to fix the wall. Figured I'd let you know. Good night. Love u!

Jayden began typing.

Good to hear. Tell Maya I said good luck on her first day at school tomorrow. Love u 2

He opened a door to the right of the kitchen and entered the laundry room with his duffel bag in tow. He grabbed his toiletry case from the bag and emptied the rest of the clothes into the hamper. He was too tired to worry about separating colored from white clothes and chose to handle this task whenever he had the energy to do laundry.

He exited the laundry room and entered the kitchen. He reached out for a stack of mail on the counter he'd left prior to the weekend and dreaded opening one envelope in particular. The return address indicated it had come from the facility that performed his recent medical testing, which had diagnosed him with a kidney stone. The kidney stone had since passed, and he'd felt much better physically.

Opening any medical bill was an anxiety-inducing experience for him. He suspected this was most likely a hefty bill because he had not yet met his healthcare deductible. He often wondered how many people developed stress-related health issues trying to pay their medical bills until they reached their deductible.

The anxiety he'd experienced dealing with medical bills stemmed from a difficult time in his life seven years ago. He and his ex-wife had been having trouble conceiving a baby. They'd worked with a fertility doctor who had confirmed the source of the problem centered around Jayden. A hormone abnormality had been impacting his ability to conceive a child. He'd tried several medications and hormone treatments, but nothing seemed to help. The doctors had given him a grim prognosis and believed his chances of ever conceiving a baby were less than five percent. This diagnosis had introduced an incredible amount of financial and emotional stress into his marriage, and after only one year, his wife had decided to leave him.

He'd remained single for a while and had been extremely reluctant to enter into another relationship after what had happened. He couldn't help but think that if he'd started another serious relationship, his partner would kick him to the curb the second she found out he was technically infertile. His fear of committing to someone all changed after he'd met Desiree, however. He'd told her he'd been married once, and it had simply ended on bad terms. Yet, he'd always been hit with a serious case of stage fright whenever he thought of telling her about his infertility issues. He had ultimately made the decision to keep it a secret.

He focused back on the medical bill, tore open the envelope, and abruptly stopped. "I'll save this for tomorrow," he whispered.

He dropped the envelope onto the kitchen counter and walked up the stairs, entering his bedroom. Although the condo was considered small from a square foot perspective, plenty of room existed in the bedroom to fit his queen-sized bed, two nightstands, and a sizable dresser.

He fell backward onto the bed and lay there momentarily. After a weekend of sharing a bed with Desiree, he looked forward to having the space to sprawl out and fall asleep. He also tried his best not to feel guilty that he could sleep soundly, without any concerns of Desiree unknowingly rising out of bed with a destination to nowhere.

Chapter 6

Two days later, Jayden fought through traffic and arrived back at Desiree's apartment after work. Although tired from another busy day of project planning, he had promised Desiree he'd come back to help put together the new dresser that had been delivered for Maya and complete the last bit of unpacking.

He entered the lobby and, for an instant, thought about bypassing the elevators and ascending the multiple flights of stairs, up to the tenth floor, to make up for his lack of physical activity during the past two days. After thinking it over, he figured assembling a dresser and squatting to search through moving boxes would provide enough activity for him during the day.

He arrived on the tenth floor, exited the elevator, and then approached the door before knocking.

A familiar voice on the other side asked, "Who is it?"

"Who do you want it to be?" he replied.

The locks shifted in the cylinder before Maya peeked her head out of the partially opened door. She opened it wider and lunged at Jayden with a tight bear hug.

His heart had always felt full whenever she displayed these signs of affection toward him. She was like the daughter he never had.

"Wow. I didn't know I'd be missed that much after only a couple of days."

"It's good to have someone else in the house now. My mom hasn't been in a good mood since yesterday."

"What did you do?"

Maya opened her mouth wide with an exaggerated look of shock. "How come it had to be *my* fault? I didn't do anything to make her mad."

Jayden engaged Maya with a high-five. "I hope you know I'm kidding." He surveyed the living room. "Speaking of your not-so-happy mom, where is she?"

"I think she's in her bedroom."

"So, tell me, how were your first two days of school?"

"Okay, I guess."

Jayden waited, expecting to hear additional details. "And?"

"And what?"

"That's all you can say about it?"

"I don't think you want to hear all the boring details."

"Sure, I do."

"Okay … here it goes. It was good seeing my friends, it was bad seeing my enemies, my teacher was boring, the lunch wasn't great, and they gave me homework on the first day." She stopped as she stroked her chin. "Now that I think about it, I would say my first two days weren't anything to write home about."

Jayden laughed. "What do you know about that saying?"

"My mom says it all the time."

"Well, sorry to hear about your challenging days at school. I'm sure things will get better for you."

Maya pointed to the hallway. "Let me show you something."

She led him into the hallway as the scent of fresh paint filled the air.

Jayden set his eyes on the wall and couldn't tell that it had ever been damaged.

"Somebody came by yesterday to fix it," Maya said.

"Looks good. And I hope it stays that way."

Jayden's vision shifted to a glimmer of silver peeking out from under Maya's shirt. "What's that around your neck?"

Maya reached under her shirt and pulled out a silver necklace with a matching silver heart-shaped pendant hanging at the bottom. "Mom gave it to me yesterday to wear."

"Look at you. Now you're old enough to wear jewelry."

Maya smiled, peeking down at the pendant. "I really like it."

Before Jayden could respond, Desiree entered the hallway, giving him a quick hug and peck on the lips. Maya mimicked putting her finger in her mouth and proceeded with a gagging motion.

"Sorry, Maya, I forgot I can't show any affection to Mr. Jayden while you're around," Desiree said.

"Yeah. I don't need to see that."

Jayden pointed to the wall. "Maya was showing me the great job the maintenance team did to fix the wall."

"It took them a while to get here, but I'm happy with the results," Desiree said.

"Maya was also showing me this nice-looking piece of jewelry you gave her."

Desiree reached for the pendant dangling from Maya's neck and gently stroked it. "It was a gift from my mom. She wanted me to wait until Maya was older before I gave it to her to wear. And now that she's about to be a pre-teen, I figured this would be a good time to give it to her."

"That's a great gift," he said and pointed to Maya. "You need to make sure you take good care of it, especially knowing it was from your grandmother."

"I will," Maya said as she patted the pendant resting on her chest.

Desiree noted the time. "Are you both hungry?"

Maya nodded emphatically.

"I'm actually not hungry now since I had a late lunch at work. It's probably best for me to start putting the dresser together. I don't want to be here too late tonight," Jayden responded.

"Can you do me a favor?" Desiree said to Maya. "We have leftover spaghetti in the refrigerator on the top shelf. Can you take it out and set up the dinner table? I'll be there shortly."

Maya did not initially respond. Her eyes were focused somewhere between Jayden and Desiree, peering down the hall. They both turned to see what had grabbed Maya's attention, but they didn't see anything.

"Earth to Maya," Desiree said.

Maya continued to stand and offered no response.

"Do you hear me, Maya?" Desiree asked, raising her voice.

Maya produced a long blink and said, "Yes. I was waiting to see if you were planning to answer the knock at the door."

Both Jayden and Desiree looked at one another before setting their sights back on Maya.

"What knock?" Desiree asked.

"I guess you both didn't hear it?"

"I guess we didn't. Were you expecting company?" Jayden asked.

"No. I don't know anyone around here yet," Desiree said.

"You both wait here and let me answer it," Jayden said.

He marched down the hallway and into the living room before arriving at the front door. He positioned his right eye up against the peephole but did not see anyone. He shifted his vision down to see if he was missing something, but with the limited field of vision offered by the peephole, he struggled to confirm if somebody was at the door. He twisted the lock, slowly opening the door, looking both left and right to view an empty hallway.

He closed the door and took a few steps away before he heard a door shut in the hallway outside. He squinted through the peephole again and spotted a woman in front of the apartment door across the hall. He pulled his head away from the peephole and made his second attempt to walk away from the front door, and that was when the knock occurred.

Jayden stood frozen, his forehead wrinkled in confusion as he attempted to process this weird sequence of events. He stepped to the door again, looking through the peephole to see a woman with dark hair, pulled into a bun, resting on top of her head. After hearing footsteps behind him, he spotted Desiree and Maya approaching.

"Well, are you going to answer it?" Desiree asked.

He put his index finger up to his lips.

"Who is it?" Desiree whispered.

Jayden shrugged and opened the door. "Hello, how can I help you?"

"So sorry to disturb you, but I'm your neighbor across the hall. My name is Paulette," she said with her hand out.

Jayden reached out to shake her hand. "Nice to meet you. My name's Jayden."

"I saw you all moving in a few days ago, and I wanted to introduce myself, but I can come back later if this is a bad time," she said.

Desiree stepped forward. "No, it's okay. I'm Desiree, and this is my daughter, Maya."

Jayden moved aside to allow Desiree to shake her hand and for Maya to wave in the distance.

"I hope you all like the apartment so far," Paulette said with a glowing smile.

"Yes, we do. And I'll like it even more once we can finish all the unpacking," Desiree said.

"I know how stressful it can be. I moved in here about a year ago, and I'm loving it so far. There's so much to do in the area."

"It seems like it. It may take a bit for me to adjust since this is the first time I'm living in the city," Desiree said.

"Where are you moving from, if you don't mind me asking?"

"We moved from Huntersville, just north of Charlotte."

"Oh, yes, I'm familiar with where that is." Paulette smiled. "Well, welcome to the neighborhood. Let me know, and I'd be happy to recommend some good restaurants and places to shop in the area."

Jayden remained quiet while listening to the discussion, occasionally nodding along.

"I know it's a weeknight, and I don't want to disturb you all anymore. Just wanted to say a quick hello. I'm sure we'll see each other around."

"Absolutely," Jayden said, finally breaking his silence.

He closed the door.

"Are you good?" Desiree asked.

"I'm okay."

"It doesn't seem like it. You're normally the extrovert when it comes to meeting new people, but you were abnormally quiet."

"I'm just tired from work," he said while seeing Maya disappear into the kitchen. "Don't worry about me. Why don't you go in the kitchen with Maya to eat, and I'll get started on building this dresser? Hopefully, it won't take me too long."

Desiree departed, and Jayden made his way back into Maya's bedroom. He stared at the large box leaning against the wall, struggling to focus on the task at hand. His mind was occupied with *The Twilight Zone* moment he had experienced while answering the door. He took out his phone to text Desiree.

Can you please come in the bedroom?

Desiree eventually appeared at Maya's bedroom door. "Were you lying to me when I initially asked if you were okay?"

"I guess so."

She reached out and stroked the right side of his arm. "I knew something was not right with you. What's going on?"

Jayden closed Maya's bedroom door. "Remember when Maya said she heard a knock at the door?"

"Yes."

"Well, when I first went to the door, there was no one there. And it wasn't until after I closed the door and was about to leave that Paulette came to the door and knocked."

"So, what are you trying to say?"

"I'm saying there is no way Maya could have heard the knock before it happened."

"Maybe Paulette had knocked on the door before you got there, left for some reason, and then came back to knock on the door a second time."

Jayden turned his head sideways. "Come on; would it make sense for her to do that?"

"That's the only thing I can think of."

"Sorry, but I'm not buying that explanation."

"What other possibilities are there?"

Jayden was about to speak, but stopped, thinking he'd heard a noise outside the door. He opened the door, confirming Maya was not in the hallway, and continued in a lowered tone. "Whether you believe me or not, I know what I saw and heard."

Desiree sighed. "So, what do you want me to do?"

"I don't know," he said while opening the dresser box. "I know it's been a long day for me, and maybe I'm overreacting. All I can say for now is to keep your eyes and ears open after I leave tonight."

Chapter 7

"I love it," Maya said as she rubbed her hands along the pine-colored, finished wood of her dresser. She produced a wide smile, looking in the vanity mirror attached to the back of the dresser.

Desiree leaned against the doorframe. "Mr. Jayden did a good job putting this together for you. I didn't think he'd be able to finish it before he left tonight."

"It looks good," Maya said.

Desiree pointed to the bed. "I'm sure you could be here all night admiring the dresser, but it's past your bedtime. I don't want to waste time tomorrow morning trying to get you out of bed to get ready for school."

Maya slid her hand along the dresser before sitting on her bed. She tilted her head upward, inhaling deeply. "Smells like wood in my room."

Desiree knocked on the top of the dresser. "That's a good thing because it wasn't cheap, so it needs to be made out of solid wood. If it's as sturdy as it looks, it should last a while."

Desiree observed Maya sitting on the bed with her legs folded under her like a pretzel. She reflected on the incident that had occurred earlier with Paulette's visit. Although she believed what Jayden had told her, she found it hard to accept the sequence of events that had led to his concerns. He admitted to having a long day, which hinted at the possibility that he could have been mistaken about the timing of Paulette knocking on the door. Even if she wanted to bring up the subject to Maya, she had no idea how to begin the discussion.

She turned her attention back to the conversation, launching herself away from her thoughts. "Any idea of what you want to put on top of the dresser?" she asked.

Maya contemplated for a second. "Maybe a few pictures and my piggy bank."

"That's it?"

"Well … not really. It would be great if I could also have a TV to put on the dresser."

"Oh, no. We're not having this discussion again. I don't want you sitting in your bedroom with a TV on all day. There are more productive things you could be doing than being hypnotized by the nonsense they have on TV these days."

Maya's gaze dropped to her hands folded in her lap, and she did not offer an immediate response.

Desiree stood at the side of the bed and crossed her arms. "Is that how you're planning to fall asleep?"

"I guess not," Maya said with a look of concern.

Desiree gently placed her fingers under Maya's chin, tilting her head up for a better visual of her face. "What's wrong?"

Maya flashed an unconvincing smile. "Nothing."

Desiree studied her with probing eyes. "Now you know you can't fool your mother. You might be able to lie through your mouth, but your face will always tell me the truth."

Maya briefly peeked up at Desiree before looking down at her lap. "I think having a TV in my room will help me sleep better."

Desiree sat on the bed next to her. "And how would a TV help you sleep?"

"It would give me some extra light in the room."

Desiree pointed to her nightlight. "Isn't your nightlight good enough?"

"Maybe, but that's not the only thing. If I had the TV on, it would also stop me from hearing the floor creaking at night."

Desiree raised an eyebrow. "What do you mean, floor creaking?"

"Sometimes if I wake up in the middle of the night, I hear the floor creaking."

"When did this last happen?"

"I heard it last night. It sounded like it was coming from the hallway."

"So, what did you do?"

"I tiptoed to my door and locked it and then went back to the bed and put the covers over my head."

"Why didn't you tell me about this earlier?"

"I wasn't sure, but I thought it was maybe another one of my dreams."

Desiree glanced over at the hallway. "If you did hear something, I think I know what it might have been."

"I hope it's not what I think," Maya said, looking toward the hallway.

"If you're thinking it's a ghost or creature roaming around at night, that's not what I was thinking."

"So, what do you think it was?"

"Since this is our first time living in a high-rise apartment, I've been told it's not uncommon to hear creaking noises from the building swaying if it's windy outside."

Maya rubbed her chin. "Okay, sounds reasonable."

Desiree laughed. "You are too grown for your age."

Maya displayed a hint of a grin before her lips leveled off. She looked at Desiree with a straight face. "Can I ask you a question?

"Uh-oh. Here we go again with Maya's famous questions. Go ahead."

"Do you believe I didn't draw on the wall?"

"If I'm being honest, I'm not sure."

"I promise you, I didn't do it."

"I get it, Maya, but there's no other explanation."

Maya focused on Desiree while gently biting her bottom lip. "Can I ask you another question? But before you answer, can you promise me you won't get mad?"

Desiree closed her eyes for a split-second to brace for whatever was going to come out of Maya's mouth. "I promise."

"Did you get up at all last night?"

Desiree fought to control any initial thoughts tinged with anger from surfacing. She immediately recognized Maya's roundabout attempt to throw blame her way.

"I usually get up to go to the bathroom during the night, but that's in my room. There's no reason for me to be walking anywhere else in the apartment."

"Oh," Maya said.

"Anything else you want to say?"

"No."

"You sure?"

"Yup."

Desiree patted the bed. "If you want, we can continue this talk another day, but it's way past your bedtime, and I already know I'm going to be fighting with you tomorrow morning to get you out of bed for school."

Maya unfolded her legs and scooted under the covers. Desiree kissed her on the forehead.

"Can you do me a favor and let me sleep with the light on?" Maya asked.

Desiree adjusted the scarf wrapped around her hair. "Or, if you want, you can sleep with me tonight?"

"It's tempting, but I think I'll be fine in my room as long as the light stays on. And if you can also please turn down the air because I'm usually freezing at night."

"Okay, it's your choice to stay in your bed, and I'll be sure to turn down the air. Have a good night's sleep." Desiree blew a kiss to Maya and closed the door.

Chapter 8

Desiree felt a slight tug on her arm and a faint voice in the background. Her eyes remained closed, struggling to jumpstart the rest of her senses.

"Mom, it's time to get up."

Desiree opened her right eye, and a blurred silhouette of Maya slowly came into focus. "What time is it?" she asked in a raspy tone.

"It's seven thirty, and I only have twenty minutes to get to the bus stop."

Hit with a jolt of energy, Desiree reached over to her nightstand and tapped her phone, which confirmed the time. "Wh-what happened to my alarm? It never went off." She looked at Maya, dressed in her red and white-checkered pajama set on full display. "Hurry up and get dressed."

*****

Desiree emerged from the bedroom, wearing navy blue sweats, a white hooded sweatshirt, and a red baseball cap with renegade strands of her hair sticking out from the side. She knocked on Maya's bedroom door. "You almost ready?"

"Yes," Maya said before opening the door, sporting a pair of dark blue jeans and a light blue short-sleeved shirt. "I need to grab my bookbag."

Desiree ran to the kitchen and snatched a granola bar. She met Maya by the front door, handing her the bar. "I'm assuming you didn't have time to eat anything, so here's your breakfast."

Desiree reached for the knob and observed a sheet of paper someone had slipped under the door. She picked it up and gave a cursory glance at the handwritten note. She initially thought it was from Paulette, who'd been the only neighbor they'd met so far.

> *Good Morning,*
>
> *I'm your neighbor downstairs, and I'm having trouble sleeping because of the footsteps I keep hearing in the middle of the night. This is the third time this week it's happened. I'm not sure what's going on in your apartment at night, but I would appreciate it if you could refrain from stomping on the floor so I can get some sleep.*

Desiree calmly folded the note and stuffed it in her pocket before locking the apartment door.

"Who's the letter from?" Maya asked.

"It's a note from maintenance talking about testing the fire alarm today." She waved Maya along to keep up as they arrived in front of the elevator.

She struggled to calm her thoughts, which had catapulted into overdrive upon reading the note. Other than the sleepwalking episode she'd experienced when Jayden had caught her in the act, she had no recollection of any further occurrences during the past couple of nights. She also realized that if no one was there to interrupt her while sleepwalking, it was quite possible she could have unknowingly ventured from the bed for a nightly stroll.

"Mom? Are you coming?"

Desiree acknowledged and stepped onto the elevator, not realizing the door had opened.

*****

A half hour later, Desiree entered the apartment after walking Maya to the bus stop with only minutes to spare before the school bus arrived. She had forty-five minutes to shower and grab a bite to eat before logging in to start her remote medical billing job.

She entered her bedroom and emptied the contents of her sweatpants pockets, including the note from her neighbor. She shuddered to think that, in her first week of moving into the apartment, she'd already managed to cause friction with her neighbor downstairs. This was most certainly not the way she had wanted to start her new living experience.

She reread the note with a new and promising theory entering her mind. She entertained the possibility that her neighbor downstairs had misjudged her location and the note was meant for the apartment next door. Anything was possible, and this would have been a welcome turn of events.

Her thoughts began to drift from one concern to another. Her stomach tensed as she considered Jayden's true feelings about witnessing her sleepwalking. She'd always admired his willingness to be up front and not hold on to his feelings if something was bothering him. She'd also appreciated his admission that he'd been disturbed about finding her sleepwalking the other night, but she wasn't sure how much of a red flag this might have raised for him in their relationship. Finding out your partner snored at night was one thing, but waking up to see your significant other swaying in the dark after violently assaulting the wall could be considered deal-breaking territory.

She could have been going overboard, thinking this one incident could cause Jayden to run for the hills. She felt like she'd known him long enough to know this wouldn't be anything close to being a deal breaker in their relationship. However, she also recognized that if the shoe were on the other foot, she would have been just as freaked out if she had found him standing by the door in a possessed stupor after using the wall as a punching bag. She could almost guarantee that after witnessing such an unsettling event, she would have taken her pillow and temporarily moved her sleeping quarters to the living room sofa for the rest of the night, sleeping with one eye open.

Maybe Jayden was trying to minimize what happened so I wouldn't worry too much about the incident, she thought. Even if it were true, she couldn't have imagined if he found out she'd been sleepwalking for multiple nights in a row, his cool and calm demeanor would stay intact, and he wouldn't have one foot out the door.

She blinked several times, attempting to snap out of the endless loop of anxiety-inducing thoughts careening back and forth in her head. She thought it still hadn't been proven that she'd participated in multiple sleepwalking episodes during the past few nights. She was innocent until proven guilty.

But her downstairs neighbor's note and Maya's mention of hearing creaky floors at night didn't bode well for proving her complete innocence.

Chapter 9

Desiree jumped at the sound of her cell phone ringing and silenced it after noting a call coming from a telemarketer. She straightened up in her office chair, staring at the monitor in confusion as the blank screen indicated it might have been in sleep mode. She tapped a key on her keyboard, which resulted in the screen saver displaying a close-up image of Maya smiling. She speculated she must have fallen asleep during her lunch break after seeing a half-eaten turkey sandwich on a plate sitting to the right of the keyboard.

She rubbed her eyes, trying to wake up from the tiredness lingering, but before she could continue working, a shot of caffeine was calling her name. She meandered into the bathroom and wet a washcloth with hot water. She gazed in the mirror, viewing a network of microscopic red veins taking root around her eyeballs. She gently pushed against the bags under her eyes that seemed to have formed during the past week.

She'd always been thankful her remote job allowed her the opportunity to forego spending time putting on any makeup. Although given the way her face looked at the moment, she was tempted to use some eyeliner and a touch of foundation to conceal the bags under her eyes.

"You look awful," she whispered.

In her younger days, she had received plenty of attention regarding her appearance, although she was never one to flaunt what she had. With an arsenal of smooth skin, curly raven-colored hair, a mouth full of pearly-white teeth, and a body repelling fat from sticking around, she was the envy of many women and the object of desire for many men. But even with all of the attention, she struggled to see herself as a desirable person. She'd never felt comfortable being in the spotlight and often tried to hide her curves and tone down her makeup to help blend in with the crowd.

Now that she had entered her upper-thirties, her body retained more fat than she would have liked, and a speckle of blemishes had started settling on the surface of her once smooth face. A part of her regretted not living her best life during her youthful years. On the contrary, another part of her recognized looks weren't everything. If she allowed herself to be consumed by this superficial world, she'd become stuck in a vicious cycle trying to impress others instead of focusing on her own well-being. And lastly, a third part of her no longer paid attention to any of these philosophical theories on appearances. She just didn't give a damn what anyone thought about her looks at this point.

A hint of a grin formed on her lips. She placed the hot washcloth on her face, gently wiping it to help wake up her senses before partaking in another round of coffee to give her an additional jolt of energy.

She made her way into the kitchen to brew her fifth cup of coffee for the day. Her normal routine included drinking four cups a day, but she found it necessary to up her intake to help combat the extra tiredness she'd been feeling during the week.

Jayden had tried on several occasions to request that she tone down the amount of caffeine she'd been consuming. He believed her caffeine consumption made her too jittery and didn't help her wallet, especially when she was out and found herself rushing to the nearest coffee shop to satisfy her craving. Although his health-conscious lectures did irritate her on occasion, she knew he was right and genuinely looking out for her best interests.

After adding a dash of cream to her mug, she took a sip, closing her eyes in delight as she reacted to the French vanilla flavor hitting her tongue. She savored the taste while thinking her coffee habit wasn't all that bad. On the bad habit scale, she believed drinking too much coffee paled in comparison to many other things she could have been doing that negatively affected her health.

She took another sip and smiled at how quickly her mind attempted to rationalize her coffee addiction. She understood this was a work in progress, and it would take much more than Jayden's lectures for her to tone down her caffeine consumption.

She pivoted and took a step out of the kitchen before abruptly stopping. She stepped back and turned her head toward the edge of the kitchen counter, setting her sights on the wooden block holding her cutlery collection. All the knife slots were occupied except for one. That was strange since she hadn't cooked any food recently that needed assistance from her butcher knife.

She peeked in the sink but did not see the knife. She opened the dishwasher, but besides a few glasses and forks, there were no other contents inside. She considered the possibility that the knife could have been lost during the moving process.

She took another sip from her coffee mug, realizing she had three hours to go before she could ask the only other person in the household who might have an idea of what had happened with the knife.

Chapter 10

Desiree stepped off the elevator with Maya trailing behind. Since the move, her twenty-minute afternoon break consisted of picking Maya up from the bus stop a few blocks away.

"When will you let me start walking home from the bus stop by myself? I'm almost twelve now. Isn't that old enough?" Maya asked.

"Maybe if we were living in our old neighborhood, I would think about it. But, since we're living uptown now, there are too many strangers walking around here, and I can't risk anything happening to you."

Desiree unlocked the apartment door, and they both stepped inside.

"Since there are more people around, at least I won't be alone. If someone tried to do something to me, I could scream, and I'm sure somebody would come running to help me."

"You might be right, but I wouldn't want to test your theory. So, for now, I'd suggest you get comfortable with the idea of me picking you up from the bus stop."

Maya sighed in disgust. "Some of my friends' parents let them walk home by themselves."

"Maybe they have no choice. But I do have a choice, and I choose to pick you up. The last thing I need is a story about you missing on the news."

Desiree motioned for Maya to follow her into the kitchen. "That's enough talking about this. I have something to show you." She stopped in front of the wooden block holding the knives and pointed. "Tell me what's wrong?"

"What do you mean?"

"Look and tell me what's missing."

Maya pointed to the empty knife slot.

"And before you ask, I already checked the sink and the dishwasher, and it's not there." She squinted at Maya. "Any chance you can help me figure out where it went?"

Maya's face grew pensive. "Um … not sure."

Desiree held in a grin, almost feeling sorry for Maya with her pitiful acting performance.

"Are you going to stand here and lie to my face?"

Maya dropped her gaze to the floor.

"I'm going to ask one more time. Where is the missing knife?"

Maya looked up, meeting Desiree's eyes for a brief moment. "It's in my room."

"*Your room*? Why did you bring it to your room?"

"For protection."

"Protection from what?"

"From the noises I've been hearing in the hallway at night."

"Didn't you tell me you thought those noises you heard were just a dream?"

"It could have been, but it made me feel better to have the knife in my room in case it wasn't."

"You didn't seem worried last night when we talked about it, since you declined my invitation for you to sleep in my room."

"Yeah, I know. I guess I was trying to show you I'm growing up now and can handle things on my own."

Desiree reached her arms out and hugged Maya. "Well, I appreciate your bravery, but there's no need for you to act all big and bad around me. I'm not one of your friends whom you're trying to impress. I'm your mother, and if you're feeling uncomfortable about something, just tell me."

Maya produced a sheepish grin. "Okay, my bad," she said before stopping abruptly and shaking her head. "Wait … I mean, my fault."

Desiree laughed. "I'm hurt that you think I'm so old that I don't know what that means. No need to translate for me. Now, let's go get this knife from your room and return it to its rightful place before you hurt yourself. And by the way, where did you hide it?"

"Under my mattress."

Maya led the way to her room with Desiree following. She entered her room and reached between the mattress and the box spring.

"Wait … Hold on!" Desiree shouted. "We don't need you blindly reaching under this mattress and potentially cutting your hand on the blade."

Desiree lifted the mattress and, as advertised, she could see the butcher knife resting on top of the box spring.

"Go ahead and grab the knife while I'm holding the mattress. But be careful and grab it by the handle."

Maya followed her instructions, gently grabbing the handle and picking up the knife.

Desiree let go of the mattress and reached out her hand as Maya gave her the knife. "I still can't believe you did this," she said, attempting to remain calm.

The sight of the knife invoked a sudden sense of fear in Desiree. Her mind flashed to all of the worst-case scenarios that could have led to Maya injuring herself attempting to handle the knife.

She glared at Maya. "I need you to promise me you'll never do this again. I don't want you coming anywhere near that knife set in the kitchen. Do you understand me?"

Maya nodded without saying a word.

Desiree continued to stare at her. "Shaking your head up and down is not an answer."

Without missing a beat, Maya said, "Yes, Mom, I understand."

Chapter 11

Jayden blew his horn, frustrated at the white sprinter van cutting him off while he attempted to merge on the highway. Although he had expected traffic at the start of the Labor Day holiday weekend, he struggled to maintain his cool as every vehicle jostled for prime position on the roads. He had hoped to leave work earlier than he had to avoid traffic, but he'd needed to finish up a few tasks before he left to ensure he wouldn't have to log in over the holiday weekend.

He eventually exited I-77, ecstatic to finally see space in front of him instead of being blinded by a kaleidoscope of red brake lights. He sighed, thinking about the next challenge of finding parking. Attempting to figure out where to legally park on the street for free was no easy task, not to mention the amount of luck needed to find an available spot. He contemplated if it was worth paying for an Uber moving forward to avoid the hassles of driving to Desiree's apartment.

After circling the area around her apartment and having no luck finding a spot, he reluctantly pulled into a parking garage, mumbling under his breath at the additional expense he would need to incur. As soon as he pulled into a parking space, his phone chimed with a text message from Desiree.

Are you still on the road?

You have great timing. I just parked. Are you tracking me?

You can call it a woman's intuition. Anyway, I have a craving for pizza. If I call in a to-go order, can you pick it up?

Pizza? That's something new you normally don't have a craving for.

I know, but I can't help thinking about having a slice now.

I can work with pizza, and I'm sure Maya would love it. Just let me know where I need to go.

There's a pizza spot I discovered a few days ago. It's walking distance from the apartment. I'll send you the information once I order the pizza.

Jayden relished the idea of having a hot slice of pizza and a cold beer to help calm his nerves after the stress-inducing car ride. He understood this would do nothing to help his health-conscious mindset, but at this point, he didn't care.

He remained in the car with the '80s XM radio station playing in the background as he waited for Desiree to text him the information for the pizza pickup.

He tapped his fingers against the steering wheel as "Maneater" by Hall and Oates blared from the speakers. He remembered hearing this song on repeat as a kid, thanks to his parents. He closed his eyes and tilted his head back against the headrest, swaying his head to the beat.

He thought about Maya and was curious about how the rest of her week at school had gone. He also thought back to his last visit to the apartment and the weird moment he'd experienced with Maya, hearing the neighbor knock on the door before it had actually happened. He'd been in communication with Desiree a few times since the incident, but she hadn't mentioned any concerns about Maya's behavior.

His phone chimed again and, as promised, Desiree provided the name and address for the pizza pickup. He shut off the engine, and then grabbed his duffel bag from the back seat before exiting the car. He eventually proceeded down the street with his phone out, following the GPS to his destination.

The sun was roughly an hour from setting as the sliver of sky within his field of vision had begun its colorful transformation with orange hues mixing into the horizon. After walking only a short distance, he could feel the dampness settling on his skin from the humid evening. The streets were busy with foot traffic on the sidewalk and the sound of vehicle horns blowing intermittently around him.

He eventually arrived in front of Al's Pizza Joint and picked up the pie Desiree had ordered. Based on the enticing aroma, it seemed like they were in for a treat. With the duffel bag strapped around his shoulder and the pizza box in hand, his ability to also hold a six-pack of beer would be a challenge. But he didn't let that deter his mission of pairing a pizza with a nice cold brew.

After picking up the beer and stuffing it in his bag, he continued walking with the pizza box toward Desiree's apartment.

*****

He entered the building and rode the elevator to the tenth floor. The once piping hot pizza had cooled to room temperature, as his fingertips were no longer stinging from touching the heated cardboard bottom.

He knocked on the door, and after a few seconds, Desiree answered. Jayden stretched out his arms to give her the pizza box. "Did you order a pizza, ma'am?"

Desiree smiled. "I believe I did." She grabbed the pizza box and gave Jayden a peck on the lips.

He entered the apartment and rounded the corner to see Maya standing with her arms wide open. He dropped his bag and gave her a tight hug. Pulling back, he peeked at Maya to see the necklace draped around her neck.

"Miss me?"

Maya offered a smirk. "Not really."

"Well, then I'll take my pizza and head on back home."

"Okay ... okay, I missed you," Maya said before laughing. "After eating that awful pizza at school, I'm happy to have the real deal."

"Before we eat, I'd suggest you warm up the pie in the oven. It got cold while I was walking from the pizza shop."

*****

Desiree took the pizza out of the oven and placed it on the kitchen table. Jayden leaned back with his cold beer and pizza, enjoying this time to de-stress from a busy work week.

Desiree reached out to prompt both Jayden and Maya to hold hands to say grace before eating.

Once Desiree finished, Jayden lifted his beer glass in the air for a toast. "Here's to the long holiday weekend." He took a sip. "So, how was everybody's week?"

"Nothing special for me. Just happy to get through my first week of school. And thank goodness, I don't have any homework to do over the holiday weekend," Maya said.

Desiree took a bite of her slice and moved her hand away from her face as a string of cheese stretched from her mouth to the tip of the pizza before it broke. Jayden turned his attention to Desiree, waiting for her to respond to his question.

She wiped her mouth. "It was another busy week for me. There's never a dull moment with medical billing."

Jayden took another sip of his beer. "Same for me in the project management world." He stopped and stared at Desiree. "Speaking of work, I did something you would be proud of. I didn't bring my laptop with me this weekend, which makes two weekends in a row of not checking in on work."

Desiree lifted her glass of water. "I'll toast to that," she said with little enthusiasm.

Jayden studied Desiree's face. "What's the matter? You look extra tired. I can see it in your eyes. They look a little red."

"I'm sure I probably look like this every Friday after a busy week."

Minutes later, Maya stuffed the last few bites of pizza in her mouth. "Nice talking with you both, but it's time for me to get in my bed, be lazy, and enjoy my long weekend."

Jayden reached out for a fist-bump before Maya left the table. He waited until she disappeared around the corner and closed her bedroom door. "How have things been with Maya for the past few days?"

"Nothing to write home about. I didn't notice any odd behavior, if that's what you're asking."

"You sure? Nothing different at all?"

Desiree's face hardened. "No, nothing different."

Jayden prolonged his stare. "Are you good? Seems like you're uptight about something."

"No, I'm good."

She lifted her glass of water to drink, and Jayden witnessed her hand shaking ever so slightly.

He set his sights on the Keurig coffee maker sitting on the kitchen counter behind her. "I'm guessing since you felt tired today, you had a few cups of coffee?"

Desiree temporarily averted her eyes to the table and rubbed her temples before focusing back up at Jayden with a harsh stare. "Why are you so fixated on how much coffee I drink?"

Jayden was about to answer, but Desiree continued, "If this is something that provides me comfort and gives me a shot of energy to get through the day, what's wrong with that?"

"Hold on. No need to get so defensive. I'm only letting you know you may not feel it, but depending on how much caffeine you have in your system, it can do more harm than good."

Desiree folded her arms. "So, what harm is it causing me now?"

"For one, I noticed your hand is shaky, and two, your eyes are red, most likely from being tired, so whatever caffeine you have in your system now is not helping. And three, if I'm being honest, you're a little on edge whenever you're tired."

Desiree let off a sarcastic laugh. "Great, just what I needed after a long week of work—a lecture from my boyfriend on everything that's wrong with me."

"I'm sorry if you're taking it the wrong way. I'm only trying to help."

Desiree opened her mouth to speak, but then stopped after seeing Maya enter the kitchen. She looked at both Jayden and Desiree before pointing in the direction of the front door. "Do you want me to get the door?"

Jayden's heartbeat ticked up a notch as a sense of déjà vu consumed him. "Did you hear a knock at the door?" he asked Maya.

"Yes," she replied.

Jayden cut his eyes over to Desiree. "Did you hear anything?"

She shook her head. "No."

Jayden jumped up. "Stay right here. Let me get the door."

He left the kitchen and arrived at the front door. He swallowed twice in succession to try to moisten his dry throat. He leaned his head toward the peephole, hoping and praying somebody would be facing him on the other side. A massive sense of relief flowed through his body after seeing a woman positioned in front of the door. For an instant, he thought it was Paulette, but this woman looked older and wore glasses, along with a blue silk headscarf wrapped around her hair.

Jayden opened the door with a guarded smile. "Hello, how can I help you?"

"I hope you can. My name is Sophia, and I'm your neighbor downstairs."

"Nice to meet you," Jayden said and raised his hand for a shake, although she did not reciprocate.

He snatched his hand back in embarrassment as an awkward moment of silence lingered in the air.

"Did you receive the note I left under your door?"

Jayden thought for a second, puzzled by her question. "I'm not aware of a note, but I can ask my girlfriend about it."

"No need. As I mentioned in my note, I've been having problems sleeping at night because someone has been walking around up here, disturbing my sleep. I can let that slide if it happened once, but this has been going on for the past few nights."

"Oh … okay. Apologies for disturbing your sleep."

"I wasn't planning on coming up here, but I have to get up and out of my apartment early tomorrow morning, and I need to get a good night's sleep. So, I'm asking if I can have some peace and quiet tonight."

Jayden turned after hearing footsteps behind him to see Desiree, with Maya a few feet to her right.

Desiree interjected. "Hello. How—"

"Did you get my note?" Sophia interrupted.

A vertical crevice formed between Desiree's eyes. "Is it too much to ask for an introduction before you start asking questions?"

"I did introduce myself to your boyfriend already. I also introduced myself in the letter I wrote and slipped under your door. How much more introducing do I need to do?"

Jayden cringed at Sophia's rude response. Desiree was already in a bad mood, and he wasn't sure what was about to come out of her mouth.

Desiree let out a long exhale. "If you had introduced yourself properly to me, I would have already known your name, but that's not the case."

Sophia opened her mouth to speak before Desiree raised her hand with her index finger pointing up. "Hold on. Let me finish. I did get your note and would have had no problem offering my apologies, but since you chose to come knocking on my door and start talking in a disrespectful manner, I'll need to put any apologies I had for you on hold."

Sophia offered a frigid stare but didn't immediately speak. Jayden could only have imagined that Desiree's venomous rebuttal might have temporarily stunned her. She looked beyond Desiree and focused on Maya.

"Is she the one walking around in the middle of the night, disturbing me?"

Desiree took a step forward, and Jayden shifted his body to the right, partially blocking her progress.

"Hold on, ladies. Let's take it down a notch."

"It's too late for that," Desiree said, raising her voice. "Don't even think about bringing my daughter into this."

"Well, since you never answered my question, I'm going to guess she's the one who's running around in the middle of the night. You need to get better control of your kid."

Desiree pushed up against Jayden's back, attempting to get past him. Sophia took a few steps back, most likely startled at Desiree's aggressive behavior. Jayden anchored his legs to the floor and extended both of his arms out to stop Desiree from advancing any further.

"Move out the way, Jayden! I need to teach this bitch a lesson."

Jayden pivoted to face Desiree and used his leverage to physically push her away from the door. "Stop it, Desiree! Nothing good is going to come out of you getting into a fight."

He quickly shifted his vision beyond Desiree to look at Maya. She displayed a blank expression on her face and didn't seem to be bothered much by the confrontation.

Jayden continued to hold on to Desiree with both arms and took a glance behind him to see Sophia, who remained by the door.

He turned his attention back to Desiree. "Please, I need you to relax and take a few deep breaths. Can you do that for me?"

Desiree finally pulled her eyes away from Sophia, focusing on Jayden. She sucked in a large dose of air before puffing out her cheeks and exhaling.

"Are you calming down now?" he asked.

She nodded.

"Can you do me a favor and stay here while I finish talking with Sophia?"

Desiree took in another deep breath before nodding again.

Jayden slowly released his grip from her arms, making sure she remained still and didn't attempt to bolt around him. Desiree took a few steps back, providing extra comfort to Jayden that she had plans to comply with his wishes.

He pivoted and took a step outside into the hallway, closing the door behind him as an extra barrier of protection in case Desiree tried to squeeze by him for a sneak attack.

Sophia crossed her arms. "You need to get your girlfriend under control."

"Please, let's calm down," he said in a lowered tone.

Although Jayden presented a calm demeanor on the outside, a part of him wanted to get into Sophia's face and call her out for the unnecessary disrespect she displayed. But he had to fight against this temptation if he had any plans to end the confrontation in a civilized manner.

"I get your frustration with the noises at night. And I apologize if your sleep was interrupted, but please understand that knocking on our door and confronting us the way you did was not going to help."

Sophia glared at Jayden. "How would you feel if a neighbor above you was walking around at three in the morning and you couldn't go back to sleep?"

"I get it. And I did offer an apology."

Sophia offered a critical squint. "As I mentioned before, I need to get up early in the morning tomorrow and could use a good night's sleep."

"I hear you. Let me talk with my girlfriend about the situation and see what we can do to stop these noises from happening at night."

"Thank you," Sophia said before walking away.

Chapter 12

Jayden closed the door, glaring at Desiree. She stood with her arms folded and a nondescript look on her face. Maya hovered a few feet to the side of her.

"What was that all about? And did you get a note from her?" he asked.

"Do you mind going to your room while me and Mr. Jayden talk?" Desiree asked Maya.

"Okay," Maya said without any pushback.

Desiree made her way into the kitchen with Jayden following. She sat and took a sip of water before tilting her head back with her eyes closed. She opened them and watched Jayden as he leaned against the kitchen counter.

"Have you calmed down now?" Jayden asked.

"Yes, I'm good."

She continued to look Jayden's way with unsteady eyes before glancing down at her hands folded in her lap.

"I don't think I've ever seen you that mad before."

"Guess I'm having a bad day."

"It must have been really bad if I had to physically restrain you from getting to Sophia."

"I'm sorry, but all bets are off once you start bringing Maya into the discussion. Nobody should ever question my parenting skills." She looked up at Jayden with her lips curled in disgust. "How's she going to tell me to get better control of my child? She doesn't know me. She doesn't know what's going on in my household. She doesn't know what I do each and every day to take care of Maya."

Jayden pumped his hands in a downward motion. "You're right, and I completely understand. But let's take it down a bit. I don't want you getting fired up again."

Desiree took another sip of water with her gaze dropping back down toward her lap.

"Now, is it true she left a note?"

"Yes. She left a note complaining about noises at night."

"Are you having trouble sleeping at night? Or do you think …?"

A look of annoyance developed on Desiree's face. "I don't know. Maybe I am sleepwalking and don't remember."

Jayden tapped his fingers on the kitchen counter. "Do you think it makes sense for us to set up a nanny cam to confirm what's happening at night?"

Desiree raised her brow in a questioning slant. "A what?"

"A nanny cam. You know the camera—"

She put her hand up. "Yes. I know what you mean now."

"So, what do you think?"

"My first instinct is to say no, but that may be the only way to see what's happening."

"I don't know much about these cameras, but I can start researching online to get an idea of what's out there. In the meantime, it might be a good idea if we talk to Maya to see how she's holding up. She appeared fine when everything was going on, but you never know what she could be thinking," Jayden said.

*****

Desiree approached Maya's room with Jayden following behind. She gently knocked on the door.

"Come in," Maya said.

They both entered to see Maya sitting on her bed with a book in her lap.

"How are you doing?" Desiree asked.

"I'm good."

"Are you sure?"

"Yup."

Although Maya seemed sincere with her response, Jayden was more concerned that she seemed unbothered by the confrontation and his attempt to physically restrain Desiree from attacking Sophia.

Desiree reached down to offer a hug. "I'm so sorry you had to see me like that. I was having a bad day and—"

"That's okay, Mom. No need to apologize."

"I don't want you worrying this woman is going to come back up here again to cause trouble."

Maya kept quiet as she blankly stared in Desiree's direction.

Desiree touched her on the shoulder. "Are you okay, Maya?"

Maya blinked several times in a row and said, "Oh, I'm not worried. And I don't think she'll be giving us any more trouble."

"Why do you say that?" Desiree asked.

"I don't know. I just have a feeling."

Chapter 13

"What did Maya mean when she said she had a feeling? Is it just me, or are you not concerned with Maya's reaction to what happened?" Jayden asked.

Desiree made sure her bedroom door was closed all the way. "I have no clue what she meant, and I didn't want to question her any further. And yes, I'm surprised she's taking it all in stride, like it's no big deal. She's normally a worrier by nature, but it seems like she's been extra calm over these past few days."

"And this is exactly what I was talking about when I said to keep your eye on her, to see if you noticed anything different about her."

"You're right. I should have mentioned it to you when you asked earlier."

"So, what do you think is going on?" Jayden asked.

"I don't know. I keep tabs on her phone, and she's not allowed on social media. I also have her password and check periodically."

"Does she have any new friends at school who could be influencing her?"

"Maybe. She just started the year, so it's probably too early to tell."

"Or do you think this move has something to do with it?" Jayden asked.

"I don't know. She seems pretty excited to be living here, and I don't think that would cause her behavior to change much."

"Guess we need to keep our eyes on her this weekend to see if anything else changes."

*****

Later in the evening, Jayden stretched out on the living room sofa with the TV remote by his side, indulging in a few late-night talk shows. Maya had been in her bedroom for a while and was most likely asleep. He was uncertain if Desiree was still awake. Although, as tired as she'd been earlier, he wouldn't be surprised if she was asleep.

He began his research to find a nanny cam. He figured he could run out the next day and browse around before purchasing a camera. In the meantime, he planned to play the role of a nanny cam during the night, which was why he'd chosen to camp out in the living room. He proposed a challenge to see how long he could stay up, with the possibility of catching Desiree in the act of sleepwalking again. He also wanted to make sure the apartment was quiet during the night to keep Sophia from coming back up again to complain and risk starting a potential brawl with Desiree.

*****

Jayden opened his eyes, realizing his goal of staying up for a while hadn't lasted long, as he had fallen asleep on the sofa. The TV remained on and had been broadcasting one of those late-night infomercials. He swung his feet to the floor, now in a seated position, still attempting to gather his bearings. Except for the dull glow of light coming from the TV, the rest of the apartment was cast in darkness.

He muted the TV to listen out for any potential movement. Other than the light humming coming from the refrigerator in the kitchen, all else was quiet. He noted a time of 3:30 a.m. He'd slept longer than expected, thinking he might have missed Desiree potentially sleepwalking.

He contemplated whether it made sense to try to stay awake for the rest of the night to see if he could catch her in the act. This would also prevent the chance of him being startled awake to potentially see Desiree roaming around aimlessly and acting out unconscious aggressions on the wall or some other part of the apartment. With only a few hours to go until sunrise, he thought he'd give it a try to see if he could stay awake, hoping the power nap he'd had was enough rest to carry him through until daylight.

*****

A dull ache radiated along the back of Jayden's neck. With his blurred vision coming into focus, it slowly became clear he had dozed off again, and his head had dropped forward as a result of him falling back to sleep while sitting up. He lifted his head before reaching for the back of his neck to try to rub away the discomfort.

With his vision cleared, he stared out into a mostly dark living room. The TV had been turned off, and only a sliver of moonlight came through the living room blinds. He touched his forehead and wiped off a bit of moisture. It was odd for him to feel warm in the apartment since Desiree liked things as cold as an icebox.

Pushing the temperature thoughts aside, his heartbeat sped up. He didn't recall shutting off the TV, and his second attempt at trying to stay awake on his stakeout mission had failed. He reached for his lap, searching for his phone, but couldn't find it, and then he heard a clicking noise in the distance, interrupting his quest to find his phone.

He stopped moving and tried to locate the direction of the noise. He leaned his head to the left, realizing the noise was coming from down the hallway. Based on the position of the couch, he could only see a small part of the hallway from where he was sitting. But even if he had been positioned in the perfect spot to see down the hall, it was a moot point now since the darkness had severely impaired his vision.

The clicking noise continued, repeating itself every few seconds. He put his hands on the sofa, searching for his cell phone or the TV remote, but came up empty. A rush of adrenaline coursed through Jayden's veins, with his ability to see now compromised and the mysterious clicking noise continuing in the distance. He'd always taken pride in being an even-keeled individual who was difficult to rattle under most circumstances. However, he couldn't deny that this moment had him a little shaken, especially based on last weekend's experience with Desiree proving that violent sleepwalking episodes were no longer a myth but an actual fact.

He continued to rub his hands along the sofa before leaning forward and reaching for the floor to see if his phone had fallen. He felt around between his legs on the hardwood floor until he made contact with an object. He probed the item with his fingers and confirmed it was the TV remote. He picked it up and turned on the TV to give him some much-needed light in the living room. Confusion set in as to why the TV had been turned off while he was sleeping. He only guessed that when the remote had hit the floor, it somehow activated the power button. It sounded like a logical explanation, and he'd only hoped his assumption was correct.

He muted the TV and looked toward the hallway, but struggled with limited vision as the light emanating from the TV barely reached the hallway. He looked to his right, searching the sofa for his phone without any luck, and then to his left with the same result. He stuck his hand between the sofa cushions and finally found his target.

He stood, taking a few steps toward the hallway, which he discovered had been devoid of any activity. He came up to the torch lamp standing against the wall near the TV and turned it on for additional lighting. He strolled closer to the entrance of the hallway as the rhythmic clicking sound persisted. He stopped at the thermostat in the hallway, shining his flashlight to see a temperature of 78 degrees. He turned down the temperature a few degrees to prompt the air conditioning to kick on.

He looked up and down along the walls but didn't see anything out of the ordinary. It wasn't until he took a few steps into the hallway that he saw Maya's bedroom door open. This was definitely something new, as he never recalled her sleeping with the bedroom door open and her lights out. He pondered if she had woken up in the middle of the night to turn off the air conditioning. Then again, Desiree would kill Maya if she'd messed with the thermostat.

Jayden continued stepping toward Maya's bedroom door and stopped after his last step disturbed a squeaky floor joist, resulting in a loud creaking sound. He winced, thinking about Sophia and hoping the noise didn't disturb her. He took another step, slowly putting his weight on the floor to try to prevent any further creaking sounds. It was at that moment he discovered the clicking noises were coming from Maya's bedroom.

Chapter 14

Jayden took his final two steps and peeked into Maya's bedroom. His vision was impaired once again with darkness. He didn't want to turn on the bedroom light, afraid he might wake her. A steady, gentle breeze greeted him as he continued to stand by the entrance.

He touched his phone and activated the flashlight. He waved the light around her room, first focusing on her bed. The lump under the covers indicated she was in bed, and Jayden assumed she was asleep. He raised the light on his phone, homing in on the clicking noise coming from up above. He took a few steps into the room and determined the clicking noise was coming from the dangling pull chain, rocking and hitting the light fixture cover as the ceiling fan blades rotated. He puffed out his cheeks and let out a large exhale after finally uncovering the source of the noise. He reached up and gently pulled on the chain to slow down the fan speed, which ultimately stopped the pull chain from rocking as much and prevented it from hitting the light fixture.

He stepped back and aimed his light on the bed again to make sure he hadn't woken Maya. With her back turned and seeing the steady rise and fall of her ribcage, he assumed her sleeping hadn't been disturbed. He backed out of her room and gently closed the door.

He scanned farther down the hallway to see Desiree's door closed. He neared, putting his ear up against the door, listening intently for any noises indicating she might have been roaming around. All was quiet, but Jayden needed visual confirmation. He wrapped his hand around the doorknob and twisted. The door slowly opened, and he aimed his flashlight on the bed, confirming it was occupied. He found Desiree positioned on her stomach, but unlike Maya, she was sprawled out on top of the covers. He took a few steps into the bedroom, moving his flashlight from right to left to confirm everything was in its rightful place.

He backed out of the room, closed the door, and then tiptoed his way down the hall, attempting to avoid the creaking land mines that existed on the wood flooring planks. With only an hour left until sunrise, he thought it made no sense to go to the bedroom to sleep. He preferred staying out on the sofa and had experienced enough excitement to keep him awake until Desiree and Maya awoke.

*****

Jayden felt a nudge on his leg as he gazed up to see Desiree standing over him. He flinched with his senses not completely alert, but attentive enough to wonder if this was the conscious or unconscious version of Desiree. After noticing her smile, he suspected it was the former.

"Did you stay out here all night?" she asked.

Jayden opened his eyes wide, attempting to clear his vision. "I guess I did."

"You must have been extremely tired to spend the whole night on the sofa."

"I must have been."

"Were you hot last night?" she asked.

"Yes. And if I was hot, I could only imagine how you felt."

"I was burning up, and it wasn't until I got up and noticed Maya's ceiling fan running that I realized it must not have been just me. I also saw the thermostat temperature was higher than normal. I hope she wasn't messing with the thermostat. She knows better than that. Unless it was you?"

"I did change the temperature after I woke up during the night and felt it was hot as hell in here, but I didn't mess with it before then."

Jayden stretched and rotated his head as far as he could to the left with a wince crossing his face. "I definitely don't recommend trying to sleep while sitting up. My neck is stiff."

Desiree reached over and briefly massaged between his neck and shoulders. "Maybe once you start moving around, your neck will loosen up."

Jayden peered down the hallway. "I'm surprised Maya isn't up yet."

"Me, too. She's usually up by now. I guess the first week of school must have worn her out."

Jayden walked over to the patio door curtains and pulled them apart as a flood of sunlight came rushing in. He squinted, attempting to adjust to the extra brightness. He studied the street below, watching the cars and people moving around, on their way to various destinations. "I'm not sure how long it's going to take for me to get used to you living in a high-rise apartment."

"I'm sure it won't take much longer. I'm getting used to it, and I'm loving the convenience of having everything within walking distance."

Jayden pulled his attention away from the busy streets below. "Let me wash up so I can make my way outside."

"What plans do you have?"

"Unless you changed your mind, I was going to do some shopping for a nanny cam. Are you still on board with doing this?"

"I forgot we talked about that. I guess I'm on board with it."

"I think it's a great idea. It will give us the confirmation we need to see what's going on, if anything, during the night."

Chapter 15

Jayden parked in the public garage and began his walk back to the apartment, with a bag holding the compact nanny cam he'd purchased. He'd made sure to pick up a model that had night vision capabilities to capture any activity while recording in the dark.

He rounded the corner and spotted an ambulance parked on the street in front of the apartment. He entered the lobby and scoped the area. He pressed the elevator button, and a familiar ding sounded, signifying the elevator had arrived. He stepped off to the side, in anticipation of anyone else who might need to get off first before he boarded the elevator. The doors opened, and two paramedics exited, rushing by Jayden while wheeling out a stretcher with a female patient.

As the stretcher rolled by him, he observed that the woman lying on it was Sophia. Although he'd only interacted with her once, it had been long enough for him to remember her face. He continued watching as the paramedics left the building and prepared to load the stretcher into the ambulance.

He pressed the elevator button again to open the doors since he'd waited too long to board the first time. He entered the elevator and was hit with a thought that almost stopped him in his tracks. The words uttered from Maya's mouth the previous evening had become hauntingly real. This couldn't have been a coincidence. His concerns with Maya had immediately skyrocketed from somewhat concerned to straight paranoia.

He pressed the button for the tenth floor and said a silent prayer for Sophia, hoping she could get the medical help she needed and recover quickly from whatever happened.

He arrived in front of the apartment door and used a key he'd borrowed from Desiree to enter. He had no idea where Maya was in the apartment, and for the first time, he deliberately wanted to avoid her. He never thought he would feel uneasy around her, as he'd only ever known her to be the sweet, lovable girl who was always happy to see him. But unbeknownst to her, their relationship dynamics were about to change, and Jayden had to figure out a way to continue to act naturally around her without giving away any of his concerns about her mysterious behavior.

He surveyed the living room for any activity before entering the kitchen after hearing a noise. He spotted Desiree pouring a cup of coffee into a mug.

She glared at him with a smug expression and put her arm out with her palm facing him. "Please, don't start."

Jayden waved her off. "I wasn't planning to say anything." He darted his eyes around the kitchen, then back behind him. "Where's Maya?"

"In her room. Why do you want to know?"

"Because I have news to tell you, and I don't want her to hear," he said, lowering his tone.

Desiree took a sip from her mug. "Okay. What's the big secret?"

"Remember when Maya said last night not to worry about Sophia causing us any more trouble?"

"Yes."

"Well … I saw two paramedics wheeling her out on a stretcher in the lobby."

"Are you serious? Are you sure it was her?"

"Definitely."

"That's horrible. I'm so sorry to hear," Desiree said while leaning against the kitchen counter. "Did she see you?"

"No, because her eyes were closed."

Desiree shook her head. "I know I didn't have the best interaction with her yesterday, but I hate to see that happen to anyone. I hope she'll be okay."

"Me, too."

Desiree's mouth dropped open. "Oh, shit! Are you thinking about what Maya said yesterday?"

"Exactly. Glad to see we're on the same page."

Desiree rested her coffee mug on the counter and stared at the floor. She remained quiet until Jayden broke the silence.

"Now do you believe me that something's not quite right with Maya?"

Desiree didn't immediately respond and continued to stare at the floor.

"Desiree? Do you hear me?"

She finally engaged Jayden with eye contact. "I'm sorry, what did you say?"

Jayden sighed. "I said, now do you believe me that something's off with Maya?"

"I never said you were wrong about your suspicions."

Jayden contemplated for a second. "I do have a theory about what's going on."

"Okay. Let's hear it."

"It seems to me this all started after you gave her the necklace to wear."

"What does that have to do with her acting differently?"

"I don't know, but we need to try to find out. Didn't you say the necklace was a gift from your mother?"

"Yes."

"Do you know where she got the necklace from?"

"She never said. It was just a gift she wanted to give to Maya."

"And since you waited until now to give Maya the necklace, where did you keep it all this time?"

"It was in the keepsake box you found when we first moved in. That's why I was so worried because I thought the box was lost and I knew the necklace was in there."

"Has Maya been wearing it the whole time since you gave it to her?"

"Not sure. I haven't paid much attention."

"I definitely know she had it on yesterday when she made the comment about Sophia, and also when your neighbor across the hall had knocked on the door," Jayden said.

"So, are you saying I should take the necklace back from her?"

"Maybe temporarily, to see if her behavior changes back to normal after not wearing it for a while."

"That might be a problem because she tells me almost every day she loves wearing the necklace," Desiree said.

"I'm not sure what to tell you. We need to figure something out." Jayden rubbed his forehead in deep thought. "Does she take it off when she goes to sleep?"

"Don't know."

"I'd suggest one of us check tonight after she goes to sleep. If we see it lying anywhere on her dresser or nightstand, I say we swipe it and act like we don't know what happened to it when she goes looking for it."

"Don't you think that would be a little cruel?" Desiree said with an arched eyebrow.

"Do you have any other ideas? Unless you can convince her to stop wearing the necklace?"

Desiree took a sip of her coffee. "I don't know. I'll come up with something."

"Hope so. But, in the meantime, we need to act as normal as possible around her, which will be a challenge for me. If I'm being honest, I'm a little freaked out with what happened between yesterday and today. There's no way this could all be pure coincidence."

"Can't argue with you," Desiree said before she quickly shifted her eyes to the right of Jayden and put the mug to her mouth.

He remained still, not turning around immediately. He didn't need a facial expression expert to tell him to shut up. Desiree had told him all he needed to know—Maya had snuck up behind them.

"There you go," Maya said from behind.

Jayden gave her a fist-bump. "If you had woken up at your normal time, you would have seen me this morning."

"Yeah, I was extra tired. That first week of school wore me out."

Jayden noted she was wearing the necklace around her neck.

She spotted the plastic bag he was holding. "Aw, you shouldn't have. What did you get me?"

"Nothing you'd be interested in."

He continued to hold the bag while being extremely thankful that the dark gray bag hid what was inside. He didn't have the energy to lie his way out of why he'd picked up a nanny cam for the apartment.

She reached for the bag. "Let me see what you have."

Jayden pulled the bag away from her.

"Hey, where are your manners?" Desiree said. "Mr. Jayden already told you it's something you wouldn't be interested in, so no need for you to reach for the bag to see."

Maya returned her hand to her side. She peered past Desiree and focused on the refrigerator. "Is it okay if I grab a bottle of apple juice? That's what I was coming in here for, anyway."

Desiree stepped aside, allowing Maya to walk to the refrigerator and grab a bottle of juice.

"Thank you," she said as she shuffled her way out of the kitchen and back to her room.

Jayden kept quiet and waited until her bedroom door closed. "Do you think she heard what we were saying?"

"I don't think so."

Jayden pointed to his neck. "I see she had on the necklace. So, what's your plan to get her to stop wearing it?"

"I guess it's time to have a nice mother-daughter talk and see how that goes."

Chapter 16

Desiree knocked on Maya's bedroom door.

"Come in," she said.

Desiree opened the door to find Maya sitting on her bed with a book in her lap.

"What are you reading?" Desiree asked.

Maya continued to gaze at the open book in her lap and initially didn't provide Desiree any eye contact. She eventually looked up and said, "One of my fantasy books."

"Well, sorry to disturb your reading, but I wanted to take a moment and talk to you about something."

Maya slowly closed her book, making sure the bookmark was sticking out so she wouldn't lose her place. She folded her legs under her on the bed, giving Desiree her undivided attention. "Am I in trouble?"

Desiree closed the door and sat on the bed next to her. "I wouldn't say that exactly."

Maya put her hands up, as if surrendering. "I didn't take the knife this time if it's missing."

A glimmer of a smile formed on Desiree's lips. "No, the knife is still where it needs to be." She shifted her vision to Maya's neck. "It's about the necklace I gave you."

Maya reached for the necklace, stroking the heart-shaped pendant on the end. "What about it? Is something wrong with it?"

"That's what we need to find out."

Maya peeked down at the necklace, then back up at Desiree, giving her a slow, appraising glance. "I'm confused."

"Let me ask you this: Have you noticed anything different about yourself since you've been wearing the necklace?"

Maya deliberated before responding. "I feel good when I have it on. Especially knowing it was a gift from Grandma."

"And I'm sure she's looking down from up above and smiling. But is there anything else that feels different when you wear it?"

Maya clasped her hands together and twirled her thumbs. "Um … I can't think of anything else."

Desiree thought it was time to take off the kid gloves and let her know what happened to Sophia to see if that would help progress the discussion along.

"Do you remember the lady who came to our door yesterday?"

"Of course. The one causing all the trouble."

"Yes. Well, something happened to her today, and an ambulance had to come and take her to the hospital."

"Oh, that's not good. I hope she'll be all right."

"Me, too."

Silence followed as Desiree made it a point to pause to see if Maya had anything else to say. After the awkward silence carried on longer than Desiree would have expected, she said, "Do you remember when me and Mr. Jayden were in your room yesterday after the woman left?"

"Yes."

"And do you remember what you said?"

"I told you not to worry about apologizing to me because you got very mad at her."

"Okay, and then you said something else," Desiree said with an exaggerated nod, as if to coax her into remembering the rest.

"And that was it. You both left the room."

Desiree puffed out her cheeks and exhaled, attempting to muster up enough patience to stay calm. She didn't know if Maya was just being difficult or somehow conveniently leaving off the most puzzling part of what she had said. With her initial plan failing miserably, Desiree had to reroute the discussion and focus on why she had come into the room in the first place.

Desiree pointed to the necklace dangling around Maya's neck. "Have you been wearing this necklace all the time since I gave it to you?"

"Yup. I only take it off when I go to sleep."

"How would you feel if I asked you to take it off for a few days?"

"Why?"

"It's because ... because we're concerned the necklace is changing your behavior."

Maya raised her eyebrow in a questioning slant. "What do you mean by *my behavior*?"

"You've been acting funny since I gave you the necklace."

"I'm still confused. What are you trying to say?"

"I'm not sure why you don't remember, but you made a comment about the lady who came to the door, saying she wouldn't be giving us any more trouble. It was as if you knew something was going to happen to her."

Several wrinkles developed on Maya's forehead. "Sorry, but I don't remember saying that."

"You definitely did, and Mr. Jayden heard it, too."

"I'm sure I would have remembered."

"I'm not going to sit here and lie to you. We know what we heard."

"So, are you asking me to stop wearing the necklace?"

"I think that would be a good idea."

"And what if I say no?" Maya asked while stroking the heart-shaped pendant.

Desiree quickly caught herself as her motherly reflex almost kicked in, ready to fend off this revolt against her authority. She forced a smile. "I think it would be disappointing. I'm just asking you to stop wearing it for a few days to see what happens."

"But it was a gift from Grandma."

Desiree closed her eyes, doing her best to remain calm and avoid this talk from escalating. "It's not permanent. I can give it back to you depending on how things go."

"I don't think that's fair. You want to take the necklace away from me for something I don't even remember doing? Do you think Grandma would like for you to take away her gift to me?"

Desiree bit her bottom lip, as she hadn't thought about looking at it from that perspective. She had to give Maya credit for how she could manipulate a discussion in her favor.

For a split-second, Desiree contemplated wielding her mom powers again to get her to take off the necklace, but decided against it. *If at first you don't succeed, try, try again.*

Desiree reached out and patted Maya on the shoulder. "You made your point. You can keep it on for now. But know we may need to revisit this discussion depending on how things go."

Chapter 17

Jayden locked the bedroom door and made his way to Desiree's closet. She'd told him about her discussion with Maya and her unsuccessful attempt to get her to stop wearing the necklace. He understood Desiree's reasoning for not pushing harder to get her to stop wearing it. He floated the idea again of swiping the necklace while she slept. Desiree wasn't completely opposed to it, but still didn't like the option, especially now knowing how much Maya treasured the gift.

Jayden put those concerns aside, with his mind now focused on something else. He wanted to find the keepsake box to see if there were any other items included that might have been of interest and could provide clues about the origins of this mysterious piece of jewelry. He was taking a risk by snooping around, but with each unexplained occurrence, his red flag count continued to grow, and he didn't want to regret waiting too long to take matters into his own hands.

Desiree had never told him where she'd kept the box, and he guessed the first place to look would be her closet. At last check, she was in the living room, taking a nap on the sofa, giving him a short window of time to search for the box.

He opened the walk-in closet door and marveled at how neat Desiree kept it. A four-tier metal shoe rack was pushed up against the wall on his left, filled with various types of footwear. On his right stood a five-foot-long wooden cubby shelf holding an assortment of handbags. Her clothes hung from a metal rod, neatly positioned according to each clothing item. All of her jeans, dress pants, blouses, and jackets were grouped together. Above the hanging clothes was a shelf containing rows of black wicker baskets.

Jayden was reluctant to start moving things around, fearing she'd notice something out of place. He grabbed his phone and took pictures of the closet to help remember where everything was positioned. He intended not to go overboard while searching for the keepsake and allotted a five-minute limit to complete his quest. He commenced with a quick visual scan, hoping to see the keepsake box out in the open so there would be no need to move anything aside.

He frowned. "I knew it wouldn't be that easy," he said after an unsuccessful attempt to find the box out in the open.

He pushed aside random articles of clothing hanging from the rod, hoping the box might have been hidden behind them. He kneeled, eventually dropping on all fours to lower his viewpoint, and scanned the floors of the closet.

With no success, he grabbed a step stool, off to the side, and positioned it by the shelf holding the wicker baskets. Although standing on the highest step, he couldn't see what was in each basket without taking them down or tilting them forward toward his face. He grabbed the first bin, which felt quite light. He pulled it down, spotting an assortment of scarves and not much else. The second bin was marginally heavier and contained a collection of baseball caps Desiree liked to wear whenever she had to run out and didn't want to bother doing her hair. He grabbed the third basket, which contained a collection of smaller handbags.

Before he could place the third basket back on the shelf, he heard a knock.

"Shit," he whispered, placing the basket back in its place.

He stepped down from the stool and put it back where he'd found it. He scanned the closet floor to make sure nothing had dropped before he exited and closed the door. "Hold on."

He unlocked the door and opened it to see Maya in the doorway.

"Am I disturbing you?"

"Uh … no. I was in bed, resting."

Maya peeked behind her. "Can we talk?"

"Sure. What's up?"

"Do you mind if I step into the room? I don't want my mom to see me talking to you."

Jayden waved her in and shut the door.

"My mom told me something happened to our neighbor downstairs, and you saw her on a stretcher in the lobby."

"Yes. That's true."

"Do you know what happened?"

"No. Her eyes were closed, and she was covered up to her neck with a sheet."

Maya looked at the floor, then back up at Jayden. "That's sad. I hope she feels better soon."

"Me, too."

Maya folded her arms behind her back and stood still for a second, as if contemplating what to say next. "Can I ask you a question?"

"Sure."

"Do you think I had anything to do with her getting hurt?"

"Of course not. Now, why would I think that?"

Maya rocked on her heels. "I don't know. I just had a feeling."

She looked around the room before focusing back on Jayden, gently stroking the pendant on her necklace. "My mom said she was worried about me wearing this necklace."

"Okay."

"She told me you were worried, also. Is that true?"

"Yes."

"Why are you worried?"

Jayden's heartbeat quickened as the discomfort he felt in this interaction grew steadily stronger. "You seem to be different since you've been wearing the necklace."

"How?"

Jayden felt like a witness on the stand being cross-examined. With his mind scattering in many different directions, he struggled to find a tactful way to explain his concerns. "I noticed you were saying things that weren't making sense."

Maya didn't respond and continued to rock back and forth. He sensed she wanted him to continue with more of an explanation.

"For example, you said our neighbor downstairs wouldn't be causing us any more trouble last night, and it seems pretty strange she had a medical emergency today."

Maya finally stopped rocking. "I thought you said you didn't think I had anything to do with her getting hurt."

"Well … I don't think you had any direct involvement with whatever happened to her. I just want to know how you had a feeling something might happen to her."

Maya sighed heavily. "I don't understand. Both you and Mom told me the same thing, but I don't remember saying anything about our neighbor not causing us any more trouble. Am I the one going crazy?"

Jayden ventured into unfamiliar waters since this was the first time he'd interacted with Maya in a contentious conversation. He didn't want to say anything he'd regret and risk upsetting Maya any further, especially not completely understanding why her state of mind had been shifting and why she couldn't remember certain parts of their discussion the previous night.

"Nobody is saying you're crazy." He sighed. "Why don't we end the discussion here? If you want, we can talk about this another day." Jayden produced a cursory smile and reached out for a fist-bump.

Maya remained silent and did not immediately reciprocate. She stared at Jayden, and after a few seconds, she turned around and left his arm hanging in the air, waiting for the fist-bump he would never receive.

Chapter 18

Later that evening, Jayden opened the box and followed the instructions to set up the nanny cam. He was amazed at how this piece of technology, which could fit into the palm of his hand, could stream extended hours of video, record using night vision, and have two-way audio capabilities. He set up the cube-shaped camera and placed it on the dresser facing the bed.

"Do you know how to work this thing?" Desiree asked as she watched him set up the camera.

"No, but that's what instructions are for."

He installed the camera app on his phone. After following the instructions and connecting the camera to Wi-Fi, he sat next to Desiree and opened the app to see a live video of them sitting on the bed. "Well, what do you know? It actually works."

He approached the bedroom light switch and turned it off. The video shifted to a black and white image with gray undertones, allowing him to clearly see the bedroom, although the room was dark. He showed Desiree the live video.

"Seems creepy. Looks like our eyes are glowing in the dark," she said.

Jayden turned back on the lights. "Yeah, I'm not going to lie, it will feel weird being recorded while we're sleeping."

"Is it going to record us the entire time we're sleeping?" Desiree asked.

"No. I have it set to record from twelve to six in the morning and only if it detects movement."

Desiree let out a huge sigh. "I'm getting cold feet now."

"What do you mean?"

"I'm worried about what the camera's going to show during the night."

"You did agree to move forward with this, right?"

"Yeah, I guess so. It's one thing to talk about it, but to actually see it set up and ready to record us sleeping is a bit unnerving for me now."

"Too late to turn back now. We spent the money on this thing, and I think it's time for us to see exactly what's been going on during the night."

*****

Hours later, Jayden woke up, feeling discomfort in his hip from sleeping on his side too long. With his mind halfway between consciousness and sleeping, he shifted on his back with his eyes remaining closed. After a few seconds, his eyes opened as a small spark in his brain reminded him this was the night they were being recorded. He touched his phone, with a time of 2 a.m. appearing. He looked over to the right to see a lump under the sheets, showing that Desiree was sleeping peacefully.

He raised his head off the pillow and peeped over at the dresser. It was too dark for him to see the camera, but he assumed it was still recording. He considered reaching for his phone to review any potential footage captured up until this point, but decided against it since they had only been asleep for a couple of hours.

*****

Jayden woke up after feeling the bed move. Daylight consumed the room, as the sun had already risen. He turned his head to see what had disturbed his sleep. Desiree had shifted her body to the side, looking half-asleep. A hint of anticipation enveloped him, thinking what the video might have captured during the night.

He propped his back up against his pillows and focused on the dresser to see the camera positioned where he'd left it. He grabbed his phone and opened the app to find five recorded files captured during the night. He only remembered waking up once, but he never left the bed. He also wasn't sure how sensitive the motion detector was on the camera and whether it only captured movement when someone left the bed.

He clicked on the first recording with a timestamp of 2 a.m. The recording showed him reaching over to the nightstand for his phone, which made sense because this was the only time he remembered waking up and performing any substantial movement during the night.

He clicked on the second file, which showed Desiree getting out of bed at 2:48 a.m. She staggered with her first few steps and eventually disappeared out of camera view, heading in the direction of the bathroom. After about ten seconds, the recording had stopped since the camera no longer detected any movement.

He clicked on the next file and noted the recording began four minutes after the first file had ended. The recording showed Desiree walking back into view and coming near her side of the bed. She lay back down and pulled the covers over her, prompting the recording to end. Jayden believed there was nothing suspicious, as it appeared to be one of Desiree's regular nightly bathroom visits.

He held off from clicking on the next recording due to seeing Desiree shift in the bed. She had her back to him, but stopped moving after a few seconds. He clicked on the next recorded file, which had a timestamp of 4:10 a.m. Desiree rose in bed before swinging her legs and putting her feet on the floor. She slowly stood and remained in the same position for a few seconds. He could tell something was off, and this was not Desiree's normal range of motion. She pivoted around and stumbled before taking a few steps. Her arms dangled down, close to her body, as she shuffled her way out of camera view, back in the direction of the bathroom. A sudden chill gripped Jayden after he realized the camera most likely captured Desiree sleepwalking. The recording abruptly ended after she had left the camera's field of vision.

Jayden's concerns increased, with thoughts of what he might see in the last recorded file. He clicked on the file and noted the timestamp indicated that twenty minutes had elapsed since the third recording had ended. Desiree had come back into camera view and stopped abruptly in the middle of the room. He couldn't completely tell, but it seemed like she was gripping something in her right hand. She stumbled toward the bed with uneven steps, as if she had a slight limp. She arrived at the edge of the bed, rocking slightly. Jayden's creep factor rose significantly, realizing how oblivious he'd been to the situation while he'd slept and at the mercy of whatever Desiree's unconscious mind prompted her to do. She eventually stopped rocking and lay down on the bed, pulling the sheets back over her.

Jayden stared at the phone, attempting to process what he'd just seen. It was unclear to him what she'd had in her hand, and it didn't appear she'd dropped it anywhere before she'd gotten back into bed. With the sheet still covering them both, he imagined it was possible that whatever she had could be found under the sheets.

He gripped the edge of the sheet resting on his stomach and gently lifted it to take a peek. He initially didn't see anything. As he continued to scan the area, he spotted a few streaks of red dotting the sheet, sparking a shot of anxiety, as he was afraid to process where those streaks could be from. He observed further, noticing red smudges on Desiree's hand, and that was when he spotted a tube of red lipstick jutting out from under her wrist.

Desiree continued to sleep, apparently clueless as to the tube of lipstick she'd dragged into bed with them.

He reached toward the lipstick and tugged on it to try to dislodge it from under her wrist. She shifted her arm, which allowed him to grab the tube and place it on the nightstand. Based on viewing the last recording, he could only surmise she'd taken the lipstick from the bathroom. With his curiosity in full bloom, he lifted the sheets and rotated his feet off the bed. He found a few smudges of red on his thigh, which he wiped off with his fingers.

He marched toward the bathroom, having no idea what awaited him on the other side of the door. He grabbed the knob, twisting it slowly, and opened the door. He switched on the light, first looking at the floor. The off-white tiles seemed undisturbed. However, his peripheral vision caught a glimpse of something written on the mirror above the sink that looked familiar.

Chapter 19

"108. What the hell do those numbers mean? This is making no sense," Jayden whispered.

He received confirmation that Desiree was indeed the culprit of the first instance of seeing those numbers written on the wall in the hallway. He studied the rest of the bathroom to make sure he wasn't missing any additional graffiti tags she might have secretly left behind.

He leaned his hands on the sink, taking a few deep breaths to try to clear his head. The red flags continued to mount, highlighted by Desiree's mysterious sleepwalking habits, her unconscious obsession with the number 108, a strange necklace, and Maya's new freaky foreshadowing abilities. He was tempted to pack up his clothes and leave until things calmed down, but he refrained from following through with that impulse. Before thinking any further about running out, he wanted Desiree to know about her nighttime activities.

He approached the bed, spotting Desiree lying on her back with her eyes closed. As he came closer, her eyes opened, prompting him to take a step back. He imagined her sleepwalking episodes had only occurred during the night. But he wanted to make sure this was the conscious version of Desiree before he moved forward with any interaction.

"What? You act like you've seen a ghost?" she said.

"You surprised me with how fast you woke up."

"I've been up for a few minutes. I heard you in the bathroom and was lying here, trying to remember a weird dream I had." She stopped and squeezed her fingers along the bridge of her nose. "I also woke up with a little headache."

She pointed to the dresser. "I'm almost afraid to see what the camera recorded. Did you already check?"

"Yes."

She winced. "Is it anything concerning?"

"I'll let you be the judge of that."

Desiree let out a huge sigh. "I'm not sure I want to know now."

"If you're curious, you can start by looking under the sheets."

Desiree rotated her legs from under the sheets and swung her feet to the floor. She quickly jumped up, taking several steps away from the bed. "Don't scare me like that. What's under the sheets?"

Her quick exit from the bed had only pulled back the sheets halfway, but she couldn't tell anything was initially wrong.

"Be my guest and pull back the sheets," Jayden calmly said.

She raised her left arm and touched Jayden's shoulder as she continued to stare with her vision transfixed on the bed. Jayden flinched and leaned to the side, away from her touch.

She broke her gaze from the bed and glared at him. "Did you pull away from my hand?"

Jayden couldn't deny he had, although it was an involuntary movement that he hadn't expected. But he also didn't want to allude to the fact that he was now a little fearful of Desiree based on her strange sleepwalking habits that probably occurred more frequently than she imagined.

"Sorry, you just scared me with your reaction."

Desiree returned her attention to the bed. She reached for the top of the sheet, slowly pulling it down until she caught a glimpse of the first red streak.

She quickly let go of the sheet, stumbling backward. "What the hell is that?"

She inspected her body and recoiled after noticing the red smudges on her hand and part of her white pajama shorts. With her mouth gaping open, she ran into the bathroom and turned on the water. Jayden did not move and waited to see what her reaction would be after seeing her handiwork on the mirror.

"What the hell is going on? Is this lipstick?" she asked.

Jayden neared the bathroom entrance to see Desiree washing her hands and looking at the mirror. She shut off the water and continued to stare at the mirror. She put her head down while taking in a few deep breaths. Jayden kept quiet, allowing her to process the moment.

She finally looked back up at the numbers. "I … I don't know what to say."

Jayden temporarily put his uncomfortable feelings aside and rubbed Desiree's back.

Her eyes watered. "I swear I'm not doing this on purpose. I don't remember sleepwalking, and I have no clue what these numbers mean."

Jayden continued to rub her back and stayed silent.

"I guess I also can't deny now that I was the one who wrote those numbers on the hallway wall last weekend." She wiped a tear escaping from her right eyelid and dribbling down her cheek. "I'm not sure why I'm so emotional now. I guess I'm just totally confused and honestly embarrassed."

She grabbed a washcloth, wetting it with hot water, and then wiped her face. She slowly pulled the washcloth away and concentrated back on the numbers. Jayden continued to stand by the door without saying a word.

"Did you find this tube of lipstick in the bathroom?"

"No. Because you kept it with you when you went back to bed. That's where the red smudges came from on the sheets."

"Is the lipstick still under the sheets?"

Jayden shook his head. "I found it under the sheets before you woke up and put it on the nightstand."

Desiree wet a handful of tissues and wiped the mirror as the numbers transformed into a blob of red streaks. She continued to wipe until the red streaks faded completely, and she could see herself clearly in the mirror without any lipstick drawn numbers distorting her face. She leaned closer into the mirror, putting her fingers along the top of her cheeks and pulling down, exposing the red flesh on the underside of her eyelids.

She focused on Jayden's reflection in the mirror. "And before you ask, I don't want to see the recording right now. Based on what I'm seeing, I have a good enough idea about what happened."

She pulled back from the mirror and pivoted toward Jayden. "Are you too creeped out to hug me?"

The initial answer in Jayden's mind was a definite yes, but he felt bad seeing how confused and vulnerable Desiree looked. He knew the morally right thing to do would be to suck it up and comfort her with a warm hug.

Pushing all of his fears aside, he opened his arms and embraced her tightly. After a few seconds, she pulled away from him and let out a small gasp.

"What? What's the matter?"

Chapter 20

Desiree did not immediately respond to Jayden's question. She made her way back to the bed. He followed and stood by her, waiting for a response.

"I'm remembering more about the dream I had, which is putting what I did in perspective."

Jayden continued to stand with his arms folded, eagerly waiting to hear about her dream and what it might reveal.

"I remember walking in the hallway of my mother's house, which was a lot longer than what I remember in real life. I saw doors on both sides of the hallway, and I tried opening the first door I came to, but it was locked. I kept going and tried opening the next door, and it was also locked," she said before stopping.

Her eyes fluttered for an instant, and crease lines formed on her forehead before she continued. "I came to the last door on my right, which I was able to open, and from the looks of it, this was my mother's bedroom. There was a desk pushed up against the wall with a sheet of paper and a pen. I remember going to the desk and writing something. Then I remembered hearing a loud bang in the hallway. I ran to see what it was, but tripped and fell, hurting my knee. I tried to get back up and run, and that's all I can remember.

Seems like I could have been acting out my dream as I was sleepwalking."

Jayden nodded. "That definitely puts things in perspective. But I still want to know what the number 108 means. This is the second time we're seeing it. It must have some significance."

Desiree shrugged. "I have no idea."

He rubbed the side of his jaw, thinking back to the previous weekend. "Do you remember anything about the dream you had last weekend when I found you sleepwalking?"

"No. I'm sorry, I don't."

His lips curled up into a small grin, trying to lighten the mood. "Of course, you don't remember your dream. It would have been nice to see what you were doing in your dream when you punched the wall."

"Sorry, can't help you there," she said before stepping in front of Jayden.

"Now that you have an idea of where my mind was while I was sleepwalking, does this mean you won't be running out on me and Maya anytime soon?"

Although the thought had definitely crossed Jayden's mind, he couldn't see himself abandoning them. Based on Desiree's dream description, he felt more at ease about the situation since it provided him with insight into the behavior he'd witnessed as she sleepwalked. He was extremely intrigued about what the dream meant, especially since Desiree hadn't talked too much about her mother since they'd been dating.

Jayden blinked several times after realizing he'd paused longer than he probably should have to answer her question. "No. I don't think I'll be running out anytime soon," he said, then opened his arms for a hug.

Chapter 21

Later that Sunday afternoon, Jayden and Desiree sat at the kitchen table, waiting for Maya to join them for dinner. For most of the day, Maya had confined herself to her room and did not have much interaction with anyone.

Jayden stared at his plate, sniffing the aroma of baked ziti with garlic bread. He drummed his fingers on the edge of the table. "I'm trying to be considerate and wait for Maya to come to the table, but if she doesn't come out shortly, I'm diving into this plate."

Desiree grabbed her phone. "I texted her to let her know dinner was ready. Not sure what's taking her so long."

She left and walked to Maya's room. Jayden heard a knock on Maya's bedroom door and muffled talking. Desiree eventually made her way back to the table.

"She's coming. She had her head buried in one of her books."

Maya shuffled her way into the kitchen and showed no interest in looking Jayden's way. She put a spatula full of baked ziti on her plate and moved a fork full of food toward her mouth to take a bite.

Desiree grabbed her wrist. "Wait! Aren't you forgetting something?"

Maya quickly put her fork back on the plate.

"You know we need to say grace before we can start eating," Desiree said before she bowed her head and reached out to both Jayden and Maya to hold hands.

Jayden followed by grabbing Desiree's hand, and as he reached for Maya, she grabbed onto his pinky finger with a flimsy grip and refused to clutch the palm of his hand.

Jayden didn't bother to correct her grip since she didn't seem interested in holding his hand.

After Desiree finished saying grace, Maya immediately dug into her food without saying a word.

Jayden darted his eyes in Maya's direction to see her wearing the necklace with the silver heart-shaped pendant swinging forward whenever she leaned over her plate to eat. The only sounds in the room were the clinking of silverware against the ceramic dinner plates.

Desiree wiped sauce from her mouth and looked around the table. "I'm sorry, everybody, but the silence is killing me. I thought we would all be happy and ready to chat, knowing we have an extra day off from school and work with Labor Day tomorrow. Am I right?"

"True," Jayden said.

Maya remained quiet and didn't acknowledge Desiree's question.

"So what do you want to talk about?" Jayden asked.

"I don't know, and I don't care, as long as I'm hearing some talking around this table," she said.

Jayden took a sip of his black cherry wine cooler. "Okay. I say we should all make plans to go out tomorrow and take a walk around the area to see what's here. Maybe we can find some good restaurants or a local park to take a stroll. I think it would do us all some good to get out of the apartment for some fresh air."

"I think that's a great idea," Desiree said. "Don't you think so, also?" she asked Maya.

Maya continued to look down at her plate, eating, and did not respond.

Desiree stretched her arm and knocked on the table beside Maya's plate. "Do you hear me, Maya? I'm talking to you."

Maya kept her head down and provided Desiree with a side-eye glance. "Fine, if that's what you want to do," she said in a cold tone.

Jayden could see Desiree's jaw clenching, sensing this dining session was about to go south.

Desiree put her fork down and gave Maya a frigid stare. "I need you to watch your tone, young lady. I'm not one of your friends from school whom you can catch an attitude with and not worry about any consequences. And if you haven't figured it out by now, if you piss me off, there will be consequences. Now, I don't know what's been going on with you lately, but you really need to get your act together and quickly." She reached over and pulled Maya's chin in her direction. "Do you understand me?"

Maya reluctantly looked at her and nodded.

Desiree continued to hold her chin. "Moving your head up and down is not an answer. I'll ask again: do you understand me?"

Maya puffed out her cheeks and exhaled. "Yes, Mom."

Jayden kept his head buried in his plate and didn't bother looking up. There wasn't much he could say to lighten the mood, and he accepted the fact that this was going to be a somber and awkward evening at the dinner table.

Maya quickly finished her food and wiped her mouth. She stared at Desiree and asked, "Can I leave the table now?"

"As long as you know to wipe your plate and silverware and put them in the sink," Desiree responded.

Maya grabbed her plate and stepped near Jayden, who continued to sit, enjoying a second helping of garlic bread. Jayden shifted his vision up as she passed. She finally looked at him and returned an icy glare, catching Jayden off guard, as he'd never seen Maya throw him a look with such a hostile undertone.

She placed her plate and silverware in the sink, rinsing them off with water before leaving the kitchen and heading down the hallway to her room. Jayden couldn't tell completely, but it sounded like her bedroom door slammed with more force than usual.

Desiree snatched her head up from her plate. "Did she just slam her door?"

Jayden knew if he said yes, Desiree would make a beeline for her room, and this evening would turn out exponentially worse for Maya. Although he believed Maya deserved some tough love, he continued to remain firm that the necklace was to blame for her change in behavior.

"She may have—"

Before Jayden could finish talking, Desiree jumped up from the table. He reached out and grabbed her arm. "Hold on, Desiree! Can you please hear me out before you decide to go in there and deliver your version of swift justice?"

Desiree let out a hefty sigh and waited to hear what Jayden had to say.

He released her arm. "I know we talked about it before, but I'm telling you, that necklace is the problem. I don't know what it is about it, but I can almost guarantee if we were to get her to stop wearing it, she would go back to being the Maya we all know."

Desiree grimaced. "I don't see how the necklace is changing her behavior. Why would my mother give her a gift that was going to turn her into a little monster? It makes no sense. Did you ever think maybe this is a consequence of her hormones changing since she's about to turn twelve and becoming one of those preteens with an attitude?"

"I would have agreed with you, but since when does a shift in attitude come with the ability to foreshadow events? That's definitely not normal. Don't you agree?"

Desiree puffed out her cheeks. "Yeah, you make a good point. I've been thinking about that, also, but I guess I didn't want to believe what you were saying."

Jayden took another bite of his garlic bread and wiped his mouth. "She didn't want you to know, but I talked with her yesterday about the necklace."

"Oh, really?"

"She said you told her about Sophia being wheeled away on a stretcher and wanted to know if I thought she had something to do with it."

"Interesting. What did you tell her?"

"Of course, I told her no. I also brought up the conversation we had when she told us she had a feeling Sophia wouldn't be bothering us again."

"I'm curious as to how she responded."

"She said she didn't remember saying that."

"That's the same thing she told me. I don't know if she's that good at keeping her lie going or if she really doesn't remember."

"I could tell she was starting to get upset, so I decided to end our little talk."

Desiree leaned her head back and then gazed back at Jayden. "She was probably trying to figure out if we were on the same page with our concerns."

"I agree. So, my next question is: since you didn't have any success with your mother and daughter talk to get her to stop wearing the necklace, are you still good with the plan to take it away from her while she's sleeping?"

"I want to say yes, but I'm afraid of how she might react once she realizes it's missing. She's going to know one of us took it, and that's going to set her off even more."

"Maybe it won't be as bad as you think once she's no longer wearing the necklace."

Desiree sat back down and fumbled with her fork. "I don't know. Let me think about it."

Chapter 22

Jayden yawned and grabbed the remote to flip the TV channel. He opted to spend the night back out in the living room, still feeling uncomfortable after receiving confirmation that Desiree's sleepwalking episodes were ongoing. He was reluctant to mention to Desiree his preference to sleep apart after seeing her confused and her emotional reaction to what had occurred the previous night. He wouldn't be able to sleep soundly if he chose to stay in the bedroom with her.

Although he wouldn't be present in the bedroom, he found comfort in knowing that the camera remained on and ready to capture any nighttime activity. He was eager to see what surprises the camera might catch. He was also interested to know if Desiree would have any additional dreams that might coincide with her sleepwalking activity, possibly providing more clues regarding the significance of the number 108.

Jayden leaned forward on the sofa, his mind now wandering to the other challenge with Maya's behavior. He learned from past experiences to always trust your instincts, and his gut was screaming that things would only get worse the longer Maya wore the necklace. It saddened him to see that their warm-hearted relationship had quickly turned sour due to such unusual circumstances.

He was tired of being an innocent bystander and wanted to take action. Even if it meant moving forward with swiping the necklace while Maya slept, without receiving Desiree's blessings. He understood this decision would upset both Desiree and Maya for different reasons, but he no longer cared.

It was a quarter to midnight, and he was almost certain Maya had fallen asleep. He muted the TV to see if he could pick up on any sounds coming from down the hallway. With his phone in hand, he started walking as the light from the torch lamp in the living room illuminated the hallway enough for him to confirm both Maya's and Desiree's bedroom doors were closed. He made it a point to step as close to the wall as possible, which he previously found would limit the floor from creaking.

He edged toward Maya's room and put his ear up against her door. He waited to confirm the silence before proceeding. He grabbed the doorknob and twisted, slowly pushing the door open. He expected to have the benefit of some light emanating from her nightlight, but he was met with total darkness instead. He activated the flashlight on his phone, making sure to initially point it to the floor. He aimed the flashlight near the bed to keep the beam from fully engulfing it. He did see the covers bunched up, indicating Maya was occupying the bed. He squinted in an attempt to figure out which way her head was positioned. He took two steps into the room and confirmed her head was facing away from him and toward the wall.

He came up to the dresser and moved the flashlight from left to right, getting a sense of where to start looking. On the edge of the dresser stood a small glass vase containing an artificial long-stemmed red rose. In addition, he noted a stuffed brown teddy bear, a picture frame, the letter *M* carved out of wood, and a glass tray filled with colorful elastic wristbands. He scoped the vanity to see several loose pictures of Maya and Desiree shoved into the edges where the mirror and frame met.

He reached for the glass tray and moved around the wristbands, making sure the necklace had not been hidden under the pile.

He rotated his head back to the bed to ensure Maya hadn't shifted her position. With the limited amount of furniture in Maya's room, the only other place Jayden figured the necklace could be was her nightstand next to the bed.

He carefully pivoted toward the nightstand. Its contents contained a pink ceramic lamp, a picture frame with a candid shot of Maya smiling, and two hardcover fantasy books piled on top of one another. He grabbed the books and shifted them over to make sure the necklace wasn't hiding. He was certain Desiree mentioned Maya would normally take off her necklace when she went to sleep, but it was nowhere to be found.

He turned his attention to Maya sleeping, and looked at the back of her neck, spotting his target. She either lied to Desiree or decided to keep the necklace on for whatever reason this time around while she slept. Jayden squinted, attempting to see exactly where the clasp was positioned around her neck. He laid eyes on the clasp in an exposed area of her neck, and available for him to try to unhook, although his mission would become much more complicated if he chose to proceed.

He rubbed his fingers together, studying Maya, and focused on listening to her heavy breathing. She appeared to be in a deep enough sleep and hadn't budged since he'd entered her room. He was also aware that the neck was a sensitive area for most people, and he'd be taking a huge risk putting pressure on the clasp to try to unhook it. Even if he managed to unhook the necklace, removing it would be more challenging since pulling it off would cause friction against her skin, which could potentially wake her up.

He bit down on his bottom lip, waffling back and forth on whether or not he should even attempt to remove the necklace. *I've come too far to give up now*. He took in a few deep breaths to relax his heart rate and steady his hands. He grabbed one of Maya's fantasy books from the nightstand and set it down on the edge of the bed. He leaned his phone up against the book to keep the flashlight angled toward his target.

He rubbed his hands against his sweatpants to remove any moisture before he reached toward the lobster claw clasp. The challenge was to pull back the lever on the clasp while keeping it steady enough to pull out the hook. This wasn't an easy task under normal circumstances, but trying to do it without putting too much pressure on Maya's skin made this exponentially more difficult.

He grabbed the clasp and gently tugged the necklace away from Maya's skin to give him slack to work with. He froze while continuing to hold the clasp to make sure Maya didn't move in response to his touch. Using the fingernail on his index finger, he tugged down on the clasp lever to pull it open. But the moisture on his fingertips caused his fingernail to slip, which snapped the clasp back into a closed position. Jayden snatched his hands back away from Maya's neck as this unexpected movement caused her head to jerk, although she remained facing the wall. He froze, hoping he hadn't awakened her. Once she settled down and stopped moving, he thought about making a second attempt to go for the clasp until her head rotated in his direction. He instinctively grabbed his phone and her book, ducking on the side of her bed. As stressful as the situation was, he almost couldn't help but smile at how stupid he must look trying to hide from her. He also thought if she found him, he'd be up shits creek without a paddle.

He kneeled on the floor with his head facing down. He had no clue if her eyes were now open, and she was peeking over the edge of the bed to see him hiding. He remained motionless, using his ears to gauge whether or not she was awake. He glanced over and remembered he'd left her door open. If she had woken up to see it, it would have definitely raised her suspicions. He held his position, and once he didn't hear any further movement, he assumed she might still be asleep.

He realized any additional attempts to continue with his mission would be foolish. He needed to accept this as a failed attempt and scurry his way out of her room to live to see another day.

He slowly raised his head, cresting the mattress, which allowed him to see her facing his way but with her eyes closed. He gently placed her book back on the nightstand before tiptoeing his way out of her room.

<h1 align="center">Chapter 23</h1>

Jayden opened his eyes, bothered by the pins and needles feeling in his left arm. He straightened out his arm, folded awkwardly under his side on the sofa. He raised into a seated position, flexing his arm to help ease the discomfort. It took him a few seconds to remember it was Labor Day and he had an extra day off to look forward to.

He observed the living room, with nothing but silence surrounding him. He held back a grin, amused at his failed attempt to remove the necklace from Maya's neck. *Things happen for a reason.* At least now, he didn't need to worry about Desiree's and Maya's predictable angry reactions about the missing necklace.

He grabbed his phone and searched for the nanny cam app, interested to see if there had been any activity recorded in Desiree's bedroom overnight. He opened the app, surprised to see only one recorded file. He clicked on the file, which showed a timestamp of 3:24 a.m. Desiree rose out of bed and swiveled her feet to the floor. She stayed still before standing with her arms hanging closely to her sides. She wobbled for a second, and then wandered toward the bathroom. She stopped in the middle of the room and pivoted her body, changing direction. She took a few steps, passing in front of the camera, and headed toward the bedroom door. The night vision accentuated the whites of her eyes, making them appear to be glowing in the dark as she passed the camera. Based on her awkward body movements, Jayden was almost certain she'd been in the middle of another sleepwalking session.

After a few seconds, the recording stopped once she moved out of view. Crease lines formed on Jayden's forehead as he struggled to figure out why there wasn't another recorded file showing her returning to the bed. He logged out of the app, and then back in to see if maybe that would refresh the screen and show additional recorded files from the evening, but that wasn't the case. The screen continued to show only one recorded file.

He leaned forward on the sofa, trying to figure out why there were no further recordings.

A rush of heat spread across his face, noting the chances she'd left the bedroom and never returned were extremely high. He scanned the living room, searching for anything that might be out of place, hinting that she'd been roaming around the area. He initially couldn't find anything concerning, which prompted him to stand to gain a better vantage point. He examined the area but didn't see anything of note. He peeked down the hallway, finding both Maya's and Desiree's bedroom doors closed.

He made his way into the kitchen, continuing his search for clues as to whether Desiree had been sleepwalking beyond the bedroom. Desiree had always been adamant about keeping the kitchen clean and organized. On top of the kitchen countertop sat a toaster oven, the Keurig coffee maker, clear canisters containing sugar and flour, a fruit bowl filled with red apples, and a wooden block holding her cutlery collection. All items were neatly pushed up against the black and white checkered ceramic backsplash, except for one. The wooden block holding her cutlery collection had been twisted away from the backsplash and teetered close to the countertop edge. Jayden examined further and noted one of the slots that should have been holding a butcher knife was empty.

"Oh shit," he whispered.

His theory on whether Desiree had been sleepwalking beyond her bedroom had been confirmed. And the worst part was that both Desiree and the knife were temporarily unaccounted for, and he had no clue what had happened while he'd slept on the couch.

He instinctively reached for one of the available knives, but stopped with his arm halfway to grab one. He winced, refusing to believe he was in any serious physical danger. He pulled his hand back, making his way out of the kitchen, and peered down the hallway.

He took a few steps and was immediately greeted by the floor creaking in unison with his footsteps. He stopped and listened for any movement. He continued, shifting his walking path toward the edge of the wall to curtail the noises coming from the floorboards. He stuck his head into the guest bathroom in the hallway and found nothing of note.

He neared Maya's closed bedroom door and halted his progress. He swung his head, looking over at Desiree's bedroom door, attempting to decide which room to enter first. After a few seconds of deliberating, he continued over to Desiree's door, putting his ear up against it with nothing but silence following. He grabbed the knob, slowly opening the door. He observed the rumpled sheets on the mattress; however, Desiree was nowhere to be found. He proceeded further into the room, scanning the area for any activity. He whipped his head to the left, spotting the dresser, and noted the camera was in its expected place and seemed undisturbed.

His next target for exploration was the bathroom. With the bathroom door cracked open, he placed his head between the frame and the door. He peered through the six-inch opening and focused on the reflection in the mirror to see if it revealed anything of concern. The mirror did not show any markings, and based on the reflection, it didn't show anyone in the shower stall. He gently pushed the door open and came up empty in his pursuit to track down any clues as to Desiree's whereabouts.

Although he didn't think she'd be there, he strolled over to the walk-in closet and took a peek, validating his assumption. That only left one room in the apartment to be checked.

He struggled mightily to believe all was well, and there would be a logical explanation as to what had happened. He'd always been a glass-half-full type of individual, although some situations made it extremely difficult for him to continue to believe and have faith in that expression. This was, by far, one of those challenging situations that he'd prayed was nothing but a false alarm.

He reached for his phone after feeling it buzz in his pocket. He hoped to see a message from Desiree explaining her whereabouts, but his phone displayed what appeared to be a spam call. After silencing the call, he tilted his head back and closed his eyes, with a glimmer of common sense hitting him. He was amazed at how stressful moments could cloud someone's judgment and prevent them from thinking rationally. He dialed Desiree's cell phone, kicking himself for not thinking of this sooner. He listened for her ringtone, but didn't hear anything.

He placed the phone back in his pocket after his idea did not yield any positive results and continued into the hallway. He stopped in front of Maya's door, saying a silent prayer and hoping for the absolute best. He puffed out his cheeks and blew out a large exhale before grabbing the knob and cracking the door open.

He was immediately greeted by seeing someone's bare foot on the floor near Maya's bed. He opened the door further and spotted Desiree sitting on the floor with her back propped up against Maya's bed and her head slouched. Beyond Desiree, Jayden spotted a lump under the sheets, which he assumed represented Maya's body occupying the bed.

He scurried over to Desiree and kneeled to commence with a quick visual scan of her body to see if he could find any apparent injuries. She was dressed in pink pajama shorts and a matching tank top, which allowed him to easily confirm there were no obvious wounds on her exposed skin. He zeroed in on her chest, elated to see the rise and fall around her ribcage, showing that she was at least breathing. It simply appeared that she was asleep.

He reached to nudge her awake, but quickly pulled his hand back after spotting the missing butcher knife resting between her legs on the floor. He leaned back away from her with his heart beating at maximum speed. He carefully reached between her legs and grabbed the knife, looking at it closely for any residue on the blade or handle. The knife seemed clean as he placed it on the dresser. He then turned his attention to Maya.

He made his way to the other side of the bed to avoid having to lean over Desiree on the floor. He swallowed in an attempt to wet his parched throat, and motioned the sign of the cross before leaning over and grabbing the edge of the sheet, slowly pulling it back. Maya's head first came into view, faced in his direction. He didn't see any injuries around her head.

He continued to pull down the sheet. He first observed the necklace around her neck, and then her torso became visible, covered by a white T-shirt. He concentrated on her midsection and relaxed after seeing her breathing. He pulled the sheet all the way down to her feet, seeing her curled in the fetal position, confirming she appeared to be physically unharmed. An overwhelming sensation of relief followed as he covered Maya back up to her neck.

This relief was only temporary since the question remained as to why Desiree would bring a knife into Maya's bedroom and sleep beside her bed, as if guarding her from someone or something.

Jayden rounded the bed, kneeling in front of Desiree again. He gently rubbed the side of her slouched head with the back of his fingers.

"Desiree?" he whispered.

Her head flinched before she lifted it with her eyes remaining closed.

"Desiree?" Jayden said in a soft tone.

Her eyes fluttered before they opened completely. She stared at Jayden, needing a moment to gather her senses. "Wh-where am I?"

"You're in Maya's room."

"But, how did I—"

"You were sleepwalking again."

She craned her neck to the side. "Am I on the floor?"

"Yes, and we need to get you out of here and back to your bed."

She put her hands out for Jayden to help her off the floor. He grabbed her hands, pulling her up to a standing position. Immediately upon standing, she swayed until she could steady her legs.

She frowned and reached for the back of her neck. "My neck is stiff," she said before turning to look at Maya sleeping. "Did you check on her? Is she okay?" she asked in a raspy tone.

"Yeah, she's fine."

Desiree reached over, hugging Jayden, presumably to use him as a crutch to help keep her balance. She faced the dresser and, without warning, pushed him away, stumbling to the point of almost falling, and put her two hands over her mouth. She pointed to the dresser before Jayden quickly discovered she was reacting to spotting the knife.

He put his index finger to his mouth to make sure she didn't follow up her scared reaction with a scream.

"Let's go outside, and I'll explain," he whispered.

She quickly stepped around Jayden and backpedaled out of Maya's room. Jayden grabbed the knife and took a quick look over at Maya to confirm she remained sleeping before he closed the door. Desiree continued to back up, appearing noticeably uncomfortable with Jayden holding the knife.

"It's okay, Desiree. Let me put the knife back in the kitchen, and then we can talk."

He entered the kitchen and placed the knife in the sink to be cleaned, especially since he didn't know where it had been. He reentered the hallway and did not see Desiree, as she'd already retreated into her bedroom. He entered the bedroom to see Desiree backed into the corner of the room by the rocking chair.

Jayden pumped his hands up and down. "Relax. It's okay."

"Why was there a knife in Maya's room?"

"I found it on the floor between your legs while you were sleeping."

Desiree's eyebrows furrowed. "Are you trying to tell me I left the bedroom, grabbed the knife from the kitchen, and walked back to Maya's room, and I don't remember any of this?"

"That would appear to be the case."

Desiree shook her head. "I'm not sure if I believe it."

"Maybe looking at the recording from the nanny cam would convince you," Jayden said as he raised his phone.

"Even if it showed me sleepwalking, we don't have any cameras anywhere else besides the bedroom, so we don't know for sure that's what happened."

"How else would you end up in Maya's room while sleeping on the floor with a knife between your legs?"

Desiree nervously tapped her right foot on the floor. "Please tell me you're not lying to me?"

"Why would I do that?"

"I ... I don't know. I just feel very vulnerable now since I have no clue what happened, and you could be telling me anything."

"Please ... please know that I'm telling you the complete truth. What sense would it make for me to bring a knife into Maya's room, anyway?"

Desiree didn't offer a response and continued to stand, staring at Jayden.

"Do you remember having a dream last night?" Jayden asked.

She held her gaze on him without speaking for a prolonged moment. "Now that you mention it ... yes."

"Do you remember what it was about?"

She pondered for a second. "Someone had broken into the apartment and was after Maya."

"Then that makes complete sense why you had a knife and were in Maya's room. You were trying to protect her. Now do you believe me?"

Desiree shrugged. "I guess so."

Jayden took a step toward her, and she backed up farther into the corner.

"What's wrong? You still don't believe what I'm telling you?"

"I ... I don't know what to believe."

Jayden backed away, giving her room with the hopes of improving her comfort level around him. "Would you agree with me if I say we should probably stop playing guessing games and bring you to the hospital for an evaluation?"

Desiree stopped rubbing her forehead and peered at Jayden. "What kind of evaluation?"

"Maybe a psych evaluation."

She grimaced. "Are you saying I'm going crazy?"

"I had a feeling you would take it that way."

"How else do you think I would take it?"

"Look, I'm concerned with what's been going on. You're not getting your proper rest because of the sleepwalking, you haven't been in the best of moods, you're having weird dreams, and now you're grabbing sharp objects while sleepwalking and don't remember any of it. I'm afraid you might wind up hurting yourself or maybe even me or Maya."

"There's no way in hell I would even think about doing that."

"And there lies the problem. While you're sleepwalking, you're unconscious and have no idea what's going on." Jayden stopped and pointed to his chest. "Do you know how freaking scared I was this morning? Knowing that you had left the bedroom while you were sleepwalking? Knowing that a knife was missing from the kitchen and not knowing what you did with the knife or if you hurt yourself or Maya? You already proved you can have violent tendencies while sleepwalking, and it makes it extra scary now if you're going to be running around with a knife. So, I hope you can understand where I'm coming from."

Desiree continued to stand with her eyes now watering, leading to tears trickling down her cheeks. "I … I'm sorry," she said, struggling to talk while the tears continued to flow. "I really don't know what's wrong with me."

Chapter 24

Desiree stepped through the emergency doors of Atrium Health Mercy Hospital with Jayden and Maya flanking her on both sides. They arrived at the registration desk and provided the necessary information for admission.

Maya had been relatively quiet during the ride over, still appearing to be confused as to why Desiree needed to make a trip to the emergency room, especially on the last day of her long weekend. Jayden had offered his best explanation of the situation, including telling her the details of Desiree's sleepwalking episode and bringing the knife into her room. Maya didn't seem all too surprised that she'd found out Desiree had been sleepwalking. She mentioned she had a hunch it was happening, but never brought up the subject. Although she did have concerns about why Desiree walked into her room with a knife.

Desiree looked around the emergency room, observing the variety of patients sitting and thinking about the reasons for their visits. Some patients appeared to be in serious pain based on their facial expressions and the low groans they would let out on occasion. Desiree had been admitted to an emergency room only once in her lifetime, and that was to treat a broken wrist when she was a preteen, close to Maya's age. She'd never thought about someone visiting an emergency room for anything other than a physical sickness or injury.

After waiting for an hour, her name was finally called. She entered the door, passing the receptionist, with Jayden and Maya close behind her. She followed one of the nurses to a bay area, which contained a rollaway bed, a counter with a sink, and various medical devices hanging from a whiteboard affixed to the wall. The room also included one chair, a stool, and a red hazardous waste bin, pushed up against a wall in the corner. Desiree sat on the edge of the bed as Jayden motioned for Maya to sit in the chair while he chose to stand. The nurse offered to bring in another chair, but he declined.

After the introductions were done, the nurse pulled the curtain dangling from a track on the ceiling shut and sat on the stool with a notepad. "What brings you in here today?" she asked.

Desiree shot Jayden a look before answering, "I guess you can say I'm having problems with my mental state."

The nurse frowned. "I'm so sorry to hear. Do you mind giving me more details on what's going on?" The nurse stopped and eyed both Jayden and Maya. "Or do you feel more comfortable talking about this without your family being present?"

Desiree hesitated a second before speaking. "No, they can stay."

The nurse turned her attention to Desiree. "Okay, ready when you are."

"I've been made aware I've been sleepwalking recently," Desiree stopped, waiting to see the nurse's reaction.

The nurse began jotting down notes. "Is this new, or have you experienced sleepwalking episodes before?"

"It's happened to me maybe once before … a while ago."

"Have there been any significant changes in your life recently that may be prompting these sleepwalking episodes now?"

"I recently moved to Uptown Charlotte. That's the only change I can think of."

The nurse continued writing on the notepad. "Has this move caused you any significant stress, besides the normal stress you might experience when moving?"

"No."

"Are you taking any medications right now?"

"No. But I've taken some melatonin tablets to help me sleep on occasion."

The nurse tapped the pen she was holding on her knee as she stared at Desiree with a stoned-face expression. "Tell me more about your sleepwalking. Do you remember anything about it? Did you hurt yourself at any point? Did you wake up in another room?"

Desiree's face flushed with embarrassment as she speculated on a response to those questions. She wasn't sure how much information she should provide. "No, I don't remember anything after it happens. And I did find myself waking up in another room."

The nurse peered at Desiree and then glanced over to Jayden. "So, is there a major concern that you might end up hurting yourself? Or is there something else going on with these sleepwalking sessions that scared you enough to make a trip to the ER?"

Desiree looked at Jayden, before focusing back on the nurse.

Jayden raised his hand in the air. "Do you mind if I jump in here?"

"Sure," the nurse said.

"I wanted to add more details. I'm worried because she's shown some violent tendencies while sleepwalking, especially the first time I caught her. She hurt her hand after punching the wall, but she doesn't remember any of it."

"That's an important piece of information to know," the nurse said.

"And this morning, she had another sleepwalking episode, and I found her in her daughter's room, sleeping on the floor with a knife between her legs."

The nurse's eyebrows rose for a second, but they quickly leveled off, as if attempting to hide her true reaction. She continued to write in the notepad at a quickened pace. She offered Desiree a critical squint. "And you have no recollection of doing any of this?"

"No, but I do remember having dreams after I wake up from sleepwalking. And it seems like the things I'm doing in my dreams, I may be acting out while I'm sleepwalking."

The nurse held a prolonged gaze on Desiree before continuing to write.

Desiree felt extremely vulnerable and embarrassed about whatever judgments the nurse had roaming around in her head. She found herself in uncharted territory, especially for someone who's always had her shit together. Typically, she was the one offering advice and helping others navigate through their various life challenges. Now, however, she found herself on the receiving end and at the mercy of medical professionals trying to help figure out her perplexing situation.

Desiree fought hard to fight off tears. She looked over at Maya, who displayed no discernible expression on her face. She had her hands folded in her lap, listening intently.

The nurse finished writing and looked at both Desiree and Jayden. "I can understand your concerns, and I think you made a wise choice to visit us today. Let me take your vitals, and we'll have a doctor come in and talk to you about your situation."

Chapter 25

Jayden left the hospital, heading back to Desiree's apartment to bring her an additional set of clothes, as the doctors had recommended she stay at least one night for observation. He'd left Maya to stay with Desiree while he made the trip back to the apartment.

He wasn't entirely surprised the hospital had decided to keep her. With Desiree's mental state in question, the hospital did not feel comfortable with releasing her, especially with her having the responsibilities of taking care of Maya. Since Desiree had no family in the area, Jayden had agreed to stay overnight at the apartment to watch Maya as a temporary solution until the doctors felt comfortable enough to release her. She'd also been assigned a social worker, who was scheduled to meet with Desiree within twenty-four hours of her being admitted to the hospital.

This raised additional fears for Jayden that she might be in the hospital longer than expected if the social worker decided she wasn't fit to return home anytime soon. Based on the possibility that Desiree had to stay in the hospital for longer than expected, Jayden planned to swing by his condo to pick up clothes and his laptop to work remotely.

Although Jayden's main concern was making sure Desiree received the help she needed at the hospital, a wave of anxiety bloomed as he thought about dealing with Maya on his own. She continued to wear the necklace, and he wasn't sure how much patience he could hold onto if she persisted with her less-than-appealing attitude. He also knew Desiree wouldn't be around, so if he chose to make a second attempt to swipe the necklace, it would be a one-on-one battle between him and Maya.

*****

After picking up clothes from his condo, he traveled back to Desiree's apartment to find another set of clothes for her. She had given him instructions on what she wanted, which entailed him going into the walk-in closet. A bit of guilt consumed him as the first thing he thought about after entering the closet was to hold off from finding her clothes and to make another attempt to find the keepsake box. He understood, in the grand scheme of things, that his wish to find the keepsake box should not have been a priority. But he also knew this would be his best chance to locate it without having to worry about anyone else walking around in the apartment.

He entered the closet, turning on the light. He grabbed a pair of blue jeans and a white T-shirt, as Desiree requested. He scanned the closet with his curiosity blossoming and decided to move forward with a second search for the keepsake box.

He placed her clothes on the stool behind him and dropped to his knees, pushing aside a few dresses she had hanging toward the back of the closet until he came upon a black hard-shell luggage carrier. He reached for the luggage and dragged it in front of him, laying it down on the floor. He unzipped it to see a few sweatshirts folded neatly, along with a lightweight burgundy nylon jacket. He thought it was odd that Desiree would have any unpacked clothes remaining in her suitcase. Her normal routine entailed immediately unpacking after arriving home from any trip. He moved aside the sweatshirts to see what else he could find in the luggage, and that's when he spotted the keepsake box hidden beneath the clothes.

His heart raced with excitement as he grabbed it and left the closet to allow more room to maneuver. Holding the box, he examined it closely while inhaling the strong cedar scent.

He remembered having difficulty opening the box when he'd first found it. He pulled it closer to his face and mashed his finger on the top, putting pressure on it and attempting to slide the door open, but like before, it didn't budge. He placed the box on the bed and tried again, using pressure from both hands to slide the door open. He snatched his right hand back after feeling a prick of pain on his pinky finger. He rotated his hand, seeing a splinter protruding from his pinky, which had drawn a speck of blood. Using the index finger and thumb on his left hand, he pinched the tip of the sliver of wood and pulled it out.

Grimacing at the annoying pain radiating around his fingertip, he walked into the bathroom and washed his finger with warm water. He opened the medicine cabinet and grabbed a small Band-Aid, wrapping it around his pinky.

He stopped for a second, thinking about the first time he'd tried to open the moving box containing the keepsake, which had also resulted in a cut, drawing blood. The superstitious side of Jayden told him this was a warning that he should put the box back in the luggage without opening it.

He observed the time, noting he'd been gone from the hospital probably longer than he should have been. He didn't want to raise any suspicions about what had taken him so long.

He grabbed the box, with plans to put it back in the luggage without opening it, but froze. With his curiosity festering, he reversed course and put the box back on the bed. He imagined he could make up an excuse if Desiree questioned what took him so long.

He analyzed the box once again to see if he'd missed anything in his quest to open it. He held the box, flipping it upside down and then on its side. He placed the box on the floor and hit the top with the side of his fist. He made one last attempt to open the box, and the top finally slid a notch. He continued sliding the top until it pushed far enough to the side to reveal its contents.

A card containing the birth announcement for Maya was the first item sitting at the top. Off to the side sat a hospital wristband that he assumed Maya wore as a newborn. Jayden carefully removed these items and placed them on the bed. The next few items in view were ultrasound images, Maya's hand and foot prints on a sheet of paper, and a sandwich bag containing several baby teeth and a separate bag containing a lock of hair. In addition, he came across a few miscellaneous birthday cards. He removed those items and laid eyes on an envelope with Maya's name and hand-drawn hearts. He opened the envelope and found a letter neatly folded.

Dee Dee,

Hope you and Maya are doing well. I wanted to wish my granddaughter a very happy first birthday. Can't believe this year went by so fast. Sorry I couldn't make it up there to celebrate with you and Maya, but I wanted to give her this necklace as a gift. I've had it for a while and was saving it for this special occasion, but there's a catch. I don't want you to give it to her right now. I want you to hold on to it and wait until she's older. And I guess your next question is, how long should I wait?

All I can say is if you have faith in your true self, your third eye will never fail you, and you'll know exactly when the time is right to gift her this necklace.

You will also see there is a second necklace that I want you to hold onto for now.

Until then, be well, and please give my granddaughter a huge kiss. And remember, the eyes only see what the mind is prepared to comprehend.

Love,
Mom

Jayden folded the note and put it back in the envelope. He focused on the bottom of the keepsake box and spotted two red velvet jewelry boxes. He picked up the first one and opened it, revealing an empty case. He imagined this was the box holding Maya's necklace. He reached for the second box, opened it, and saw a silver necklace with a heart-shaped pendant resting comfortably inside. It appeared to be a mirror image of the one Maya had been wearing.

Jayden quickly closed the second jewelry box and struggled to make sense of what he'd found. He was happy to confirm Desiree wasn't lying about her mother giving the necklace to Maya as a gift and her wish to wait until she was older to present it to her. But the presence of a second necklace that Desiree had never mentioned elevated his concerns. It was bad enough having one mysterious necklace in the household, but now there were two. Since Desiree's mother never alluded to it in the letter, he thought about who this necklace was meant for and whether it would provide the same type of foreshadowing abilities that Maya now possessed.

Putting those thoughts aside, Jayden experienced an additional sense of uneasiness with the odd references used by Desiree's mom in the letter. Having faith in her true self and trusting her third eye was not language Jayden would call normal. And the last sentence she wrote in the letter made this even more mysterious. Desiree never spoke about what her mother did for a living or her religious beliefs, so he struggled to interpret what she'd meant by these references in the letter. Whenever he'd tried to bring up the subject of her mother in the past, Desiree had never seemed interested in carrying on the conversation, and he never pushed her to talk about it.

He noted the time again, realizing he needed to get moving and head back to the hospital. He carefully placed the items back in the keepsake box, doing his best to remember exactly how everything had been positioned. He slid the cover back on top and entered the closet to put the box back where he'd found it in the luggage. He went into Desiree's nightstand, grabbed the undergarments she'd requested, and placed them with the outerwear he'd picked from the closet. He ran into the bathroom, picked up her toiletry case under the sink, and dropped it in a plastic bag, along with her clothes. He retraced his steps to the closet, confirming everything was in its proper place and nothing had been left out in the open. Once satisfied with his quick inspection, he left the apartment to make his way back to the hospital.

Chapter 26

"I thought you were never coming back," Desiree said as Jayden arrived.

She remained in the same bay area where he had left her. She'd been given a hospital gown to wear and was sitting upright on the rollaway bed with a thin sheet covering her.

He gave her the plastic bag with her clothes. "It took a while for me to go home first and pick up clothes and my laptop. And then you can add the time it took for me to go to your apartment for your clothes, and then pick up a few burgers for us, since I'm thinking you all were hungry."

He reached into a paper bag and handed a hamburger contained in a brown wrapper to Maya.

She smiled and said, "Thank you."

It seemed like forever since Jayden had seen her smile. He hoped this was the start of a turning point, although he remained leery because she continued to wear the necklace.

He reached into the bag to grab a hamburger for Desiree, but she waved him off. "I'm not hungry now."

"You might want to save this for later. Not sure how good the hospital food is going to be."

Desiree shook her head, declining to take the burger for later.

Jayden took a bite of his hamburger. "Did any doctors come in to talk with you?"

"Somebody came in about an hour ago to give me a cognitive test. They asked me some basic questions, checked my memory, and gave me a few simple problems to solve. They also drew blood, and I'm waiting for those results."

"I'm sure that's standard protocol for them to check."

"They were also waiting for a room to become available so they could move me out of this emergency bay area."

"Hopefully, that will happen sooner rather than later so they can get you somewhere quieter," he said.

Jayden focused on Maya, sitting comfortably and eating her hamburger. He felt this was a good opportunity to generate a bit of small talk to see how she would respond. "How you making out over there? Is the burger good?"

Maya nodded while chewing with her mouth full. Jayden didn't want to worry much about her nonverbal response since her mouth was full of food. There would be plenty of other chances for them to talk once they left the hospital.

*****

A couple of hours later, they had found a room for Desiree and were planning to move her, but there were a few unexpected delays. Jayden had planned to wait until she had been moved before leaving, but Desiree suggested they go back to the apartment since it was later in the afternoon and their long Labor Day weekend was coming to a close.

Jayden left the hospital with Maya trailing behind. After arriving in the visitor's parking lot, Maya finally broke her silence.

"You think my mom's going to be all right?"

"Absolutely. This trip to the hospital was all for precautionary reasons. The doctors want to make sure she's feeling okay before they allow her to come home."

Maya didn't offer a response as they neared Jayden's car and she reached for the rear passenger side door.

"You can sit up front if you want. You'll make me feel like I'm your chauffeur if you sit in the back," Jayden said.

Maya hesitated before opening the front passenger door.

Jayden started the car and thought about what he could say to remove the awkward silence. He couldn't have imagined ever coming to a point where he struggled to have a natural conversation with Maya. He had no clue what was going on in her head, or if Desiree was right and she was going through one of those preteen phases. But after reading the note her grandmother had left, it didn't do anything to calm his suspicions that she wore no ordinary necklace and that it was responsible for her new foreshadowing abilities.

"So, it's you and me until your mother comes back home from the hospital," Jayden said as he put the car in gear and drove off.

Maya offered a slight nod and rubbed the heart-shaped pendant while staring straight ahead. She finally twisted her head in Jayden's direction.

"Can I ask you a question?"

Jayden could see her looking his way based on his peripheral vision. He was trapped in the car with her for the next half an hour and at the mercy of whatever question was about to come out of her mouth.

"Of course," Jayden said, attempting to sound calm and confident.

"Do you want to marry my mom?"

Interesting question. "Would you be more upset if I said yes, or no, or I don't know?"

"It doesn't matter. Just curious."

"How about this answer. I would like to see how things go, and we'll see what the future holds."

"You still didn't really answer my question."

Jayden hoped he'd get away without answering the question directly.

"How about if I say I wouldn't be against marrying her, but we need to see how things go in the future. Is that a better answer for you?"

She rolled her eyes. "I guess so."

Jayden stopped at a red light. "Now, can I ask you a question?"

"Yup."

"Did your mom ever tell you much about your grandmother?"

Maya pursed her lips. "Why do you want to know?"

"Because your mom never talks about her, and I was curious to know who she was and what she was like."

Maya smirked. "Would you be more upset if I told you I don't know much about her or if I do know but don't want to tell you?"

A laugh escaped Jayden's lips. "Are you eleven going on thirty?" He pushed his foot on the accelerator as the light turned green.

"Well? I'm waiting for your answer," Maya said.

Jayden pondered coming up with a witty response. "It doesn't matter. I was just curious," he said with a thin smile.

"As my mom would say, touché."

Jayden laughed. "I'm speechless you even know how to use that term in the right manner. I bet you don't even know how to spell touché."

Maya shrugged. "Maybe … maybe not."

Jayden merged onto the highway.

"Well? I'm still waiting for your answer about your grandmother," Jayden said.

"Sorry, but I don't have much to tell you. My mom told me I was about two years old when she died, so I don't remember much about her."

"Did your mom tell you where she was living before she passed away?"

"She was living in a town near New Orleans. I don't remember the exact name."

"And did your mom tell you what she did for a living?"

"I have no clue."

Jayden imagined Maya wouldn't have known the answer to the question, but he believed it had been worth a shot to ask.

Maya rubbed her hands on her knees. "And that's about all I can tell you for now."

"How about her name?"

Maya cocked her head sideways. "Wait. My mom never even told you her name?"

"No, she didn't."

"That's a shame. I was told to call her Grandma Isy. It's short for Isabelle."

"Thanks. Good to know. Anything else about her?" Jayden asked.

"Nope. I'm all out of answers for you."

Jayden continued driving, feeling optimistic that he would soon learn more about Maya's grandmother. For now, he was content that he'd had a civilized talk with Maya without any hint of an attitude coming through. She seemed to be mostly back to her normal self, although Jayden was unsure of how long it would last.

Chapter 27

Desiree flipped through the channels on the TV, searching for anything interesting to watch as she settled into bed. She'd been moved to a room and, luckily, didn't have a roommate. The room was relatively empty except for the bed and a nightstand pushed into the corner. A folded wheelchair had been pushed up against the wall on the opposite side of the room. Sporadic beeping noises emanated from a monitor she'd been hooked up to, which tracked her heart rate and pulse. She'd been told the on-duty nurse would be observing her closely through the night as she slept.

She yawned, unsure how much longer she could last watching TV. She had taken medication to help reduce the chance of her sleepwalking for the evening, and one of the major side effects was drowsiness. She rubbed her eyes, trying to ward off the sleepiness.

Now that things were quiet, a pinch of anxiety had crept in as she thought about whether Jayden would have any issues dealing with Maya's attitude change, especially since she was no longer there to act as a buffer.

She wondered if her overnight stay in the hospital would serve as a wake-up call for Maya, temporarily putting her cranky attitude on hold. But it was difficult for her to gauge Maya's true feelings, given her calm demeanor during the hospital visit. She couldn't tell if that had all been an act or if she'd simply been distracted by the situation.

Desiree also had to consider the possibility that Jayden was right and the necklace had something to do with Maya's shift in behavior. *Maybe my timing was off and I should have waited longer to give Maya the necklace, or given it to her even earlier.* She'd had discussions with her mother before she'd passed regarding when to give the necklace to Maya, but her mother's only answer to Desiree had always been to trust her third eye. It was almost as if her mother had been testing her.

As instructed, she'd followed her mother's advice and used her intuition to help figure out when the timing was right. Desiree's intuition paled in comparison to her mother's, yet she was confident she'd learned enough from her to trust her instincts, which told her the timing was now to present the necklace to Maya.

She tilted her head up to the ceiling. "Please give me a sign, Mom, that I didn't make a mistake by giving Maya the necklace now," she whispered.

Desiree stopped after seeing the third shift nurse in the doorway.

"Sorry to disturb you, hon. I was just checking in on you," the nurse said.

"I'm a little sleepy, but I'm good."

"It's the medicine kicking in, but there's no need to fight it. If you're tired, go ahead and close those eyes and start counting sheep."

Desiree exhibited a half-smile. "Thanks for checking in on me."

The nurse waved and walked out of sight.

*****

Within the next half hour, Desiree had drifted off to sleep and was soon greeted by a familiar dream. She found herself in the hallway of her mother's house again. She struggled to see because of the dim lighting, but there was enough for her to make out the row of doors scattered along both sides of the hallway. A powerful scent of cinnamon, cloves, and sweet cedar emanated throughout the hallway, which revealed to her the burning of incense somewhere in the area.

She took a few steps as the ground gave way slightly, indicating unsteady ground beneath her feet. She squinted down at her feet, struggling to see through the haze, which prevented her from determining the type of surface she was walking on. She continued her march until she came upon the first door on the right. She placed her hand on the rose-colored crystal doorknob and attempted to twist it clockwise. It didn't budge. She rattled the knob and twisted again with no success.

She studied the lightly distressed pine door and rotated her eyes to the bottom before lifting her head to the top. She stopped above the door as she spotted a silver plaque affixed to the wall with the number 101. She reached up and touched the raised numbers, and then tried again to open the door with no luck.

She continued to walk down the hall while attempting to remain steady on the soft surface. She approached the next door on the left, which appeared to be identical to the previous one. She twisted the rose-colored knob and experienced the same result, as this door was also locked. She directed her vision to the top of the door, observing another silver plaque showing the number 102.

A breeze picked up, sending a chill through Desiree as she continued to walk. She came across another pine door, but this one had a jade-colored crystal knob. Also, unlike the others, this door did not have a plaque with a number. She twisted the knob and successfully opened the door.

Upon entering, she recognized the area as her mother's bedroom. A king-sized sleigh bed was positioned in the middle of the room, but her mother was nowhere to be found.

She focused her attention on a desk in the corner with a sheet of paper and a marker lying on top. She came up to the desk and grabbed the marker, lowering her hand toward the paper. She slowly guided her hand along the page and wrote the letter *J*. She stopped after hearing knocking sounds from the hallway and dropped the marker, running over to the door to close it. She immediately jumped back after hearing three loud bangs outside the door.

Desiree's eyes shot open, and she let out a scream. She clutched her chest, coming in contact with her damp hospital gown. Shallow, fast breaths accompanied her racing heartbeat as she sat up in bed.

The third shift nurse ran into the room. "Are you okay, sweetheart?"

Desiree didn't immediately answer as she attempted to work on catching her breath. After a few seconds, she responded. "It was only a dream."

Chapter 28

Jayden leaned against the doorframe as Maya tucked herself into bed. The evening had been uneventful since they had arrived home from the hospital. Maya seemed to have reverted to her old self, although the necklace remained around her neck.

"You promise you'll be up on time to walk me to the bus stop?" she asked.

"Yes. It's not like I have nothing to do tomorrow. After I take you to the bus stop, I need to come back and log in for work."

"Okay. My mom wouldn't be happy if I missed the school bus."

"Well, at least we would have a backup plan."

"What do you mean?"

"Since I have a car, I can always drive you to school if you miss the bus."

"I didn't even think about that. Well, I'd say we go with plan A and have me not miss the bus."

"You got it," Jayden said, glancing down at Maya's necklace.

He lifted his eyes, spotting Maya looking directly at him. He was certain she caught him looking at her necklace, but he ignored the awkward moment, carrying on like nothing had happened.

He reached out for a fist-bump. "Have a good night's sleep."

Maya extended her arm and touched fists with Jayden. "I hope you have a good night's sleep, also, and sweet dreams."

He walked to the door, shutting off the lights. He started to close the door when Maya said, "You can leave the door open."

Jayden stopped with a puzzled look on his face. "But you rarely sleep with your door open."

"I thought I would try something new tonight."

"All right."

He left and entered Desiree's bedroom. It felt strange for him to know he'd be sleeping in the bedroom without her. He thought about how she was doing in the hospital and whether the nurses would have a chance to witness her sleepwalking. If she did sleepwalk, at least it comforted him knowing the medical staff would be monitoring her and could hopefully stop her from wandering too far from the bed.

A sense of relief consumed him, knowing that he'd have the room all to himself with no need to worry about Desiree roaming around the apartment in the middle of the night.

He scrolled through his phone as it neared the ten o'clock hour. He would normally be wide awake if he were home, but the eventful day with him shuttling to the hospital, and his broken sleep on the sofa the previous evening, had contributed to his sudden onset of sleepiness.

His phone eventually slipped out of his grasp, settling alongside his hip on the bed as he fell asleep.

*****

Later in the night, Jayden's sleep was disturbed by an unconfirmed noise in the background. As his senses sharpened, he homed in on a rhythmic creaking noise in the room. He remained on his side, thinking the noise was coming from behind him. He rubbed his eyes, trying to clear his vision. Desiree's nightstand and her closet door were the first things developing in his line of sight.

He remained still, listening intently to confirm the source of the noise. After listening further, the noise continued at the same pace without breaking rhythm. With heightened senses, Jayden knew this couldn't be Desiree since she was at the hospital.

He shifted his weight off his right hip and moved his body until he lay flat on his back. The creaking noise persisted even after he changed positions.

He stared up at the ceiling, refusing to immediately twist his head to the left, as he didn't want to make any sudden movements. He finally worked up the nerve to cautiously rotate his neck. There was enough moonlight coming in from the blinds for him to make out the silhouette of an unidentified individual sitting in the rocking chair. The person appeared to be a female based on the outline of hair flowing down to the shoulders. This person continued to rock in the chair and seemed to be facing the bedroom door, not looking Jayden's way.

He kept his body still and squinted, carefully studying the shape, trying to determine if this was Maya. But based on the larger shape, he could tell this was an adult occupying the chair and not Maya.

A scent of cedar infiltrated his nose, similar to the smell from the keepsake box, but on a stronger level. He wanted to reach for the baseball bat, but it was located under the bed. This meant he'd need to lean over and reach under the bed to grab it, losing sight of the mysterious figure, which was the last thing he wanted.

Instead of moving forward with that option, he covertly rotated his hand from side to side, feeling for his phone on the bed. After a few seconds, his thumb brushed up against his phone.

As the person continued to rock, he grabbed his phone, keeping it close to his body, with the intent of snapping a picture of this unconfirmed person. He took several deep breaths to help control his racing heart. The next challenge was unlocking his phone and positioning the camera in the person's direction.

Using his right arm, he slowly lifted the phone onto his chest, and at about the same time, the rocking stopped. He cut his eyes to the left, noticing the person's head slowly rotating his way.

Jayden had always heard stories of people who were frozen with fear and hit with the deer-in-the-headlights syndrome, but he never understood how that could happen … until now. His mind told him to roll off the bed in the other direction and get the hell out of the room, but he couldn't move. He was stuck to the bed as if someone was holding him down.

He continued to cut his eyes to the left, trying to keep sight of the unidentified person. He closed his eyes tight for a few seconds, and then opened them, hoping the person would be gone. As expected, that didn't work.

As if his body had finally figured out how to move, he carefully shifted about a half a foot to the right to create distance between him and the figure. He couldn't see their face, but he could tell this person's head continued to angle in his direction. He nudged his body another half a foot and was about to roll off the bed, away from the figure, when the person bolted out of the rocking chair with their arms extended and immediately latched on to his neck. The person's nails were sharp as they dug into his neck and began choking him.

He was powerless and unable to move as he struggled to breathe. He tried calling for Maya but couldn't get any words out, as the pressure on his windpipe prevented any sounds from escaping. His vision flickered in and out as his oxygen supply dwindled, and he was on the verge of losing consciousness.

His eyes snapped open while he grabbed his neck, gasping for air. He spun his head around from right to left, but the mysterious figure had disappeared. He quickly rose on his elbows, frantically looking around the room, and set his sights on the rocking chair, which was empty. He plopped his head back on the pillow after realizing he'd experienced a nightmare.

He fought to control his breathing and heart rate while pulling the covers off of him to cool down his damp body. The room remained dark as he reached for his phone and unlocked the screen to see the time of 1:08 staring him in the face.

Chapter 29

Jayden woke up and quickly lifted his head off the pillow. He surveyed the room to see daylight poking through the blinds. He tapped his phone, noting he had woken up thirty minutes before his alarm was scheduled to go off at 6:30.

He'd been awake for roughly two straight hours after the nightmare and had trouble getting back to sleep. He couldn't recall how long it had been since he'd experienced a nightmare of that magnitude, and one that seemed so real.

The time of 1:08 continued to circle in his head. He'd experienced a few coincidences in his lifetime concerning numbers; however, this scenario was by far the most noteworthy. He believed the chances of Desiree writing this number down during two separate instances of sleepwalking, along with him waking up from a nightmare at exactly 1:08, must have been influenced by something beyond normal reality. It also put him on high alert for the next time the clock was scheduled to display this combination of numbers, which would be at 1:08 in the afternoon. To make sure he didn't forget, he grabbed his phone and set his alarm to go off at that exact time.

He peeked over at the rocking chair to see it empty and sitting in the same position as it always was in the room. He massaged his neck and could almost feel a hint of soreness. He couldn't deny the nightmare had been spawned from him rummaging through the keepsake box and the thoughts of Desiree's mother in his head. He could almost guarantee the figure presented to him in his nightmare was none other than Grandma Isy, as Maya called her.

He winced, thinking he should have followed his gut and never opened the keepsake. He most certainly learned his lesson and had no plans to go near it again, especially now knowing there was a second necklace waiting to be claimed by its yet-to-be-identified owner.

He rotated his head, still bothered by the slight discomfort in his neck. He looked over at the dresser, and it hadn't occurred to him until now that he'd never disconnected the nanny cam. He reached for his phone, pulling up the app to see a notification of four recorded files. He expected to see a few files after being startled awake by the nightmare and struggling to fall back to sleep, so this was no surprise to him.

He clicked on the first file with a timestamp of 1:07 a.m., which was a minute before he had awoken from the nightmare. He carefully studied the video showing him sleeping on his back. He focused on the rocking chair, which was empty. He was completely puzzled as to why the recording had started with no movement being captured. He continued watching, and once the timestamp hit 1:08, his head moved from side to side in the bed, right before he reached for his neck and propped up on his elbows. The video showed him frantically looking around the room and staring at the rocking chair before putting his head back down on the pillow. Seconds later, the recorded file ended.

He clicked on the next file with a timestamp of 1:30 a.m., which showed him sitting up in bed, and looking back over at the rocking chair.

The last two files did not show anything of note other than him tossing around while he couldn't sleep. He went back to the first video and analyzed it, paying special attention to the rocking chair. He paused it right at the point before he reached for his neck at the 1:08 timestamp and could have sworn he saw the rocking chair push back ever so slightly.

He went back a few seconds and watched again. The video wasn't the highest of quality, particularly when viewing it in night vision mode, but he still believed the chair might have moved. He tried to rationalize that the poor video quality might be playing tricks on his vision.

He sighed, placing his feet on the floor, and cupped his face with his hands. No matter what was going on in his head right now, he had to push forward with his responsibilities for the day, starting with making sure Maya was up and ready to walk to the bus stop.

*****

After showering and getting dressed, he arrived in front of Maya's bedroom. He peeked in to see her under the covers. He neared her bed and could tell she was sound asleep. He wasn't certain if she'd set her alarm.

He reached over, tapping her on the shoulder. "Maya? Time to get up and get ready for school."

She rolled over on her back. "What time is it?" she asked in a broken whisper.

"Ten minutes to seven."

She sucked her teeth. "You woke me up too early. I have my alarm set for seven."

"Sorry. I wasn't sure if you put on your alarm. Go get your extra few minutes of sleep, but you need to make sure you get out of bed when your alarm goes off."

Maya quickly shifted back on her side.

Jayden left her bedroom and entered the kitchen, searching for something to eat. He picked up an apple and a bottle of water before sitting at the kitchen table. He hoped Desiree was doing okay and had been able to get some sleep during the night. He had plans to call her during his lunch break. He also contemplated whether or not to tell her about his nightmare regarding her mother. Since she had no clue he'd opened the keepsake box, he imagined it would be odd for her to hear he had a dream, seemingly out of the blue, about her mother. Even if he didn't tell her about the dream details, he was sure she would have found it interesting that he had woken up at exactly 1:08. He didn't expect her to have an answer as to what this meant, but at least they could be confused together in their efforts to try to figure it out.

He took a sip of water and peeked into the hallway, watching Maya walk out of her room and stumble to the bathroom with her shoulders hunched and head hanging low, looking like she could use a few more hours of sleep.

*****

Maya eventually strolled into the kitchen with her dark blue jeans and a blue and white striped T-shirt. "Good morning," she mumbled. She grabbed a box of Honey Nut Cheerios and poured them into a bowl before joining Jayden at the kitchen table and shoveling a spoonful into her mouth without any milk.

"You can eat your cereal dry?" Jayden asked.

"I do it sometimes. I didn't feel like putting any milk in the bowl today."

Jayden shot a quick look at her neck as she continued to proudly wear the necklace. He darted his eyes away before she noticed.

"Did you hear from my mom?"

"Not yet. I'm planning to call her during my lunch break. Hopefully, she was able to get some rest during the night."

"I hope so, too," Maya said, continuing to eat her cereal.

She snatched her head up from her bowl with an inquisitive look on her face. "Did you come into my room last night?"

"No, definitely not. Why?"

"I could have sworn I heard footsteps in the hallway coming toward my room at one point during the night."

"Wasn't me. I didn't get out of bed all night."

"That's weird, although my mom did say because we now live in a high-rise building, we might hear creaking noises during the night if it's windy outside. Do you believe that?"

"I didn't think about it, but that could be a possibility."

Maya shoveled the last spoonful of cereal into her mouth. "I'm ready when you are."

*****

Jayden entered the lobby after walking back from the bus stop. The discussion with Maya during the walk had been uneventful. She had mostly professed her displeasure

187

about having to go back to school after the long holiday weekend.

The elevator ascended to the tenth floor, and as he exited, he noticed a figure standing in the hallway. As he came closer, he spotted Desiree's neighbor, Paulette. She was dressed in a pair of yellow nylon shorts and a white tank top with her hair pulled into a ponytail.

She greeted him with a warm smile. "Jayden?"

"Yes. And if I remember correctly, Paulette?"

"Absolutely," she responded. "How have things been for you guys since the move-in?"

"It's going about as well as can be expected. I'm sure you know it's an adjustment period, but we're getting used to it."

"That's good. How's your wife doing? And I apologize if I don't remember her name."

"No problem. It's Desiree, and she's actually my girlfriend."

"Oh. I'm sorry."

"I don't blame you for assuming because I don't think I ever confirmed our relationship when we first met."

A brief silence followed before Paulette spoke up. "I hope you don't think I'm being too nosy, but I overheard you and your girlfriend having a disagreement last week with our neighbor downstairs, Sophia."

Jayden displayed a sheepish grin. "I'm not surprised you heard it. Sorry if we were being a little too loud. The last thing we want to do is cause problems with our neighbors."

"That's okay."

"Speaking of Sophia, are you friends with her?" Jayden asked.

"Yes. We're in the same yoga class," Paulette said as her once cheerful demeanor quickly faded. "I don't know if you know, but she had a stroke last week, and last I heard, she'd just woken up from being in a coma for a few days."

"I'm so sorry to hear. I did see her being wheeled out on a stretcher but didn't know what happened."

"It was definitely a shock. She's always been very health-conscious, and it doesn't make any sense to me that she would have a stroke."

Jayden put his hands together in prayer. "We're praying for her."

"Me, too," she said, and then noted the time. "I'm sorry, but I'm running late to get to the gym, so let me get moving. It was nice seeing you again." Paulette left and jogged to the elevator.

Jayden felt extremely guilty that he and Desiree's first and only interaction with Sophia hadn't been a pleasant one. He decided to keep the news a secret and not let Desiree know, to help limit the amount of stress consuming her.

After entering the apartment, he took his laptop out of the case and placed it on the kitchen table, listening to the complete silence in the apartment. He thought back to what Maya had said regarding the footsteps she might have heard in the hallway overnight. Since he could remove Desiree from the picture as a possible reason, he was at a total loss as to what Maya could have heard. He was ninety-nine percent sure the nightmare he'd had was simply just that. It wasn't real, although it had sure felt like it to him.

His pulse quickened, thinking his decision to open the keepsake box might have opened the door to something beyond his comprehension. It also didn't help for him to think about the weird references Desiree's mom had used in the letter, which added to his anxiety. Or maybe it was a problem for Jayden because he simply didn't understand what she was trying to say. As the saying goes, *"People fear what they don't understand,"* and in Jayden's case, this couldn't have been more accurate.

He cupped his hands around his face, feeling disappointed that his long weekend hadn't turned out to be as restful and stress-free as he'd wanted. He never thought he'd say it, but he was looking forward to logging in to work and getting his mind off the drama that had been inundating his life.

*****

Jayden was satisfied with completing a few productive hours of work and had intentions of giving Desiree a call. As soon as the thought crossed his mind, his phone buzzed with a call from her.

"Your ears must be ringing. I was going to call to check in on you. How are you feeling?"

"All right, I guess. Didn't sleep too well during the night."

"Do you think you—"

"According to the nurse on duty, they didn't witness me sleepwalking. I'm assuming that's what you were going to ask?"

"Yes."

"I didn't think it would, but maybe the meds they gave me actually did work. But I'm still feeling drowsy, which is one of the side effects."

"Any updates from the doctors on what they think is going on, or if they have any plans to release you today?"

"I was told my blood work came back mostly clean. They mentioned my stress hormone was a little high, and so was my blood pressure."

"I'm not surprised based on what's been happening with you."

"But I am worried because a social worker is scheduled to see me in about an hour to go over my situation. I have no idea what questions they're going to ask or if they're going to think I'm crazy and refuse to release me."

"The best thing you can do is remain calm and be truthful with your answers."

"Easier said than done. I'm already stressed out about being in the hospital. And if they say I need to stay longer, I'm going to have some serious problems with that."

"If it makes you feel any better, me and Maya are doing fine over here. I had no problems with her last night and got her to the bus stop on time."

"Good. And please don't forget you should be at the bus stop by three thirty to pick her up."

"Don't worry; I got it covered."

Desiree let out a long sigh.

"Can you do me a favor and relax? I'm sure the meeting with the social worker will go fine. Just know they're not your enemy and are only looking out for you and Maya's best interest."

"I know … I know. I'll try to keep that in mind," Desiree said, followed by a yawn.

"I don't want to hold you up any further from getting some rest. Please give me a call back after the meeting to let me know how it went. Love you, stay strong, and I'll talk to you later."

Jayden hung up the phone and tapped his fingers on the table. He was also concerned about this meeting with the social worker, but there was no way he was going to let Desiree know. He understood she needed all the encouragement she could get at this point.

He stepped away from the table and decided to take a break and eat lunch.

*****

An hour later, Jayden had finished eating leftover beef lo mein for lunch and had been working for a short time before his cell phone alarm went off. Confusion set in as he reached for his phone and was quickly reminded that he had set his alarm to go off at 1:08. He shut off the alarm and paused a webinar he'd been viewing for work, taking in the silence. The only sound he could hear was the mild humming coming from his laptop fan. He had no clue what to expect or if he'd even notice anything different that might coincide with this specific time. But he figured it was worth a shot to investigate based on something he now felt went beyond pure coincidence.

He peered down the hallway to see that both Desiree's and Maya's bedroom doors were open. That was an odd sight for him because he was used to both of them being home with at least one of their bedroom doors closed.

He walked down the hallway with the creaking noises sounding extra loud over the hushed silence. He arrived at Maya's bedroom door and took a peek inside. Her bed was nicely made with two oversized white decorative pillows as the focal point, resting on top of her covers. He studied the room and didn't see anything unusual.

He left Maya's room and headed to Desiree's bedroom. As soon as he cleared the doorway, he immediately placed the rocking chair in his field of vision. Before last night, the rocking chair had simply been a standard piece of furniture taking up space in the corner of the room. Now, his perception of the chair had completely changed.

He stared at it with flashbacks in his mind of who he believed to be Grandma Isy occupying the rocking chair in his nightmare. He took another step closer and reached out with his right foot, gently kicking the chair to get a sense of its rocking motion. The chair glided on its rockers, as the rhythmic creaking noise reminded Jayden exactly of how it had sounded in his dream.

He backed away from the chair and walked around the bed, opening the closet door. Everything appeared normal from a visual standpoint, although a faint smell of cedar lingered in the air, prompting him to take a step back. He couldn't recall if this scent had always been present in the closet or if he happened to be paying more attention to it now after what he'd experienced in his dream.

He closed the closet door and glanced over at the rocking chair while shaking his head. "What the hell is the matter with me? I'm letting this nightmare get into my head too much. There's no one else here but me."

Unconscious Impulses

With renewed confidence, he exited the bedroom to continue watching the webinar, attempting to put the dream way back in the recesses of his mind.

Chapter 30

Desiree swallowed to moisten her dry throat after seeing a young woman appear at her hospital room door. She was dressed in beige slacks, a white blouse, and had dark brown hair cut into a bob, stretching an inch below her jawline. Desiree had expected someone older to show up. Regardless of this woman's age, it did nothing to calm her nervousness.

"Am I speaking to Ms. Campbell?" the woman asked.

"Yes, that's me."

She extended her hand for a shake. "I'm Olivia, the social worker assigned to your case. Nice to meet you."

Desiree shook her hand.

Olivia pulled up a chair and sat with her legs crossed, resting a notebook on her lap. "Now, before we begin, I wanted to make sure you were aware I was coming to talk with you today."

"Yes."

"Good to hear. I can't tell you how many times I first met with a patient and they were looking at me like I had two heads."

"No, I'm only seeing one head," Desiree said, attempting to inject some humor into the situation, mostly to help calm her nerves.

Olivia let out a small laugh and tapped her pen on the notebook. "I want to start by saying I'm not here to cause you any trouble. I'm not here to make things difficult for you and your family. I don't want you feeling worried, anxious, or angry. I'm only here right now to have a conversation with you. I want to know how you're feeling and find out information regarding your family situation. And, most importantly, please know I'm not doing this for fun and trying to get all up in your business. I simply ask if you could give me your honest feedback; it will go a long way in helping me do my job, which in turn allows me to help you. Does that sound good to you?"

"Sure."

"Perfect. Before I begin, I did want to point out that everything we talk about in this room will be confidential. Although I will say certain situations may require breaking this confidentiality, and that's if I feel there's a potential threat of harm to someone, or if there are any instances of child abuse or neglect found. I want to make sure you understand."

"Yes."

"Great. So my first question is: how are you feeling? And I don't mean physically, but how are you feeling mentally? How's your mood right now?"

Desiree sucked in a large dose of air and then exhaled before answering. "Other than feeling tired from the medication they've been giving me, I feel good. Although it's a little stressful being in the hospital right now, so I wouldn't say I'm in the best of moods."

Olivia nodded and wrote down a few things in her notebook. "That's understandable. I would say that's a normal reaction for anyone who had to spend a night in the hospital."

Olivia flipped through a few sheets of paper in her lap. "I understand you have a preteen daughter in your household."

"Yes. Her name is Maya, and she's about to turn twelve, but going on twenty-five."

"I know what you mean. My daughter turned fourteen, and she gets confused sometimes, thinking she's the mother and I'm her daughter."

Desiree let out a small laugh. She was relieved to hear Olivia also had a daughter, so she could relate to the mother-daughter dynamics.

"It says here you're a single mother and you have a boyfriend who stays with you on occasion."

"Yes. Jayden has been such a huge help to me. And the best part is my daughter absolutely loves him."

"I love to hear that," Olivia said, jotting down additional notes. "Is Maya's father a part of her life?"

"No."

"If you don't mind me asking, is that by choice?"

"Her father is an ex-boyfriend of mine who ran out on me after he found out I was pregnant, and I have no clue where he is."

Olivia put her hand over her chest. "I'm so sorry to hear."

"No need to feel sorry for me. I was hurt in the beginning, but I realized I have the most amazing gift in my daughter, and because of that, I don't regret what happened one bit."

"That's definitely the best way to look at it. Can you tell me if you had any issues with Maya's father before he left?"

"There was no verbal or physical abuse, if that's what you're asking. We had our arguments here and there, but nothing more than any other couple might go through."

"Does Maya know the situation with her father?"

"She knows. But since she's never met him, it doesn't bother her too much. She used to ask about him when she was younger, but I don't remember the last time she mentioned him."

"It's so unfortunate when men run away from their responsibilities," Olivia said, leaning forward. "And between you and me, if this weren't a professional setting, I would be saying that a lot differently."

Desiree grinned, happy to see Olivia had a little spice bottled up in her and not afraid to provide a glimpse of her personality.

"On a scale of one to ten, how happy would you say Maya is at home?"

"I would say a nine. She pretty much keeps to herself and stays in her room to read her fantasy books."

"Now that's impressive. Hopefully, that trend continues, and she can stay away from having her head buried in her phone like my daughter."

"If I have anything to do with it, that trend will continue. I do my best to limit her time on the phone," Desiree said.

Olivia flipped through additional sheets of paper in her lap. "How's Maya doing in school?"

"She's doing fine. She may not enjoy going to school, but she gets her work done and gets good grades."

"I don't know many kids who look forward to going to school, so she falls right in line with the rest of them," Olivia said. "And how have things been for you at home lately? Meaning, have you had any issues or conflicts with either Maya or Jayden?"

"It's been challenging lately dealing with my daughter's attitude. But I'm hoping it's a temporary phase since she's now approaching those teenage years."

"Have you had any verbal or physical confrontations with her?"

"Yes to verbal, but a no to physical."

"Have you had any physical confrontations with her in the past?"

"Thankfully, no. She's been a great kid up until this point and mostly listens to what she's told."

Olivia continued to furiously write in her notebook after Desiree responded to each question.

"How have you been dealing with her attitude change? Does it make you mad when she's going through one of those moments?"

"I'm dealing with it the best way I can. Of course, I get frustrated, but who wouldn't as a parent dealing with a child who's throwing attitude your way?"

"What do you do to help blow off steam during those times?"

"I take a few deep breaths, focusing on those moments of Zen, and that helps relax me."

"And has she displayed the same attitude with your boyfriend?"

"She has lately, but there's been no verbal or physical confrontations between them."

"Have there been any verbal or physical confrontations with you and your boyfriend?"

"Oh, no. We've had a few minor disagreements, but nothing that escalated into anything noteworthy."

"And I understand your boyfriend is currently looking after your daughter while you're in the hospital. Correct?"

"Yes. I have no family around, so he was the only logical choice to watch her."

"Do you feel comfortable with him watching her without you there?"

"Absolutely. He's been nothing but an angel since I've been with him, and I trust him to take care of her like she's his daughter."

"You're a lucky woman to have somebody like that."

"Thanks."

Olivia looked down at her notes once again. "Oh, I almost forgot to ask, but what do you do for a living?"

"I work from home as a medical biller."

"And how long have you been doing that?"

"About three years."

"Is it stressful?"

"It can be, but since I've been doing it for a while, it's easier now than it was when I first started."

Olivia smiled. "It sounds to me like things are going pretty well in your household."

"I guess you can say that."

Olivia rotated her eyes around the room. "Were you able to get any sleep during the night?"

"A little. The medication made me tired, but it's hard to sleep anywhere else but my bed."

"I understand. I'm the same way," Olivia said.

She stared at Desiree, almost as if this was the first time she had taken a real good look at her instead of paying attention to her notebook. "Do you know if the medication helped with your sleeping situation?"

Desiree thought for a second, attempting to interpret what Olivia meant. She imagined Olivia was aware of her sleepwalking issues from the medical notes and assumed that's what she was referencing.

"If you're talking about me sleepwalking, I was told it didn't happen last night."

Olivia tapped her pen on the notebook in her lap. "Did anybody talk to you yet about taking precautions in your house to make things safer for you and your family?"

"What type of precautions?"

"Maybe moving things out of the way or out of reach so you won't hurt yourself or anyone else if you continue sleepwalking."

Desiree had a feeling she was referring to the knife incident. A flicker of anger sparked within her. She felt like a baby whose house needed to be child-proofed for safety reasons. She took a deep breath to help suppress any anger threatening to derail this otherwise pleasant dialogue. She knew deep down that what Olivia said made complete sense. She just needed to put on her big-girl pants and accept this as a smart recommendation if she continued to sleepwalk.

"Yeah, you're probably right."

"I'm also sure if you do your research, there are devices you can use that will wake you up before you stray too far away from the bed."

"I can check on that. Thanks for the information."

"I do have another suggestion. Have you ever thought about participating in a sleep study?"

"I've heard of it, but I don't know too much about it."

"I'm by no means an expert on this, but it sounds like you would be a perfect candidate for it. My husband participated in a sleep study last year to treat a sleeping disorder. His experience was pretty much stress-free and painless unless you have a phobia about being hooked up with a bunch of wires and sensors while you sleep."

"Did the sleep study help him?"

"Because he participated in the study, the doctors were able to properly diagnose him and prescribe medication that pretty much cured his sleeping disorder."

"Good for him. Was it covered by insurance?"

"You can check with your insurance carrier, but as long as you have medical records showing you have a sleeping disorder, they'll usually cover the cost of the study."

"Great to know. I appreciate the information you've given me."

Olivia glanced at her notebook. "I think that's all the questions I have. Do you have anything for me?"

Desiree was dying to get Olivia's opinion on what she thought about the answers she provided. She felt like a student handing in a final exam and wanting to immediately know her grade. However, she couldn't think of a tactful way of communicating this to Olivia.

"Um, so what are the next steps?"

"I'm going to summarize these notes I wrote down and determine if any further meetings are needed with you or your family. I'll also consult with your doctors to come up with a plan on how we need to proceed."

Desiree opened her eyes wider, waiting to hear if Olivia had anything else to say.

"Any other questions?" Olivia asked.

"Do you have any information on whether I'll be discharged today?"

Olivia tucked her notebook under her arm. "No, I don't have any information yet, but let me talk to your doctors and see what we can do."

Desiree bit her bottom lip, struggling to remain calm and not move forward with the urge to get dressed and sprint out of the hospital.

Olivia extended her hand for a shake. "Thanks for your time. Hang in there, and I'll be in touch."

Chapter 31

Jayden stood at the corner, scrolling through the work emails on his phone as he waited patiently for Maya's school bus. The bus was running later than the time Desiree had said it should arrive.

A warm breeze ruffled his light blue, wrinkle-free collared shirt, though the humidity levels led to a bit of sweat escaping his pores. He lifted his right arm, glancing under his armpit to make sure no sweat stains were forming.

He tried his best not to be distracted by the ice cream shop located across the street. He'd normally save any sweet treats for the weekends, but between the heat and the oversized pictures of ice cream sundaes plastered against the windows, he wasn't sure how much longer he could deny the temptation.

He twisted his head to the left after hearing the rumble of an approaching vehicle. "Finally," he mumbled after seeing Maya's school bus pulling up to the corner.

She exited the bus as he reached out, greeting her with a fist-bump.

"Was the bus running late?" he asked.

"Yeah, I guess a little. There was an accident that happened on one of the streets we had to go down."

"How was your day?" Jayden asked.

"Fine, nothing special."

"Did they give you any homework?"

"Yeah, but not much. I started doing some of it on the bus to try to get it out of the way."

Maya began her trek down the block, but Jayden didn't follow.

"Aren't you coming?" she asked.

He pointed to the ice cream shop. "Let's stop and get ice cream before we go back to the apartment."

"Really? I thought you didn't like to eat anything sweet during the week."

"Me, too, but after sweating on this hot corner, waiting for your bus, I feel like I have no choice."

Maya laughed. "Okay, fine with me. You know I'm not going to say no since you're buying."

*****

They each left with two scoops of vanilla ice cream stuffed into a waffle cone.

"Did you talk to my mom?" Maya asked while attempting to lick the sides of the cone to prevent any melted ice cream from running down to her fingers.

"I talked with her earlier, and she didn't know if they were going to release her today. She said she was going to call me back later to give me an update."

Maya continued licking her ice cream. "If they don't let her go today, hopefully it will be tomorrow."

"I hope so, too," Jayden said.

Maya looked at the time on her phone. "Aren't you still supposed to be working?"

"Yes. I was responding to emails while I was waiting for you."

"You know I could have walked home by myself."

"I'm sure you probably could have, but you know your mother wouldn't let you do that."

"I don't know why. I keep telling her I'm old enough now to walk a few blocks by myself, but she doesn't want me to do it."

"I think she needs to get used to the area first. Maybe she'll loosen up a bit as the school year goes on."

*****

They eventually arrived at the apartment. Jayden didn't want to jinx anything, but the old Maya was definitely back in his mind. Although she continued to wear the necklace, her odd behavior seemed to have temporarily disappeared.

"Any idea what's for dinner?" Maya asked.

Jayden entered the kitchen and opened the refrigerator. "Based on what I'm seeing, we'll probably need to order takeout."

"I can go for pizza," Maya said.

"Sounds good to me. Give me about a half hour, and I can place an order."

Maya gave a thumbs-up. "I'll be in my room, finishing up homework," she said, and then left.

Jayden looked down after feeling his phone vibrating and saw Desiree's name appear on the screen.

"How did the meeting go with the social worker?"

"Better than I expected. The questions weren't bad, and it was actually a decent discussion."

"Are you getting discharged today?"

"Don't know. The social worker needs to meet with my doctor first, and I don't know if that's happening today."

There was a brief pause before Desiree continued, "I'm assuming you picked up Maya?"

"We walked in the door not too long ago."

"Any problems getting her?"

"Other than the bus being late, I had no problems."

Jayden opened his laptop. "After I'm done working, we can swing by the hospital for a visit."

Desiree sighed. "No. Let me save you a trip. Don't want you fighting through traffic to get here. I also don't want you and Maya to see me looking pitiful and sitting in this hospital bed for two days in a row."

"Okay, if that's what you want."

A few seconds of silence elapsed before Desiree spoke up. "That's it? You're not even going to fight me about coming to the hospital to see me?"

Jayden shook his head. "Why? I now know you're uncomfortable with us seeing you in a vulnerable position, so I figured I wouldn't force a visit on you if you don't want us to come."

"Okay. Good answer," she said.

Jayden heard a brief bit of talking in the background.

"Sorry, they were bringing me my dinner."

"I'm almost afraid to ask what they're serving."

"It said meatloaf on the menu, but after looking at it, I'm beginning to question if that's what it is."

"I'm about to order pizza since there isn't much in the refrigerator."

Desiree sighed. "Now, why would you tell me that after I just told you my concerns about eating this mystery meat in front of me?"

Jayden winced. "Sorry. I'll make sure to save you some slices for when you come home.

Silence followed as Jayden could hear Desiree breathing in deeply. "I'm telling you right now, if they don't release me by tomorrow, I'm walking right out of here with no questions asked."

"Don't worry; I'm sure you'll be back home before you know it."

"I sure hope so. Anyway, I guess I at least need to attempt to eat something. Please take care of my baby. Hopefully, she's not giving you too much trouble."

"No. Everything's good here. She's in her room doing homework."

"Call me if she's not acting right."

"I will. Make sure you call me the minute you find out when they're going to discharge you."

*****

Two hours later, Jayden had finished working and Maya had completed her homework. A large pepperoni pizza had been delivered, and they were sitting at the kitchen table eating.

"Are you used to being back at school?" Jayden asked.

Maya picked a pepperoni slice off her pizza and stuffed it in her mouth. "I guess so. It would be better if they weren't giving us so much homework."

"Homework is good for you. It builds character. It keeps your brain sharp."

"I beg to differ."

Jayden laughed. "Let me guess; is that another one of your mother's sayings?"

"Yup."

"You're like a sponge, observing everything your mother says or does. I need to tell her to be careful what she says around you."

Jayden grabbed a second slice of pizza and put it on his plate as the talking temporarily ceased. He grabbed a napkin and dabbed his pizza slice to absorb the excess grease layered on the top.

"What do you think of your teachers?" Jayden asked as he continued to clean up the excess grease.

He didn't receive any reply from Maya, which prompted him to look up. He observed her staring down at her plate and rubbing the pendant dangling from her necklace. *Oh no. Things have been going so well. Please don't start acting weird on me now.*

"Maya?"

She slowly returned her gaze up at him, her eyes appearing distant.

"Earth to Maya. Did you hear me?" he asked.

"Sorry, what did you say?"

"I asked what you thought of your teachers?"

"Oh, they're all right."

Jayden leaned forward, waiting for her to say more. "That's it? You don't have anything else to say about them?"

She stared at Jayden before speaking. "No, I don't have anything else to say about my teachers, but I do have a question for you."

Oh shit. I don't like the way that sounded.

"Are you sure you weren't in my room the other night?"

Jayden's heartbeat spiked. "What are you talking about?"

"I'm pretty sure someone was in my room two nights ago when I was in bed."

Jayden wanted to continue to play dumb, but Maya seemed pretty convinced about her beliefs. He imagined she could have potentially seen him when he had ducked alongside the bed, or she had been up and acting like she was asleep. Even if that were the case, Jayden was puzzled as to why she hadn't previously mentioned it and had waited until this moment to do so. At this point, it didn't matter. He had to make a quick decision on whether or not to confess.

"Why do you think I was in your room?"

"Because I'm sure someone was tugging at my necklace while I was in bed, and I don't think it was a dream."

Jayden could no longer continue to deny. He was guilty as charged and knew he needed to fess up and face the consequences.

"Okay. I admit I was in your room the other night."

"And were you trying to take my necklace?"

Jayden responded with a defeated nod.

Maya watched him with a blank expression. "Why would you want to do that?"

"We already talked about it before. You've been acting different ever since you put it on, and I assumed if you were no longer wearing it, maybe you would go back to your old self."

"I'm still confused why you and my mom keep saying that. It was a special gift from my grandma. I don't know how or why this would cause me to act different."

Jayden could feel the heat rising in his body. He let out a large exhale to ward off the tinge of impatience blossoming within him. "I don't know, either—that's why we're worried."

"Did my mom know you were trying to take my necklace?"

"No. I was the one who decided to do it on my own."

She remained quiet and took another bite of her pizza. She looked back up at Jayden with disappointment in her eyes. "What happened to you? I thought I could trust you."

Jayden felt like he'd been hit by a speeding truck. The honeymoon phase was over. He feared he might have lost the little girl who had once adored him. He had no one else to blame since he had acted on his own to try to swipe the necklace before getting Desiree's approval.

"I thought it was the best way to deal with the situation. But I can admit I was wrong for trying to take it."

Maya did not respond but continued eating. Her silence concerned Jayden more than anything since he had no clue what she was thinking. He figured it was best to stay quiet.

She finished her last bite and offered Jayden a withering stare. "I'm not the only one you should be apologizing to. I don't think Grandma Isy appreciated what you tried to do, either."

She emptied her plate into the garbage and left without saying another word.

Chapter 32

With the midnight hour approaching, Jayden had been dozing while sitting on the sofa with the TV on. Maya had turned in for the night a couple of hours ago and was asleep in her bedroom. He had done what he could to avoid her after their tension-filled dinner chat. As much as he didn't want to admit, he'd been rattled by Maya's last statement before she'd left the dinner table. This might have been a different story if he hadn't experienced the nightmare last night, but he couldn't deny the dream continued to run through his mind more than he would have liked. So much so that he had decided the sofa would be his bed once again for the night. He no longer felt comfortable sleeping in the bedroom with the rocking chair sitting in the corner and the keepsake box tucked away in the closet.

He flipped through the channels, hoping to find something to make him laugh and forget about the current situation. He hadn't heard back from Desiree, which meant another night at the hospital was necessary. He'd hoped this would be the last night for her in the hospital since he was concerned with her mental state and how she'd handle being there for an extended period. He also didn't want to deal with Maya on his own any longer than he needed to, now that the Mr. Hyde version of her persona had revealed itself once again.

*****

Jayden eventually fell asleep, and after a few hours, a gut-wrenching scream rattled him awake. He surveyed the living room, hoping he hadn't been dropped into another nightmare. He leaned forward, listening out for any further sounds. His phone chimed as a text from Maya appeared.

Are you up? Can you please come to my room now!

Jayden received confirmation that what he'd heard wasn't a dream, and he wasn't looking forward to seeing what awaited him in Maya's room. He marched down the hallway, opening her bedroom door.

"Can you turn on the light?" she asked.

He flicked the switch to see Maya sitting up in bed with the covers pulled up to her neck, breathing heavily.

"What's the matter?"

"I had a dream someone was standing in the corner of my room," she said, frantically looking around. "At least, I think it was a dream."

"Were you able to see who it was?"

"No. It was too dark for me to see a face. The person just kept standing in the corner and didn't say anything."

Jayden struggled to remain calm. He didn't want to jump to any conclusions, but he thought it was too much of a coincidence that both he and Maya had had nightmares on back-to-back nights about someone in their room.

He took a step into her bedroom, twisting his head from side to side. He approached the closet and opened it, seeing nothing out of the ordinary.

"Can you check under my bed, please?"

Jayden turned on the flashlight from his phone and kneeled, lowering on all fours to peek under the bed. He rotated the flashlight from left to right but didn't see anything.

"I can confirm nobody is in your room now, so it had to be a dream."

Maya puffed out her cheeks, still attempting to control her breathing. "It seemed so real. There was also a smell, almost like some type of wood that I can't really explain."

Jayden didn't need to hear anything further about the smell. He was confident Maya was referring to the same cedar odor he had experienced in his dream. But he didn't want to mention anything about his dream to make Maya more nervous. This helped solidify his theory that Grandma Isy had paid both of them a visit in their dreams on consecutive nights for reasons unknown.

His mind drifted to Desiree as he thought about if she'd also experienced any vivid dreams about her mother recently. He no longer wanted to keep any of this a secret and decided that he needed to let Desiree know what had happened. He'd hoped this would also prompt her to be more forthcoming about her mother's background, though he didn't want to go so far as to admit that he'd gone searching for the keepsake box and opened it.

Jayden scanned the room once again. "If you want, you can come out to the living room and watch TV to help get your mind off the dream."

"I think I'll be okay staying in the bedroom if you keep the light on for me."

"All right. I'll be outside if you need me again."

He stepped into the hallway, looking in the direction of Desiree's bedroom door, which he'd made a point to keep closed. He neared her door and placed his hands on the knob. He twisted it, but then stopped. He opened his phone and clicked on the nanny cam app. It was still set to record any movement during the night. He launched the app, and to his horror, one recorded file displayed.

His hand shook as he hovered his finger over the *play* button. He finally tapped the button, and an image of the bedroom came into view. It was unsettling for him to see the bed made up with no one in it. He studied the rocking chair, looking for the slightest movement as the recording played. After fifteen seconds, the recording ended, and he hadn't seen any movement. He played the recording back once again, focusing on other areas in the room to see if he could find anything unusual. Although he didn't detect anything from a visual standpoint, his ears came to another conclusion.

He turned up the volume on his phone and played the recording once more. Seconds before the recording ended, the rocking chair creaked. Although it was subtle, he heard it.

A part of him had hoped the camera was defective and randomly recording things even if no movement had been detected. He figured that could be a possibility, but hearing the sound at the end of the recording threw a huge monkey wrench into his theory. Though his eyes did not detect any movement, he was convinced something, or somebody, was present at the time of the recording.

He put his hand on the doorknob, contemplating whether or not he should enter to investigate further. He desperately wanted to retreat and refrain from entering, but if he didn't go in, his conscience would remain in overdrive, wondering what would have happened if he had opened the door. Not to mention his ego would take a hit with thoughts of him being a coward.

Before the next string of doubts entered his mind, he threw caution to the wind and promptly twisted the knob, opening the door.

He switched on the light and instantly directed his attention toward the rocking chair. There didn't seem to be anything unusual about it. He scanned the rest of the room, hesitating about walking in and exploring further. He decided to move forward, reluctantly stepping into the room and surveying the scene.

With his anxiety heightened, he felt as if he were being watched. He turned in a complete circle, making sure he hadn't missed anything. He made his way to the closet and opened it, turning on the light. Everything appeared to be in its place and, as he noticed previously, the cedar smell continued to linger in the air.

He closed the door behind him, twitching from an unexpected chill tickling his skin. He ducked his head into the bathroom but didn't see anything. Exiting the bathroom, he continued eyeing the rocking chair. If this were an ordinary rocking chair that Desiree had found at a flea market, he could almost guarantee he would have immediately tossed it out on the street. But, since it was an heirloom that had significant sentimental value to Desiree, he had to quickly remove the thought from his head.

After glaring at the rocking chair for what seemed like an eternity, he decided he'd had enough of this staring contest with an inanimate object and promptly left the room.

There was no way he'd feel comfortable falling back to sleep for the remainder of the night. Not only was he concerned with Maya's state of mind after her nightmare, but he also imagined the odds of him having a bad dream were suddenly higher, and he had no interest in meeting up with Grandma Isy again.

Chapter 33

The following day, Jayden pulled up to the hospital lobby entrance, waiting for Desiree, who had been discharged. It had passed the noon hour when Jayden had driven out to get her on an extended lunch break.

She entered the car, holding a plastic bag containing her clothes and a folder tucked under her arm, and hugged Jayden. "I can't tell you how happy I am to see you and to finally be able to leave this place."

"You were definitely missed," Jayden said, putting the car in gear.

"I see you survived without me," Desiree said.

"I'm still standing."

"Is everything good with Maya?"

"She's good," Jayden said, keeping his response short, not wanting to immediately get into the drama that had occurred.

He peeked over at the folder in Desiree's lap. "What was the doctor's verdict about your sleepwalking?" he asked, attempting to divert their talk.

"They weren't too concerned about the fact that I was sleepwalking, but more about my actions while I was in that state." Desiree opened the folder sitting in her lap. "Based on what I have in this folder, we have reading homework to do. We need to rearrange things in the apartment, and have a few things we need to purchase."

Jayden shot her a look. "Sounds like a lot. What are we rearranging and what do we need to buy?"

"For one thing, we need to move the cutlery set from the kitchen counter and out of my reach. And that goes for anything else that could be potentially dangerous for me to get my hands on."

"That could be a lot of things in the apartment."

"Yes, I know. These are the kind of things I used to do when Maya was a baby. I can't believe I need to do this for myself. I'm a grown-ass adult. This makes no sense."

Jayden stopped at a light and tapped her on the leg. "As much as you might hate doing it, you gotta admit this is a smart move."

"I guess so."

"What kind of things do we need to buy?"

Desiree flipped through a few of the pages in the folder. "There are different alarms and sensors that can be used to wake up anyone who sleepwalks. We'll need to do some research because I was told there are a lot of things to choose from on the market."

"Would any of those things really work?" Jayden asked.

"That's where our research comes in. And before I forget, we need to swing by the drug store and pick up a prescription for pills they want me to take at night to help limit my sleepwalking."

Jayden stopped at another light and adjusted his GPS for directions to the local drug store near the apartment.

"That'll be helpful for you to finally get a good night's rest."

"Yes, that would be nice because I didn't sleep all that great in the hospital."

"Was that because you had another sleepwalking episode?"

"Not that I'm aware of. But I do remember having another dream about being in the hallway of my mother's house. It was similar to the first dream I had, but this time the doors in the hallway had numbers above them. The first one had the number 101, and the second one had 102. But they were both locked."

Jayden's eyes widened. "Do you recall seeing the number 108 anywhere?"

"No. But something is telling me if this pattern continues in my dreams, I'll eventually make it to door number 108. And I'm almost afraid to think what I might find behind that door if it opens."

"Not much we can do now. Just need to wait and see if those dreams continue."

Silence followed as Desiree flipped to another sheet in the folder. "I was also given the option of participating in a sleep study."

"Sleep study?"

"Yeah. The social worker first mentioned it to me. Based on my research, it's a diagnostic test that would record how my mind functions while I sleep."

"Sounds interesting."

"It seems like something out of a sci-fi movie where they hook you up to all kinds of sensors and wires that monitor you while you sleep."

"What's the goal?"

"Doctors can find out what's going on with my brain while I'm sleeping and would have a better understanding of how to potentially treat my condition."

"Is that something you'd be interested in doing?"

"I don't know. It depends on whether the medication does its job and stops me from sleepwalking. But I also don't want to be on any medication for the rest of my life."

Jayden grabbed Desiree's hand and gently stroked it. "I know this is a lot, but I'm happy you agreed to go to the hospital. You're now getting the help you need to improve your sleeping situation."

Desiree smirked. "I must admit I didn't want to go at first, but I see the benefit now."

"And you were so worried about meeting with the social worker, but it turned out fine. The answers you gave were obviously convincing enough that they agreed it was safe for you to come back home."

"Thank God! Two nights in the hospital were enough for me," Desiree said as she yawned. "I still have some medication floating around in my system, and it's making me tired."

Jayden looked at the GPS. "We still have about half an hour of driving, so feel free to close your eyes. By the way, I want to talk with you about a few things later, and I want to make sure you're awake."

Desiree had closed her eyes, but briefly opened them to respond. "We can talk about it now."

Jayden rubbed the back of his fingers along her cheek. "Just close those beautiful eyes of yours, and we can talk about this when you're more awake back at the apartment."

Chapter 34

They arrived back at the apartment, and Desiree immediately shuffled into the bedroom, collapsing on the bed to continue her nap. Jayden opened his laptop to check in on anything he had missed at work while away.

There were roughly two hours to go before he planned to leave and meet Maya at the bus stop. He hoped Desiree would wake up before then so he could express his concerns about the dreams he and Maya had experienced and see if she'd be willing to talk about her mother. He also figured it would be smart to admit to trying to take Maya's necklace. He wanted to make sure this came from his lips first, instead of Maya being the one to tell her.

*****

An hour later, Jayden hung up from a Zoom meeting as Desiree entered the kitchen.

"Good timing. My meeting finished a minute ago. Did you enjoy your nap?"

Desiree stretched her arms out. "Absolutely. I feel rested now. I'll leave in an hour to pick up Maya from the bus stop."

"No, don't worry about it. I can go out and get her. After spending two days in the hospital, you can use more rest."

"Okay. I won't argue with you on that," she said as she sat at the table. "Do you have another meeting coming up?"

"No."

She placed her elbows on the table and stared at Jayden, giving him her undivided attention. "So, what was it you wanted to talk to me about?"

Jayden leaned back in the chair. "I have to make a confession."

Desiree leaned forward and raised an eyebrow. "I'm listening."

"Remember when we talked about taking Maya's necklace away from her while she slept?"

"Yes."

"Well, I went into her room a few nights ago and tried to take it off of her while she was sleeping."

"You what?" Desiree said with her eyes sharpening. "I know we talked about it, but I never agreed for us to do it."

"I know. I was just very impatient with the situation and didn't want to wait any longer."

Desiree folded her arms. "Does she know you tried to take the necklace?"

"She didn't initially, but she knows now."

"And did you tell her I agreed to this?"

"No. I told her it was all my plan."

Desiree gazed at Jayden as if she were struggling to figure out what to say next. "Let me get this straight. You tried taking the necklace from her, and I'm assuming you didn't succeed. She now knows what you tried to do, which will only add fuel to the fire and make her attitude worse. You also now gave her reason not to trust you, not to mention you're going to have me looking at you sideways, wondering if there's anything else you need to tell me."

"I get that you're upset, and I don't blame you. The only thing I can say right now is I'm sorry. I admit it wasn't a good decision, and now I need to deal with the consequences."

Desiree sighed. "This is not what I wanted to hear after spending two days in the hospital."

Jayden remained quiet and contemplated whether he should even move forward now with mentioning the dreams he and Maya had experienced.

"Was this it, or do you have something else to tell me?"

Here's the opening I needed.

"I have something else, but we can talk about it another time if you want."

"I'd rather talk about it now instead of having to wait."

Jayden attempted to figure out the best way to start this discussion. He decided to get straight to the point. "Maya woke up screaming last night after having a nightmare about someone standing in the corner of her room."

Desiree's face softened. "It's been a while since she woke up from any night terrors. She used to get them more frequently when she was younger. Did she say anything else about the dream?"

"She said she couldn't see who it was because it was too dark. She also said something about smelling a wood odor, but she couldn't describe exactly what it was."

"Was she able to go back to sleep?"

"Eventually. She wanted me to keep the light on and the door open."

"I thought she'd outgrown these nightmares. I hope they're not coming back."

Jayden rubbed the side of his cheek. "And she wasn't the only one who had a nightmare."

Desiree snatched her head up. "You, too?"

"Yes. But my dream happened two nights ago. It was the first night you spent in the hospital."

"I'm afraid to ask what your dream was about."

"I was sleeping in your bedroom and started hearing creaking sounds. I saw someone rocking in the chair, but it was too dark for me to see a face. I'm pretty sure, though, it was a woman. I also remember smelling a strong cedar odor. I was planning to sneak a picture with my phone, and the person suddenly jumped up and choked me, and that's when I woke up."

Desiree continued to watch Jayden with steady and measured eyes.

"It took me a while before I could calm down and go back to sleep."

Desiree kept quiet.

"I find it strange that me and Maya had a similar dream about somebody in our rooms on back-to-back nights. And I can't even begin to tell you how long it's been since I had a nightmare."

Jayden grabbed his phone. "Let me show you something." He opened the nanny cam app and played back the recording before waking up from the nightmare.

"What's the problem?" Desiree asked.

"Look at the timestamp when it first starts."

He played the recording again.

"1:07. What's so special about that time?" she asked.

"What would you say if I told you I woke up exactly a minute later?"

Desiree's mouth gaped open for a moment. "No way."

"Now, some people could see that as pure coincidence, but something tells me that's not the case."

"What the hell is going on? That's gotta be a sign," Desiree said.

"But a sign for what? What does that number symbolize?"

"I wish I knew."

Jayden played the recording once again. "See anything else weird?"

Desiree shook her head.

"Let me help you out. Why did the nanny cam start recording a minute before I moved?"

"Now that you mention it, that's a good question."

"And tell me if I'm going crazy, but did you see the rocking chair move before I woke up?"

Desiree watched the recording again. "The footage is not too clear with this night vision, so I can't honestly say if I saw it move."

Jayden was tempted to mention the mysterious recording from last night when no one was in the room, but decided against it. He didn't want to throw too much Desiree's way since she'd just been released from the hospital.

Desiree leaned back in her chair. "Did you get a look at the person who was trying to choke you?"

"No, though I have my suspicions."

Desiree squinted. "Don't tell me you think it was my mother."

"Bingo."

"What sense would that make? Why would you have a dream about her choking you?"

"I have no clue. I've never been good at trying to interpret dreams."

"This is all a little too much for me. I'm confused and don't know what to think. Although I don't think it was my mother in your dream."

"You did say the rocking chair was given to you by your mother, didn't you?"

"Yes. But that doesn't mean she was the one sitting in the chair."

Jayden folded his arms, giving Desiree a slow, appraising look. "I know you haven't talked much about her, but do you realize I never knew your mother's name until Maya told me while you were in the hospital?"

"Are you sure I never told you?"

"I'm absolutely sure."

"I know I haven't said much about my mother, but I have my reasons. Don't get me wrong; she was a great mother to me, but if I'm being honest, there are things in my childhood I don't like talking about. And before you even think it, there wasn't any type of abuse going on in my household while I was growing up."

"Thanks for clearing that up, because that's where my thoughts were about to go." Jayden peered at Desiree. "Now that I think about it, not only did I not know your mother's name until recently, but I have no clue what she did for a living."

"Why is that important for you to know?"

"Because I'm concerned about trying to figure out what the dream meant, and I feel like if I know more about your mother, then maybe it can help me interpret the dream a little better."

"You still don't know if that was my mother in your dream."

"True. I understand it's only my theory, but I can't figure out who else it could have been."

Desiree shifted her eyes away from Jayden, focusing them on the tabletop. She returned her gaze to him. "If it'll make you feel any better, I can one hundred percent say my mother would have adored you if she were still around now."

"That's nice to know. But it's a little concerning to think my reward for being adored by your mother would be a good old-fashioned choking session."

Desiree displayed a dampened smile. "Contrary to what you think, I'll let you know my mother was a very generous and empathetic person. Always willing to give a helping hand, and down to earth by nature." She let out a small laugh. "However, you didn't want to get on her bad side. While she loved like no other, she also despised like no other. I can't even begin to tell you the stories of my mom almost getting into fist fights with people who she felt wronged her or messed with our family."

"I guess I can see where you get your feistiness from."

"Exactly. I learned from the best."

Jayden figured he'd take advantage of the opportunity to see how much more information Desiree was willing to give up about her mother.

"You still didn't answer me about what she did for a living?"

"Oh, she held down many different jobs during her lifetime. She was a short-order cook, a seamstress, and a small business owner."

"Sounds like she kept herself busy."

"Yup. Because she was a single mother, she had to hustle."

"Was she a religious person?"

"I'll say she believed in God, but she wasn't a church-going type of person, if that's what you're asking."

"Did she practice any specific form of religion?

Desiree let out an exasperated sigh. "How many more questions do you have for me?"

Jayden was surprised to see Desiree's abrupt attitude shift. "I have more, but I can see you're getting annoyed. Although, it would be nice if you could at least answer the last question I asked."

A frown developed on Desiree's face. "Do you mind if we stop talking about this now?"

Jayden wanted to keep prying but didn't want to press too hard and chose to respect Desiree's wishes. "Okay. No problem."

Desiree stretched her arms out wide and observed the time. "Maya's bus should be at the stop in the next half-hour. By the way, I changed my mind about you picking her up. I'm awake now and have no problems getting her. Besides, I miss my little girl and want to see her as soon as I possibly can."

Chapter 35

Desiree focused her vision down the street, hoping to see Maya's bus approaching. Between the long holiday weekend and the two days spent in the hospital, it felt like forever since she'd picked Maya up from the bus stop.

She lifted her baseball cap to wipe the moisture gathering where the brim of the cap met her forehead. The humidity levels were extremely high, and she longed for a cool shower.

She looked across the street, setting her sights on the ice cream shop calling her name. The line didn't appear to be too long, and she imagined this would be a nice surprise for Maya.

She flinched after feeling a bead of sweat roll down her side. She regretted not letting Jayden pick Maya up, but those thoughts went out the window after seeing the bus coming down the street. Desiree could feel a smile breaking through as the bus neared the corner. The customary stop sign extended alongside the bus with the flashing red lights. The door opened, and Maya stepped off the bus.

Desiree opened her arms. "There's my baby girl."

Maya slowed before she reached Desiree.

"Why are you slowing down? Come give your mother a hug."

Maya glanced behind her to see the bus pulling off. Once the bus had left, Maya opened her arms and gave Desiree a warm hug. "Sorry, Mom. I didn't want to be teased tomorrow by my friends seeing you get all mushy."

"Is it that bad?"

"Yes. They already tease me because you pick me up from the bus stop since they normally walk home by themselves."

"Well, I'm sorry for being such a caring and responsible mother."

Maya patted Desiree on the shoulder. "Glad to see they released you from the hospital. How are you feeling?"

"Much better now that I'm home."

"So, what did the doctors say?"

"Not much. They gave me medication to help with the sleepwalking. They also want me to remove anything in the apartment that might be dangerous for me to get my hands on."

"That's it?"

"There were other things we discussed, but nothing you'd be interested in. Anyway, enough about that. I have a surprise for you," Desiree said.

Maya opened her eyes wide. "I like surprises. What is it?"

Desiree pointed to the ice cream shop across the street. "You up for ice cream?"

A mischievous grin formed on Maya's face. "Of course. Why would you even ask?"

Desiree held her gaze on Maya. "Why are you giving me that look?"

"What look?" Maya asked, struggling to hold in a smirk.

"The same look you give whenever you're trying to hide something from me."

"How come you're so good at reading my face?"

"Because that's what mothers do. So, what's the big secret?"

"Mr. Jayden treated me to ice cream after he picked me up when you were in the hospital."

"What a shock. He normally doesn't eat sweets during the week."

"I was surprised, too," Maya said as her smile leveled off. "Does this mean no ice cream since I already had some?"

Without saying a word, Desiree grabbed Maya by the arm and led her across the street. "Does this answer your question?"

*****

They both left the shop, enjoying soft serve ice cream to help cool down.

"I can get used to this," Maya said.

"Sorry to burst your bubble, but this will not be the norm."

"I'm not surprised."

"I'm assuming you have homework to do tonight?"

"Of course."

Desiree licked the side of her cone to catch the ice cream starting to run down. "Are you keeping up with your studies so far this year?"

"Yes. I'm getting a lot of homework, but it's not hard."

Desiree's thoughts shifted from school to the necklace Maya continued to wear. She still couldn't believe Jayden had gone behind her back and tried to swipe the necklace while Maya was sleeping. Although she did give him credit for admitting he'd tried to do it, she thought about how this would affect Maya's relationship with him moving forward. She also wondered if Maya would ever mention what Jayden had attempted to do. She seemed okay now, so Desiree didn't want to stir the pot by talking about it.

"Don't know if you heard yet, but I had a nightmare last night," Maya said.

"Mr. Jayden told me. I was hoping you had outgrown those night terrors."

"This was different. I never remembered what was going on when I had the night terrors. But this time, I remember what happened. There was someone definitely standing in the corner of my room because I could see the shadow. They never said anything. They were just watching me."

"Could you tell if it was a man or a woman?"

"I couldn't see their face, but if I had to take a guess, I'd say it was a woman. And there was also a strong smell of wood. Almost like how my dresser smelled when Mr. Jayden first put it together."

"Are you sure it wasn't your dresser you were smelling?"

"No. That smell isn't as strong as it used to be in my room, so I'm sure it wasn't the dresser. It almost smelled a little sweet."

Desiree thought back to Jayden's nightmare, as he'd mentioned a similar smell. He had never said whether he'd told Maya about his dream, and she didn't want to bring it up in case he hadn't. Desiree could no longer deny what she'd heard from both Maya and Jayden. The odor they had both described was similar to the way her mother's clothes would smell after burning her incense sticks. She realized this was no longer a coincidence that they both had dreams on back-to-back nights. The questions now were why her mother had visited them in their dreams, and why she had resorted to violence during Jayden's nightmare.

Chapter 36

Desiree inspected the kitchen. The countertops were practically wiped clean, with only the bowl of apples remaining. Jayden had been tasked with hiding everything else, including all silverware and kitchen utensils that were no longer in the drawers.

She clapped softly. "Very impressive. Everything is out of sight except for the plastic fruit bowl. I guess I can't do too much damage with an apple."

"I sure hope not."

She strolled into the living room, noticing he'd also hidden all of the glass figurines resting on the coffee table and end tables.

"I see you're not playing around," she said.

"I'm doing what the hospital suggested. I may have gone overboard, but until we can find a device that can send an alert when you're sleepwalking, it's better to be safe than sorry. I also cleared out anything in the bathrooms I felt could be dangerous and removed the bat from under the bed."

Desiree scoped the area in front of her. "Where the hell did you put everything?"

"That's for me to know and for you not to find out."

Desiree approached Jayden with a hug. "It's a shame we need to go through this just because of me. Thanks for doing this. And thanks again for watching Maya these past few days."

"Hey, we're a team, and this is what teammates do."

She focused her attention on a bed sheet folded on the living room sofa. "Is that your way of telling me you'll be sleeping on the couch again?"

"Yes. I hope you don't mind?"

Although Desiree understood his concerns, she couldn't help but feel like she was infected with some type of contagious sickness that prevented Jayden from sleeping in the same room. She also had to consider whatever trauma Jayden had been dealing with regarding the nightmare. She could only imagine he no longer wanted to go anywhere near the rocking chair.

"That's fine."

"Also, I'm planning to work remotely here for one more day, and then I'll be heading back home."

An uncomfortable silence followed before Desiree spoke up. "Anyway, let me say goodnight to Maya. I doubt she's asleep yet since she just got into bed."

Desiree entered Maya's room to see her kneeling by her bed in prayer. She remained quiet to let Maya finish. After a few seconds, Maya noticed Desiree staring at her.

"Oh, didn't know you were there," Maya said.

"I didn't want to disturb you."

Maya sat on the bed with her legs crossed under her.

"I didn't know you still said your prayers at night," Desiree said.

"I normally say them silently in my head before I go to sleep, but I had extra prayers I wanted to say, and I thought it was better to kneel like I used to do."

"Okay. Makes sense." Desiree kissed Maya on the forehead. "Are you going to be all right sleeping in your bed tonight? Because I have a vacancy in my room since Mr. Jayden will be sleeping on the couch again."

"I think I'll be fine as long as you leave my bedroom light on."

"You got it. Try to have a good night's sleep," she said, blowing Maya a kiss before she left the room.

She stepped into the hallway and peered into the living room, spotting Jayden watching TV. She paused, looking at him for an extended moment before she walked into the living room.

"I'm about to take my medication and get ready for bed," she said.

"Try to have a good night's sleep."

Desiree gave him a peck on the lips. "Same for you and, hopefully, no more nightmares."

*****

A few hours later, Desiree shifted in her bed as another dream sequence intruded upon her sleep. She once again found herself in the hallway of her mother's house. The ground was shrouded in a thick mist, with doors lining both sides of the hallway. She took a few steps as her feet sank into the mysterious soft ground surface.

She neared the first door on the right with a rose-colored crystal knob. She attempted to twist the knob, but the door did not open. She raised her head and found the number 103 written on the plaque above.

She continued until she came upon the next door on the left, which also had a rose-colored crystal knob. She twisted it, but the door did not open. She looked up above the door, seeing the number 104.

She walked in front of another door on her right, containing a jade-colored knob with no plaque above it. She twisted the knob and pushed the door open. A cherry-wood sleigh bed was positioned in the middle of the room, along with two nightstands on both sides of the bed. She turned her attention to the desk pushed up against the corner of the room. She neared the desk to see a sheet of paper with a marker resting on top. She flipped the sheet and spotted Jayden's name written in bold letters. Without hesitation, she raised her fist in the air and swung down, striking the desk with such force that it collapsed.

She opened her eyes while clutching her chest after waking up.

Chapter 37

The following morning, Desiree had finished walking Maya to the bus stop and entered the apartment. Other than the dream sequence she'd experienced, she was unaware of any sleepwalking episodes or anything else that might have disrupted her sleep during the night. She had been grateful for the medication, which had kept her in a deep sleep. She didn't even recall getting out of bed to use the bathroom.

She hadn't had an opportunity to speak with Jayden in the morning yet since he was still asleep when she had left to take Maya to the bus stop.

She made her way into the living room, noticing an empty sofa. She confirmed Jayden's whereabouts after hearing running water in the bathroom.

Last night had been the third time she'd experienced this recurring dream sequence in the hallway of her mother's house, and she could clearly see a pattern developing. However, this had been the first instance she remembered Jayden's name appearing in her dream, and her violent reaction to seeing it was even more puzzling. She could no longer ignore the fact that a message was being sent from these dream sequences, and she had no clue how much time she had left to decode the message.

She entered the kitchen to grab a bottle of water and looked up when Jayden appeared.

"Good morning. How did you sleep?" Jayden asked.

"Okay, for the most part. I don't think I left the bed once unless you know something I don't know."

"If you were sleepwalking, I didn't know. From what I can see, everything appears to be in order around the apartment." He reached for an apple from the fruit bowl on the counter. "I'm assuming you dropped Maya off at the bus stop without any problems?"

Desiree nodded.

Jayden held his gaze on Desiree. "Are you good?"

"Not really."

"What's going on?" Jayden asked as he stepped closer.

She instinctively stepped back.

Jayden's forehead wrinkled in confusion. "What's wrong?"

"I'm sorry. I didn't mean to take a step back. I'm just a little frazzled from the dreams I've been having."

Jayden pulled up a chair and sat in front of his laptop at the kitchen table. "Did you have another dream last night?"

She nodded with her eyebrows knitted together.

Jayden continued to stare at Desiree intently. "Why are you looking at me like I'm crazy?"

She took a sip from her water bottle and held her gaze on Jayden for an extended period before speaking. "I feel like I should know you pretty well after being together for two years. Wouldn't you say so?"

"Yes, I would agree with that."

"And I should be able to trust that you're not hiding anything from me about you now or in the past?"

"What are you talking about? Why are you acting all suspicious like I did something wrong?"

Desiree folded her arms. "I'd act even less suspicious if you can just answer my question on whether or not I should trust you're not hiding anything from me."

Desiree's heart rate sped up after seeing Jayden hesitate before offering a response. "You're not helping your case right now by being slow to respond. And the longer it takes for you to answer, the more worried I'm getting."

Jayden swallowed the lump in his throat. "I do have something I can share about my past. Something I contemplated telling you for a while, but I honestly never had the courage to talk about it."

Desiree's nostrils flared as her mind immediately drifted to the worst-case scenario.

"It's about how my marriage ended. I never told you the complete story."

Desiree rested her elbows on the table and leaned forward.

"Me and my ex-wife were having issues trying to conceive a baby, and after visiting fertility doctors and taking tests, it turned out the problem was with me," he said while nervously tapping his foot on the floor. "Without going into too much detail, I have a hormonal issue that's affecting my ability to become a father. And the doctors only gave me a five percent chance of ever conceiving a baby." He stopped talking, refusing to provide Desiree with any eye contact.

Desiree's face softened.

"Between all of the financial stress from medical bills and the emotional roller coaster we experienced dealing with this, our marriage suffered. And there's nothing worse than coming home from work one day and finding a note on your bed from your spouse who suddenly decided to pack up their things and ask for a divorce. The same person you thought was going to be your partner for life. The same person you thought would be with you through sickness and in health. The same person you hoped would offer you much-needed support during difficult times, but instead, this person decides to run out on you."

Desiree's eyes watered as she processed what she'd heard. She gave Jayden a gentle hug. "I'm so sorry to hear."

"It is what it is. Can't do anything about what happened in the past, but I can tell you one thing; going through something like that really does toughen up your skin. I'll admit I was broken for a while, but I was able to eventually pick myself off the ground and keep moving forward."

Whatever ominous suspicions Desiree had floating around in her head about Jayden had momentarily faded away. This was far from the secret she'd expected to hear.

"Sorry if I ruined any happy vibes you were trying to generate for the day."

"I'm happy you at least told me. I'm sure it's a relief to get this out in the open and off your chest."

Hearing this news tightened the pressure on Desiree to be forthcoming with Jayden regarding her own past. She could only imagine the amount of courage Jayden had needed to muster to tell his story.

She sighed, now feeling guilty about shooting down Jayden's prior attempts to find out about her mother's background. She had a feeling this moment would eventually come, and she figured there was no better time for her to start talking than now.

"I guess it's my turn," she said.

"What are you talking about?"

"It's my turn to tell you about my mother."

"I don't want you to feel obligated to tell me now after what I told you."

"It's okay. I think this is the perfect opportunity for me to talk."

"All right. I'm not going to argue with you if that's what you want."

She remained silent for a few seconds, attempting to figure out where to start.

"Isabelle Campbell was her birth name, but people in our town outside of New Orleans knew her as Madam Isy. My mother was born with an incredible intuition and had a way of connecting with people and their emotions within the first few minutes of talking to them."

Jayden continued to focus on Desiree, listening attentively.

"She was what people referred to as a mystic. She could feel things beyond the conscious world that we know. This gift of hers came with its privileges, and also some criticism. There was a group of people in our town who respected her, some who feared her, and some folks who didn't believe in her abilities. It was always her dream to be a small business owner, so she moved forward with opening a tarot card reading business in town." Desiree smirked.

"The name, Madam Isy, hung on a sign above the door. I remember her being so proud of the sign because I helped with the design.

"Her business wasn't too far from the house, so I would go there after school if I didn't have too much homework to help clean up or run errands for her while she was working." Desiree smiled. "During those times when she didn't have a customer, I would be off on the side, playing with the tarot cards, acting like I had my own imaginary clients." Desiree stopped to see if Jayden had anything to say.

"Wow. That's deep. I never knew anybody who was a tarot card reader. I mean … I've seen tarot card reader businesses before, but I was always curious if anyone actually went inside. Did your mother get a lot of business?"

"She did in the beginning. I think people were more curious about her business since it was the first of its kind in our town. After that, she had a few repeat customers and maybe some tourists who found their way to our town from New Orleans."

"How long did she have the business?"

"Maybe a couple of years. It should have been longer, but things went downhill after her first year."

"What happened?"

"Once the rumors and gossip started around town, she began losing clients. Some people said she was a fake, and other people thought she was some kind of witch. She heard it all, but that didn't stop her because she believed in her abilities. It wasn't until her shop was vandalized that we knew things were getting serious. But if you knew my mother, this made her even more determined to keep the shop open and not let those people run us out of town.”

“How old were you when all of this was happening?”

“Around thirteen.”

“Must have been tough on you.”

“That’s an understatement. It was by far the worst school year of my life. Word got around that I was Madam Isy’s daughter, and I had to deal with all kinds of bullying and teasing in school. I couldn’t even begin to tell you how many fights I had. My mother would come up to the school sometimes to talk to my teachers, which normally didn’t end well. There were a few times where I thought she was about to get into physical fights with them because she felt they weren’t doing enough to protect me.”

“So sorry to hear about all of that.”

“And you still haven’t heard the worst part.”

“We can stop right here if you want. I can see you’re getting agitated.”

“I’ve come this far talking about it, might as well finish the story.” She swallowed a gulp of water. “My mom’s business closed after only two years because some lunatic, or lunatics, decided to burn down her shop in the middle of the night. She lost everything she worked so hard for, and they never found out who did it.”

“That’s horrible.”

Desiree gritted her teeth, attempting to calm down from the anger building. “And this is why I never wanted to talk about it, because it still pisses me off.”

“I can now see why you avoided the subject. Does Maya know everything you told me?”

"She knows the basics about the tarot card business and someone burning it down. But I told her not to say anything to anyone about it. So, I'm happy to know she didn't mention it to you when you were talking with her."

Jayden leaned forward in his chair. "I will say this is making a lot more sense to me now with the necklace and your mother being a tarot card reader. Did she ever show an ability to tell the future?"

"If she did, I don't recall knowing about it. But she didn't actually market herself as a fortune teller." Desiree put her hand up. "Hold on, I know what you're thinking. I know my mother had some unique abilities, but she didn't practice witchcraft. I definitely wasn't aware she had any type of supernatural ability to be putting spells on things or people, or telling the future."

"So, how do you explain Maya's ability to foreshadow the future since you gave her the necklace?"

"I'll admit I don't have an answer for you."

"I'm sorry, but after hearing your mother's story, I'm even more convinced that's no ordinary necklace. I'm curious if she ever gave you a necklace like that when you were younger?"

"No. I guess I wasn't special enough. And speaking of the necklace, it's been a while since Maya has foreshadowed anything that I'm aware of," Desiree said.

"True. I don't remember anything recently."

"Does this change your mind about wanting to take the necklace away from her?" Desiree asked.

"I guess, for now. Although I still think she's acting a little strange with the necklace on."

"Don't know what else to say. We can continue to monitor her and see what happens in the future," Desiree said.

Jayden shifted his eyes to his laptop as an email appeared. "It's been nice chatting with you, but I need to start working."

"Same for me. I'm sure I have some catching up to do since I missed the past two days."

"Thanks for the talk. It was a lot more information than I ever thought you would give me," Jayden said.

"You asked for my truth, and I gave it to you. And thank you for speaking your truth."

"No problem," Jayden said with apprehension. "Now I'm thinking I was better off not knowing what you told me about your mother."

"Why? Are you scared because I told you about her background, and you think she's coming back to haunt you for some reason?"

"That's a damn good question. Too good, if you ask me."

Chapter 38

Jayden finished typing up an email, responding to a request from his coworker. He'd struggled for most of the day to concentrate on his work, as the discussion with Desiree had continuously floated in and out of his mind. Learning about Desiree's mother was a true eye-opener, along with everything she had gone through while trying to run her tarot card business.

As much as Desiree didn't want to believe anything supernatural was going on, Jayden had come to a different conclusion. He was absolutely convinced the mysterious events that had occurred over the past couple of weeks had not been the result of coincidences but were manifested by Grandma Isy.

He didn't think attempting to take the necklace from Maya and opening the keepsake box would warrant such a violent reaction from Grandma Isy in his dream. But he couldn't think of any other times in his relationship with Desiree where he'd done anything else wrong that would have put him on Grandma Isy's hit list.

Now that Desiree had enlightened him on her mother's background, he could no longer picture spending the night in the apartment without having real concerns. It also didn't help to know a second necklace existed in the keepsake box, waiting for its future owner to wear. It bothered him that Desiree had decided to keep the second necklace a secret. Though, if he hadn't been snooping around, he never would have found it.

For some reason, he wasn't welcome and had no problem heeding the warning. But he also didn't want to feel like he had abandoned both Desiree and Maya.

He realized there was still unfinished business concerning what type of device to buy for waking up Desiree during any future sleepwalking episodes. Although he did find comfort in knowing they had at least taken precautions to limit the chances of Desiree hurting herself or Maya if she continued to sleepwalk. He also hoped the medicine Desiree had started taking would continue to work and keep her from wandering from the bed at night.

Desiree had left to pick up Maya from the bus stop, and he expected them to come walking through the doors shortly. Outside of the brief interaction he'd had with Maya after her nightmare, there hadn't been much talking between them since she'd found out about his failed attempt to take her necklace. He continued to regret his decision and hoped this didn't put a permanent scar on their relationship.

The front door unlocked, and Maya came walking in with an agitated expression on her face. She didn't even bother to look his way and stomped straight to her room with her bookbag dragging alongside her. She entered her bedroom and closed the door.

Desiree entered the apartment and approached Jayden with a blank expression on her face.

"I'm almost afraid to ask what happened."

Desiree stretched out her arm and opened her hand to reveal the necklace sitting in her palm.

Jayden flinched, seeing the necklace. "Did you take it from her?"

"No. The necklace fell off while she was playing around with her friends at school. The clasp broke and needs to be fixed."

Jayden couldn't help but feel a sense of relief that his wish had finally been granted, though this wasn't the way he'd expected her to stop wearing the necklace.

"I can tell she's not too happy about it," Jayden said.

"She's also upset with me because I told her we can take it to a jewelry store to have it fixed, but it probably wouldn't be until the weekend, and she doesn't want to wait that long."

As much as Jayden was relieved to know Maya was no longer wearing the necklace, he imagined this could be a golden opportunity to reverse the bad karma he'd felt surrounding him. He could hopefully appease both Maya and Grandma Isy if he offered to bring it to a store to have it fixed after he finished working.

"If you want, I can find a jewelry store after I log off from work to see if they can fix it."

Desiree tilted her head to the side. "I thought you'd be happy she was no longer wearing the necklace and not be in such a rush to have it fixed?"

"A part of me agrees with what you're saying. But I feel it's the least I can do after what happened this past week."

"Are you feeling guilty now for what you tried to do?"

Jayden smirked. "I guess you could say that. I also don't want any more trouble with your mother."

Desiree shook her head. "I keep telling you it hasn't been proven that was my mother in your dream."

She put the necklace on the table in front of Jayden. "If you want to get it fixed, be my guest. I'm sure Maya will be thrilled."

Desiree walked out of the kitchen, leaving Jayden alone with the necklace sitting on the table. This was the first time he could remember being so close to the necklace. It didn't appear to be anything other than a standard silver necklace with a charm attached. Although now knowing the history behind the person who had gifted it to Maya, he felt like he was staring at an ancient artifact with supernatural abilities. He slowly moved his finger toward the necklace but stopped short of touching it. His mind had shifted into overdrive as he imagined he would receive a shock if he put his finger on it.

He opened a cabinet above the sink to grab a sandwich bag. He flipped the bag inside out while placing his fingers in it. With his fingers covered by the plastic, he reached down, grabbed the necklace, and pulled it into the bag before flipping it back to its normal position and sealing it shut.

Out of the corner of his eye, he found Desiree standing there with her arms folded, shaking her head.

"Are you afraid to touch it?"

Jayden offered a sheepish grin. "Maybe." He looked behind Desiree and into the hallway. "Do me a favor and don't tell Maya what I'm doing. I want it to be a surprise."

Desiree let out a chuckle. "Oh, I see you're really trying to gain brownie points with her."

"If that's what you want to call it. I hope she'll appreciate what I'm about to do."

*****

Two hours later, Jayden was lucky enough to find a local jeweler who could replace the clasp and complete the necklace repair. After the necklace was fixed, Jayden continued his conscious effort to avoid touching it and kept the necklace in the sandwich bag.

He entered the apartment, listening for any sounds that might reveal Desiree or Maya's location. There was no one present in the living room or the kitchen. He peered down the hallway to see both bedroom doors closed. He walked down the hallway and stopped in front of Desiree's bedroom, lightly tapping on the door.

"Come in," she said.

He opened the door and spotted Desiree sitting in front of her computer. "It's almost six thirty, and you're still working?"

She continued to type without glancing Jayden's way. "This is what happens when you're playing catch-up after being out for two days." She stopped typing and swiveled her office chair around. "Did you get the necklace fixed?" she whispered.

Jayden reached into his pocket, grabbed the sandwich bag, and then placed it on the desk.

Desiree opened the bag, pulling out the necklace. She examined the clasp, confirming the necklace had been fixed. "Look at you playing the superhero of the day. Maya is going to be shocked." She put the necklace on the desk.

"Next question is: do you want me to give it to her, or do you want to do it?"

"I'll do it. But do you mind putting the necklace back in the bag?"

Desiree shook her head. "Still can't muster up the courage to touch it on your own?"

"What do you think?"

She put the necklace in the bag. "Good luck."

"Thanks," Jayden said as he left the room.

He stood in front of Maya's door, taking in a deep breath before knocking. He didn't receive any response and knocked again.

"Yes," Maya said from beyond the door.

"It's Mr. Jayden. I need to show you something."

There was a pause before she spoke up. "Come in," she said in a somber tone.

Jayden cracked open the door. Maya was sitting on her bed, writing in a notebook.

Jayden took one step into her bedroom and stopped. "Are you doing homework?"

Without looking up, she nodded and continued writing.

"I don't mean to disturb you, but I thought you'd be interested in seeing what I have to show you."

"I doubt it," she said in a matter-of-fact tone, continuing to look down at her notebook.

Without saying anything, Jayden raised his arm, dangling the sandwich bag from his fingertips. He purposely remained quiet to see how long it would take for Maya to be curious enough to lift her head.

After what seemed like a long few minutes, she finally looked his way. "Is that my necklace?"

"Yes."

"Is it fixed?"

Jayden held back a grin. "I just came back from getting it fixed."

She opened her mouth wide and jumped up from the bed. She reached for the bag, grabbed it from Jayden, and then opened it. She studied the clasp, proceeding to open and close it to confirm it worked. She placed the jewelry around her neck and, after a few tries, closed the clasp to secure it.

She opened her arms for a hug. "Thank you, Mr. Jayden."

Jayden reached forward, giving her a tight hug. A sense of relief flooded his body as he, at least for the moment, had Maya's loving attention. She held on for a few seconds before she let go and retreated to her bed with a broad smile.

She patted the necklace and pointed at Jayden. "You did good."

Jayden laughed. "Is that another one of your mother's sayings?"

"You got it."

Jayden gave her a thumbs-up and took a few steps back toward the door. "I don't want to disturb you any longer from doing your homework. I guess I'll see you shortly for dinner."

Jayden closed the door and immediately spotted Desiree leaning up against the wall by her door. She patted her heart, mouthing the words, "*Thank you.*"

Chapter 39

Jayden pressed the remote to open the garage before pulling his car forward. He'd left Desiree's apartment after eating dinner and arrived back at his condo. He shut off the car, leaning his head back against the headrest. A mild throbbing pulsated around his forehead, which normally indicated a headache was brewing. He closed his eyes as a slew of thoughts infiltrated his mind.

He was optimistic that the medicine Desiree was taking would continue to prevent her from sleepwalking. He also hoped Maya would sleep well and avoid any more nightmares.

He felt a sense of relief to finally make it back home to clear his head and welcome some peace. The unexpected overnight stays at Desiree's apartment had thrown him off his schedule, even though he had enjoyed the opportunity to work remotely and avoid commuting to work.

He sent a text to Desiree, letting her know he'd made it home safely, and then exited the car. He entered the condo and was happy to see that he at least remembered to shut off all the lights this time while he was gone. He took a step into the laundry room, placing his overnight bag on top of the washer with the intention of washing his clothes the next day. He walked up the stairs and into his bathroom for a quick hot shower.

After the shower, he stretched out on his bed to unwind. Up until now, he'd kept his mind busy during the day to avoid thinking about the interesting family history lesson Desiree had given. With no rocking chairs or keepsake boxes to worry about in the room, he hoped for a restful night's sleep.

*****

Jayden woke up, staring into the darkness. He could have sworn his phone chimed. He listened out further to make sure he wasn't hearing things. Seconds later, his phone lit up, showing that a text had come through at 3:30 in the morning.

He grabbed his phone to see who was texting in the middle of the night. He squinted and saw Maya's name appearing as the sender.

Sorry if I'm waking you up, but we have a little problem here.

Jayden began typing.

What's wrong?
I woke up when I heard a knock, and I now see my mom standing by my door.
Is she up? Did she say anything?
No. She's just standing by my door while I'm typing now.
It sounds like she's sleepwalking again. Sit still for now, and let me know if she starts moving.

There was a thirty-second pause, and Maya hadn't responded.

You still there?
Yes. She's not doing anything. Still standing in the same spot. This is the first time I'm seeing her sleepwalking, and it's creeping me out.
Don't worry. It may seem weird seeing her like that, but she's not going to hurt you. Just relax and keep still.

Another twenty seconds had passed before the dots displayed on Jayden's phone, showing Maya was typing another message.

I'm starting to panic. She got down on the floor and is crawling around.
Stay calm. Is she coming near your bed?
No. She's crawling by the door like she's looking for something.
Sit tight.
Should I throw a pillow at her? Maybe that will wake her?
No. As long as she's not in danger of hurting herself or you, just leave her alone.

Another few seconds had passed before Maya responded.

Help me! She's starting to crawl closer to my bed. I'm freaking out and about to run.
It's okay. Stay where you are.

Jayden had remained calm throughout the text message exchange up until this point. But his comfort level dropped when Maya stopped responding to him.

Are you still there?
Maya? Are you ok?

"Oh shit. What the hell is going on over there?"

He tried calling Maya, but she didn't pick up. He jumped up from his bed, reaching for a pair of jeans to throw on, along with a T-shirt. He looked on the nightstand but didn't see his key fob. He thought that was where he'd left it when he'd come in last night.

He swiveled his head around, looking at his dresser and the nightstand on the other side of the bed. He dropped his head, examining the floor to see if the fob had fallen.

"You gotta be kidding me. Where the hell is my key?"

He dialed Maya's number again, receiving no answer.

He darted out of the bedroom and ran downstairs, almost tripping in the process. He lunged for the handrail and grabbed it to keep steady. When he arrived on the first floor and entered the kitchen, he scanned the counter, but had no luck locating the fob. He took a few steps toward the laundry room and approached his overnight bag on top of the washer, and that was when he spotted the fob nestled in the folds of the bag. He imagined he must have inadvertently let go of the fob as he was tossing his bag on top of the washer.

He tapped his phone to wake it up, confirming he hadn't missed a text or call from Maya. Upon opening the garage door, a ringtone played on his phone as Maya's name appeared on the caller ID.

"Maya! Are you all right?"

"Yes. I'm in the living room right now. I didn't feel safe staying in my room with her, but I had to wait for her to move out of my way so I could leave," she whispered.

"Where is she now?"

"Still in my room. Sounds like she's banging on something."

"That's not good. Can you go back to your room to see what she's doing? I want to make sure she's not hurting herself."

"Do I have to?"

"Yes. We need to make sure she's okay."

Maya let out a loud sigh. He waited as he listened to her shallow breathing coming through the phone.

After a few seconds, she whispered, "She's banging on my closet door pretty hard."

"I'm going to need you to do us both a big favor and wake her up."

"I thought you told me to leave her alone?"

"I did, but now she's in a position where she might hurt herself."

Silence followed as Jayden could hear the rhythmic knocking in the background.

"Can you do that for me?" Jayden asked.

"What do I do? Tap her on the shoulder?"

"Maybe you won't need to. Turn on your phone flashlight and shine it in her face to see if that wakes her. It worked for me when I found her sleepwalking. But before you do that, put your pillows on the floor around her and get ready to try to catch her if she starts to fall."

"What are you talking about? I'm not strong enough to hold her up if she falls."

"That's why I asked you to put pillows on the floor."

"Wait … she stopped banging."

"Good. Now put those pillows around her and turn on your flashlight."

"I … I can't do that right now."

"Why not?"

"Because she turned her head in my direction."

"Does she look like she's up now?"

"No. She's not saying anything, and she looks creepy. I'm sorry, but I'm not going near her."

Jayden could hear shuffling going on through the phone.

"I'm back in the living room, and I really wish you were here now."

"I got dressed before you called and was going to make my way out there. I can still come, but it will take about twenty-five minutes."

"I don't care. Can you please come as soon as possible?"

Jayden put the phone on speaker and opened the garage. "I'm on my way. Stay on the phone with me and give me updates on what she's doing."

Jayden reversed out of the garage, closed the garage door, and put on the GPS. This was the first time he could recall not seeing any traffic on the map, but it made complete sense based on the early morning hours.

"Are you good, Maya? Still with me?"

"Yes."

"What's she doing now?"

"She came out of my room and is standing in the hallway."

"Do you have any lights on?"

"In the living room."

"Is the hallway light on?"

"No."

"Can you go and turn it on to see if the light might wake her?"

"That means I need to go near her."

"Or you can turn on your phone flashlight and shine it on her. That way, you don't need to come too close to her."

"Hold on."

Jayden heard more shuffling.

"My flashlight is on."

"Now you'll need to go closer to shine the light in her face."

Jayden stopped at a light. He scoped the intersection and, after not seeing any cars, he ran through the red light, hoping no police were hiding out anywhere. He continued following the GPS, which placed him half a mile from entering the ramp to the highway. He then heard Maya gasp.

"What happened?"

He received no response but could hear what sounded like Maya on the move.

"Maya?"

"I'm in the kitchen," she whispered. "Before I could put the flashlight on her, she started walking in my direction. You sure she can't hear me when I'm talking?"

"Not that I know of."

"Where are you? Are you close?"

"I'm about fifteen minutes away. Where's your mom now?"

"I guess somewhere in the living room. I'm letting you know now, if she comes in the kitchen with me, I'm going to scream," Maya said, continuing in a whispered tone.

"I know it's not easy seeing your mother like this, but she's not going to hurt you."

"You keep saying that, but how do you know? Isn't that part of the problem? We don't know if she might start acting violent while she's sleepwalking?"

Jayden always found it difficult trying to rationalize with Maya. She was too smart for her age and always seemed two steps ahead.

"Trust me; I'm sure she won't bother you," Jayden said, attempting to sound confident with his words, though he couldn't completely guarantee her safety.

He merged onto I-77 with only a scattering of car lights joining him on the highway. He pressed the pedal harder than normal and prayed there were no speed traps set up anywhere.

"I'll be there shortly. Where's your mother now?"

He didn't receive a response.

"Come on, Maya. You make me nervous when you take too long to answer."

"I'm here. Since I can't see her where I'm standing, I was trying to listen out to see if I could figure out where she was. Hold on a second."

Jayden heard rustling over the phone.

"Oh crap!"

"What? What's wrong?"

"I think she walked out of the apartment."

"Are you sure?"

"I heard a door slam, and it didn't sound like one of our bedroom or bathroom doors. I also don't see her anywhere in the living room."

"Shit," Jayden mumbled. "Do you see her out in the hallway?"

"Hold on a second. I'm looking now and don't see her."

Jayden's heart rate spiked at the thought of Desiree now aimlessly wandering around outside the confines of her apartment.

The GPS indicated he would arrive in five minutes, but a lot could happen in that short amount of time, especially with Desiree being oblivious to what she was doing.

"Stay in the apartment and keep peeking out in the hallway to see if you see her. I'll be there in a few minutes."

Jayden exited the highway and blew through two additional intersections with red lights, free from any vehicular traffic.

*****

Jayden arrived at the apartment, ignoring the no-parking sign in front of the building, and turned on his hazard lights.

"Still no sign of her?" he asked.

"No."

"I just parked. I'll be there in a second."

He ran into the lobby and mashed the elevator button. He entered the elevator, pressed the 10th floor button, frantically pushing the button to close the door. He stood, nervously tapping his foot on the floor, wishing the elevator could move faster.

The doors finally opened, and he stepped out, searching the hallway, but he didn't see Desiree. He sprinted to the apartment and spotted Maya with the door cracked open. She immediately lunged at Jayden and wrapped her arms around him in a tight hug. She wiped a tear trickling down her right cheek.

"Please, find my mom."

Jayden glanced beyond Maya and into the apartment. "Are you sure she's not in the apartment?"

"Yes. I ran back in and checked all of the rooms."

"Go back inside, but keep the door cracked open to see if you spot her. I'll be back."

Jayden peered down the hallway. Based on the L-shaped hallway, his vision was limited. He hoped she had walked around the bend.

He jogged down the hallway, praying that once he rounded the corner, he'd see Desiree. He cleared the corner, but there was no trace of her.

"Where the heck did she go?" he whispered.

He rotated his head from side to side, analyzing the doors on the floor. He approached what appeared to be a utility closet. He tried opening it, but it didn't budge. He made his way farther down, passing a few apartment doors, and continued to the end of the hallway until he arrived in front of a window. He looked out of the window; however, it was too dark to see down below. He studied the edges of the window but didn't see any way to open it.

His phone chimed with a text from Maya.

Did you find her around the corner?

No.

Should we call 911 to report her missing?

No. Not yet. She couldn't have gone too far. Let me keep checking.

Jayden focused on the carpeted floor to see if he could find anything indicating Desiree's presence. He figured she'd likely been walking around the floor barefoot since she was not someone who normally slept with socks on.

He marched back around the corner and stopped by the elevator. *Could she have used the elevator*? This hadn't crossed his mind until now. If she had used the elevator, he imagined his search area would need to expand exponentially.

He put his hands on top of his head, trying to think of where else she could possibly be. His quick brainstorming session paid off as he bit his bottom lip, upset for not thinking about this earlier.

He jogged over to the stairwell door and cracked it open. It was at this moment that the excessive pressure sitting on his chest was released.

Desiree was sitting on the floor of the stairwell with her back against the wall and her head slouched down. As he figured, she had no socks on, and the bottom of her feet contained a sprinkling of dirt she'd picked up from walking around barefoot. He was relieved to see she at least had on long pajamas, so the back of her legs weren't touching the cold floor.

He kneeled in front of her, examining the exposed skin along her arms and neck, but he didn't see any visible injuries. He rubbed the side of her cheek with the back of his fingers. She flinched, lifting her head. Her eyes fluttered as she squinted at Jayden.

"I … I thought you left. What are you doing back here?" she said in a muted tone.

"Let's get you back in the apartment first. Then we can talk."

She rotated her head, looking at her surroundings. "Where are we?"

"In the stairwell of your building."

Her eyes widened as if she had received a jolt, waking her up. "How did—" She stopped speaking abruptly, shaking her head. "I answered my own question. This is crazy."

Jayden reached out and grabbed her by the arms, slowly pulling her up. She wobbled for a second, and then caught her balance.

"Where's Maya?"

"She was patiently waiting for me to find you, so let's get you back into the apartment and make your daughter happy."

Chapter 40

Desiree held on to Jayden's shoulder to keep steady as they shuffled down the hallway. They neared the door, and Maya opened it, taking a step back.

"It's all right, Maya. She's awake now," Jayden said.

Desiree opened her arms for a hug. Maya hesitated before obliging and proceeding with a hug. Maya let go as Desiree continued to hold on longer.

"I'm so happy you're okay," Desiree said.

They entered the apartment, and Desiree took a seat on the sofa. "My mouth feels dry," she said.

Before she could say anything further, Maya ran into the kitchen and returned with a bottle of water.

Desiree took a gulp. "I can't believe I walked out of the apartment." She grabbed Maya's arm. "I'm so sorry if I scared you."

"I'm fine. I'm just happy Mr. Jayden found you."

A group of wrinkled lines developed on Desiree's forehead. "I was having this crazy dream we were in the apartment sleeping, and I woke up smelling smoke. I went to Maya's room, and there was a bunch of smoke, but I couldn't see her. I remember getting down and crawling around to try to find her bed."

Both Jayden and Maya locked eyes.

Desiree stopped. "What's the matter?"

"Keep going on with your dream. I'll tell you after," Jayden said.

Desiree shrugged and continued, "I remember banging on a door because I wasn't sure if Maya was hiding. Then it sounded like I heard her voice in the room. I tried to follow her voice, but then I lost track of the sound, and then I ran out into the hallway to get help. That's the last thing I remember."

"That makes a lot more sense," Jayden said.

"Why do you say that?"

"Maya called me because she found you sleepwalking and didn't know what to do. I was on the phone with her on my way over here, and she was describing what you were doing while you were sleepwalking. And it's exactly the same as what you described in your dream."

"Are you serious?"

"Yes. And it wasn't fun seeing you like that," Maya said.

Desiree took another gulp of water. "That's wild. It's amazing what your mind can do while you're sleeping."

"Looks like we confirmed your medicine doesn't always work and stop you from sleepwalking," Jayden said.

Desiree shook her head. "Not true, because I fell asleep before I could take my medicine."

"Oh. Well then, there's still some hope with your medication. You need to remember to take it before you go to sleep," Jayden said.

Desiree peeked down at her feet. "My feet are cold," she said. She rolled her ankles, looking at the soles of her feet. "They're also dirty. Can someone get me a wet paper towel and socks?"

Maya left the room.

Desiree gazed at Jayden. "I feel so bad you had to come right back here in the middle of the night for me."

"No problem. That's what concerned boyfriends do."

She leaned forward to give Jayden a hug. "What time is it?"

"A few minutes after five."

"What are you going to do about work? I'm sure you can use more sleep, and you don't even have your laptop with you to work remotely."

"I honestly haven't even thought about it with everything going on." He stopped talking as Maya came back with a wet paper towel, a plastic bag, and white ankle socks.

Desiree wiped the dirt from the bottom of her feet and placed the soiled paper towels in the plastic bag.

Jayden rubbed his chin. "Now that I think about it, I can't remember the last time I called out sick for work. This may be a good reason to do so."

"It's going to make me feel guilty you're calling out sick because of me," Desiree said.

"Don't feel bad. I need a break from work, anyway."

"How you holding up?" Desiree asked Maya.

"I'm tired."

"Well, why don't you go back to bed and try to get a couple of more hours of sleep so you won't be too tired for school?"

Without saying a word, Maya walked to her bedroom.

Desiree rolled the socks on her feet. "I'm afraid to go back to sleep now." She pointed down the hallway, toward the bedroom. "You're welcome to go into the bedroom and take a nap. I think I'll turn on the TV and stay up until Maya's ready for school."

Jayden let out a small laugh. "I think I'll pass. After all this excitement, I'm not even close to being sleepy. Also, please don't take this the wrong way, but I'm not eager to be sleeping back in your bedroom for a while."

"Why?" Desiree asked, but before Jayden could respond, she waved him off. "Forget it. I know why. Dumb question on my part."

"I think the best thing for us to do now is for you to lie down on the sofa and try to get some sleep. Since I'm wide-awake, I can stay here in the living room and make sure you don't go wandering off the couch. And then, when the time comes, I can walk Maya to the bus stop. I'll make sure you're awake before I leave."

Desiree smiled, wondering what she had done to deserve such an unselfish man. "I don't want you to go through all of this trouble for me. You did more than enough coming out here in the middle of the night to rescue me from wandering to God knows where and to make sure Maya was okay. But I can't lie, that sounds like an offer I can't refuse."

"Then we have a deal."

"I guess so."

Desiree proceeded to lie down on the sofa. Jayden kissed her on the forehead before strolling over to the recliner.

"You sure you're not going to fall asleep on the recliner?" she asked.

"No. I'm up and will keep my eyes on you."

*****

Desiree drifted off to sleep. In what seemed like an instant, she found herself back in a familiar setting. She stared down the hallway and took a few steps through the heavy mist covering the floor. She came to the first door on her right and noted a plaque with the number 105. Based on her past experiences with this dream, she recalled that any doors with a rose-colored crystal knob indicated it was locked. She moved forward with testing her theory and twisted the knob. As expected, the door didn't open.

She neared the next door down the hall on the left and saw a plaque with the number 106 above it. She quickly grabbed the rose-colored crystal knob to confirm that this door was also locked. She peered down the hallway, noticing that the next door on the right was located a longer distance away. She walked, picking up her pace to get to the door. With each step she took, the mist dissipated, revealing a plush mat of green grass, which explained the soft surface she'd been stepping on.

She stopped in front of the door, which looked different from the others. This was a solid metal door with no plaque above it. The jade-colored crystal doorknob indicated it should be unlocked. Desiree grabbed the knob, twisted it, and pushed the door open.

A familiar setting appeared, showing the apartment kitchen with Jayden sitting at the table and Maya walking to the refrigerator. She could see their mouths moving but couldn't hear what was being said.

Maya grabbed a half-gallon bottle of apple juice from the refrigerator, opened it, and then placed it on the counter. Maya continued to talk while reaching up to take a red plastic cup from the cabinet, and as she lowered her arm to grasp the bottle, she inadvertently knocked the bottle off the kitchen counter. The bottle hit the floor with the juice contents spilling out.

Maya placed her hands over her mouth before lunging to grab some paper towels and passing them to Jayden. He kneeled and wiped the tiled floor, attempting to soak up the liquid. Maya gave him additional paper towels to clean up the rest of the juice on the floor.

The scene faded as Desiree's eyes fluttered, and she squinted with her vision revealing Jayden sitting on the recliner, watching TV.

"Are you good?" he asked as he spotted her looking his way.

Desiree continued to squint at Jayden but did not respond.

"I can see you're still half-asleep. It's only six. It will be another hour or so before Maya's alarm goes off, so go get some more rest. I'll make sure to wake you before we leave for the bus stop."

Chapter 41

Jayden tried to fight off the sleepiness overcoming him. He'd managed to stay awake since Desiree had fallen asleep on the sofa, but the drowsiness started to catch up to him. The sun had been up for a while, and he expected Maya to come walking out of her room and into the bathroom at any moment. He'd already moved forward with sending his team an email, confirming he'd be out sick for the day.

Other than Desiree waking up for a brief second earlier, she'd remained in a deep sleep and had barely moved on the sofa. He imagined she had to be exhausted these past couple of weeks from the various sleepwalking interruptions, especially with this latest episode, which had been the most eventful disturbance yet. They needed to move quickly on finding an alarm or another device to wake her up, now that she'd proven a sleepwalking stroll outside of the apartment was possible.

As expected, Jayden spotted Maya leaving her room and stumbling her way into the bathroom. He felt bad that he had the option to call out sick from work, but Desiree didn't say anything about Maya staying home from school today.

*****

A short time later, Jayden stretched his arms and yawned. He walked into the kitchen, grabbed a bottle of water, and then took a seat at the table. The sound of footsteps approached behind him, and Maya passed, giving a quick wave in the air.

"I guess you're too tired to say good morning?"

Maya stopped and looked at Jayden. "Good morning."

"Don't worry; I have sympathy for you. I know you're tired after what happened earlier."

She frowned. "It's not fair."

"What's not fair?"

"You get to call out sick from work, and I still need to go to school."

"I can't say I disagree with you. But your mother is the one making the call."

She walked toward the refrigerator and grabbed a half-gallon bottle of apple juice. She opened it and placed the bottle on the counter. "I can't wait until I'm older and can make my own decisions," she said, reaching up to the cabinet to grab a red plastic cup.

She lowered her arm from the cabinet, and her elbow made contact with the bottle, pushing it off the counter and onto the floor.

"Oh crap," she said while covering her mouth.

"Quick, grab a few paper towels," Jayden said as he jumped up from the table.

She reached for the paper towel holder and pulled, ripping a few sheets off the roll. She gave them to Jayden as he kneeled and used the paper towels to help soak up the juice that had splattered on the floor.

"Did you get any on your clothes?" Jayden asked.

Maya inspected her pants, and then her shirt. "No, I don't think so."

"Good. I need more paper towels," Jayden said.

Maya handed him a few sheets as he continued to wipe up the liquid.

Jayden wiped up the last bit and then backpedaled to peek into the living room. "I thought your mom might have woken up from all of this commotion, but she's still asleep."

Maya smirked. "This never would have happened if I weren't up so early in the morning to go to school."

"Hey, I'm not arguing with you. But the person you need to talk to is still sleeping."

"Don't we need to wake her up before we leave for the bus stop?"

"I was planning to wait until a few minutes before we left to give her more time to sleep." Jayden peeped into the living room again. "I'll leave it up to you if you want to wake her up now and tell her you're too tired to go to school."

Maya thought for a second. "Forget it. I'm already up and showered. I also know my mom is never in the best of moods when you first wake her up, so it probably won't work out for me, anyway."

*****

Maya ran back to her room to make sure her book bag was packed with everything she needed. Jayden closed in on Desiree, who had been sleeping peacefully on the sofa. He contemplated whether he should wake her; however, he couldn't afford to let her sleep while he escorted Maya to the bus stop. He speculated it would be his luck that she decided to rise from her slumber and begin another sleepwalking episode while he was gone.

He squatted and rubbed her cheek gently. "Desiree?"

She didn't budge initially. He continued to rub her cheek, causing her to stir.

She opened her eyes and flinched.

Jayden moved back to give her space. "Sorry if I scared you. I'm about to take Maya to the bus stop and want to make sure you're up before I leave."

She continued to stare at Jayden with a furrowed brow. She reached for the bridge of her nose, scrunching up her face as if she were in some type of pain. Seconds later, a drop of blood escaped her right nostril. She instinctively reached her hand up, swiping her nose, and gasped after seeing the streak of red smudged on her finger.

"Why is your nose bleeding?" He motioned for her to stay put as he ran into the guest bathroom and grabbed a few tissues.

He returned, giving her the tissues. "Pinch your nose and tilt your head back," he said.

She followed his instructions as Maya entered the living room. "What's wrong?" she asked.

"Your mom woke up with a nosebleed."

Maya peered over at Desiree, holding her nose. She immediately ran into the kitchen, wet a paper towel, and returned. She gave it to Desiree to wipe the blood smear on her finger.

"How did that happen?" Maya asked.

Desiree shook her head. "I don't know. I just woke up like this," she said with a nasally tone as she continued to hold her nose and breathe in through her mouth. "Don't worry about me. I'll be okay."

Desiree held her nose for another minute before sitting up. She removed the tissue from her nose, looking at the bloodstains left behind. She sat still, waiting to see if the nosebleed had stopped. She gestured with a thumbs-up. "I'm good now."

"You sure?" Jayden asked.

Desiree nodded.

Maya kissed her on the forehead. "Feel better, Mom."

*****

Jayden arrived back at the apartment after walking Maya to the bus stop. He didn't see Desiree in the living room or kitchen. He walked down the hallway, into her bedroom, and heard the shower running in the bathroom. He figured her nosebleed was no longer an issue if she was in the shower.

He was curious to know if she had plans to log in for work since she'd never mentioned anything about it. Although knowing Desiree, he wouldn't have been surprised if she moved forward with working since she'd missed a couple of days.

He cut his eyes over to the rocking chair, making sure to keep his distance. He was amazed to think how a dream could change his perspective on a simple piece of furniture. He struggled to think if he would ever feel comfortable sleeping in the bedroom again. He did have hope that his kind gesture to fix the necklace had helped in appeasing Grandma Isy and deter any more violent visits from her in his dreams.

He heard the shower stop and expected Desiree to be coming out momentarily.

"I'm back."

"Okay," she said from beyond the door.

He made his way back into the living room, perched on the recliner, and turned on the TV.

Desiree eventually made her way into the living room. "I'm assuming the drop off was fine?"

"Yeah. How are you feeling?"

"I'm fine. No more issues with the nosebleed."

Desiree walked into the kitchen without saying another word. Jayden followed her, still showing some concern about why she'd woken up with a nosebleed. Before he could say anything, Desiree stopped by the kitchen counter and looked down at the floor. "Why is the floor sticky?"

"Because your lovely daughter spilled some juice this morning."

Desiree immediately froze and continued staring at the floor. "What kind of juice?"

"It was apple juice. Why?"

"How did she spill the juice?"

"What do you mean? It was a simple accident," Jayden said with an edge of impatience creeping into his voice.

Desiree lifted her head to stare at Jayden. "Please, tell me exactly how this happened?"

"What's going on with you? Are you good?"

"That will depend on how you answer my question."

Jayden pointed to the countertop. "She had the bottle of juice on the counter, she reached up to grab a cup from the cabinet, and when her arms came down, she knocked over the bottle."

Desiree took in a few deep breaths.

"You're starting to scare me. Are you feeling all right?" Jayden asked.

"Did she grab a red plastic cup from the cabinet?"

"Yes."

"Did she also put her hands over her mouth after it happened?"

Jayden thought before answering. "Yes, I believe she did."

"And did she give you paper towels to wipe up the spilled juice?"

"Wait … were you up when this all happened?"

Desiree didn't immediately answer.

"Desiree? I asked if you were up when this happened?"

"No. At least, I don't think so."

"So, how do you know exactly what happened?"

"I'm not sure you're going to believe me if I tell you."

"Try me."

"Remember when I woke up on the couch and you told me to go back to sleep?"

"Yeah."

"I had just woken up from a dream about you and Maya being in the kitchen and her spilling juice on the floor."

Jayden stood with his hands on his hips. "Are you sure you weren't up when this actually happened and you thought you were dreaming?"

"I'm positive. And even if I was up, I couldn't see what was going on from the living room if I was lying on the sofa."

Jayden's mouth hung open. "That doesn't make any sense. Are you trying to tell me you saw the future in your dream?"

"I think that's exactly what happened."

"That's crazy. This is definitely something new, unless you remember this happening to you before?"

"I don't remember anything like this before."

A long moment of silence hung in the air. Jayden rubbed his chin and continued to stare at Desiree. "Are you thinking what I'm thinking?"

"About what?"

"Maybe you didn't know or, for whatever reason, denied that your mother had some type of psychic ability to see into the future, and your dream proved you inherited this ability? And your mother also passed this ability down to Maya by way of the necklace?"

Desiree raised an eyebrow. "And you thought of this wild theory on your own that quickly?"

"Well ... not really. I've had thoughts running through my head recently, trying to figure out an explanation for everything that's been happening. I guess, with these things already weighing on my mind, this made it easier for me to come up with that conclusion."

Desiree paused a while before responding, "I ... I don't know what to say, but that's an interesting theory. Although I must admit, with the way things have been going recently, your theory may not be as wild as it sounds." She sighed and took a seat at the kitchen table. "I knew my mother was gifted with an incredible intuition, but I guess I always denied the fact that she could have possessed abilities that went far beyond that. Truthfully, it hurt me when I was younger, and people called my mother a freak or some kind of witch. I remember crying myself to sleep many times, wishing she could be seen as a normal mother so we could just live our lives in peace and blend in with all the other families."

Jayden reached out, gently rubbing her back.

"I guess I'm at the point now where I can no longer argue with your theories and need to accept them as real-life possibilities." She rubbed her forehead. "Do you mind grabbing me a bottle of water? I'm feeling a little lightheaded."

Jayden grabbed a bottle of water from the refrigerator and gave it to her.

"Are you good? Do you feel like you're going to pass out?"

"No. I'll be okay. Give me a moment."

Jayden continued to monitor her, making sure her facial expressions didn't provide any clues that she was on the verge of passing out.

After a minute, she looked up at Jayden with worried eyes. "So, what does this mean for us?"

"What do you mean?"

"Is this a deal breaker for you now, knowing me and Maya may be"—she stopped, raising her hands, and signed in air quotes—"'different.'" She took a sip of water. "Does this not scare you?"

Jayden couldn't deny that it did. But there was no way he could see running out on both Desiree and Maya at this point, especially after all they'd been through. "I'd be lying if I said I'm completely fine with it. But it doesn't mean I'm going to run out on you and Maya. I've been on the other side of the fence, and it's not fun having a significant other run out on you when things get tough. So, like it or not, I'm planning to stick around."

Desiree's face lit up with a beaming smile. She stood, wrapping her arms around Jayden, and whispered, "Thank you."

After a long embrace, she sat back down. "I think this is a sign that I need to move forward with the sleep study. I know we have our theories as to what's going on, but I'm curious to see if there's maybe a scientific explanation as to what's happening in my head when I'm sleeping."

Chapter 42

A few weeks later, Desiree sifted through her overnight bag to make sure she had everything packed. Her scheduled sleep study date had arrived, and she was eager to move forward with the testing to see what it would reveal.

She was only aware of two sleepwalking events during the past few weeks, thanks to her medication. And the two times she had sleepwalked, she hadn't wandered far from the bed due to the flashing lights from the alarm system installed that had woken her up. Also during this time, she hadn't experienced any recurring dreams in her mother's hallway or any bizarre episodes with predicting future events. These preventative measures relieved a great deal of stress she'd been experiencing, but she didn't want to develop any long-term dependencies on both the medication and alarms to help her sleep soundly every night.

The sleep center was located a half-hour away from the apartment, and Jayden was on his way to drive her to the facility. Since the test had been scheduled on a Tuesday night, they had made plans for Jayden to stay at the apartment overnight to watch Maya.

Jayden's overnight stays at the apartment had been limited over the past few weeks. Desiree figured it was a combination of him being less concerned with her and

Maya's safety since she'd been sleeping better. She also imagined he was still spooked by the nightmare of who he believed to be her mother choking him.

Maya's questionable behavior had also improved during the past few weeks, even though she continued to wear the necklace. In addition, Desiree hadn't noticed any odd foreshadowing abilities displayed by Maya recently.

Although Desiree's sleep situation had been trending in a positive direction, her stress levels had been heightened as she prepared for the sleep study. She'd been instructed to refrain from taking any medication twenty-four hours before the study, which also included no alcohol or caffeine consumption. The caffeine withdrawal had put her on edge, and her energy levels had been depleted more than normal. She'd also been advised not to put on any lotions that could interfere with the sensors being applied to her skin while she slept. With all of the prep work, she felt as if she were being admitted to the hospital for a major surgical procedure.

*****

A short time later, Jayden arrived. "You have everything you need?" he asked.

She pointed to the overnight bag sitting on the floor next to her. "I'm all set. I even brought my pillow."

"Do you need it? I'm sure they'll have a pillow for you."

"It's my choice after they told me I can bring it. I already know I'll have problems sleeping on any other pillow but mine."

"Whatever works for you. So, how are you feeling about the testing?"

"I'm anxious. I know it's not going to hurt or anything, but I'm trying to picture myself strapped up with all kinds of wires hanging from me while trying to fall asleep. I'm also worried since I'm not taking the medication that there's a good chance I might have another sleepwalking episode."

"I don't think that would be such a bad thing. At least you would be in a controlled environment, and they can monitor what's going on in that pretty little head of yours. That's exactly what we want to know, anyway."

"Yeah, I guess you're right."

*****

Desiree stepped into the sleep study facility with Jayden and Maya trailing. She checked in and was told to wait in the lobby until called.

She peered at both Jayden and Maya. "It's up to you, but you don't need to wait until they take me. I'll be fine waiting in the lobby by myself until they call me."

"We'll wait. We're in no rush," Jayden said.

"And just so you know, I already finished my homework," Maya chimed in.

"That's my girl." Desiree pinched Maya's cheek.

Maya leaned back away, swiping at Desiree's hand. "Come on, Mom; I'm getting too old for that type of behavior."

Both Desiree and Jayden laughed.

"You are truly one of a kind," Desiree said.

"We're ready for you now, Ms. Campbell," the receptionist said.

Desiree motioned for Jayden and Maya to join her for a group hug.

"Good luck, Mom."

She smiled. "Thanks."

Jayden proceeded with another hug and kiss on Desiree's lips as Maya turned her head away.

"Hope you have a decent sleep, and we'll see you tomorrow morning," Jayden said.

Desiree watched as Jayden and Maya left through the revolving doors. She experienced a flashback to when she had been in the hospital, though these circumstances were entirely different, and she understood this would only be a quick overnight visit.

A young man dressed in beige khakis and a white-collared shirt led Desiree down the hall. She entered a room, which contained a full-sized bed, pushed up against a dark brown, floor-to-ceiling curtain. The only other pieces of furniture in the room were a desk and chair on the opposite side of the bed, and a tall, narrow cabinet. To the left of the bed were a sink and two shelves affixed to the wall.

The young man pointed to the cabinet. "Here is where you can put your clothes and any of your other personal belongings. And don't worry; this cabinet does lock to make sure you're belongings are safe." He walked to the door and stopped. "Do you have any questions for me?"

"No, I'm good."

"Great. The doctor should be in any second."

As he finished talking, Desiree heard a knock and spotted a middle-aged woman wearing a white lab coat and horned-rim glasses standing by the door with a wide grin.

"Hello, Ms. Campbell. I'm Dr. Grayson, and I'll be in charge of your sleep study for this evening."

Desiree waved and greeted her with a nervous smile.

Dr. Grayson approached, holding a chart. "Is this your first time doing a sleep study?"

"Yes."

"Well … have no fear. I can tell you this will be an absolute painless experience unless you find sticking sensors to your skin a problem."

"No. I'm good. I already read through the paperwork, so I'm aware of what to expect," Desiree said.

"Perfect. I'm assuming this included the prep work you needed to complete for the study?"

"Yes, indeed. I can tell you that, without my coffee these past twenty-four hours, I'm already tired and should have no problems falling asleep." She reached into her overnight bag. "I even brought my own pillow."

"Perfect. You can put your pillow on the bed. I'll leave the room so you can change. I'll come back shortly to start prepping you for your sleep."

*****

Desiree finished changing and sat herself on the bed, wearing ankle socks, a pair of long, sky-blue pajama pants, and a white T-shirt. She had placed her belongings in the cabinet, as instructed, and waited for Dr. Grayson to return.

Minutes later, Dr. Grayson entered the room, wheeling a cart with a large assortment of wires attached to a rectangular-shaped device. "Please don't let this scare you. It may look a little intimidating with all of these wires sitting on top of one another. But there's nothing on this cart that can hurt you."

Dr. Grayson pushed the cart in front of Desiree. "This is where the fun begins with hooking you up to these wires.

But I've done this so many times that it shouldn't take long to finish."

In what seemed like only a few minutes, Desiree had been hooked up to a multitude of wires affixed to her head, chest, arms, and legs. She felt like she was about to take part in a secret government scientific experiment. Dr. Grayson had been careful to explain the purpose of each connection and how it would be used to monitor her body activity as she slept. She showed Desiree the camera tucked in the corner of the room near the ceiling that would keep track of her movements throughout the night. She also informed Desiree that she would be in a room across the hall with two other staff members, watching her as she slept.

Desiree pulled the sheet up to her waist and adjusted her head on the pillow with Dr. Grayson watching.

"Do you have any questions?" Dr. Grayson asked.

"Um … what would happen if you see me sleepwalking during the night?"

"The second we see you trying to get out of the bed, me or another staff member will be ready to come in the room to gently wake you up if necessary." She offered a reassuring smile. "Believe me, Ms. Campbell, we've studied your medical records and have contingencies in place in case you decide to get up from your bed unexpectedly."

"Okay. You're the expert. I'm trusting you," Desiree said.

Dr. Grayson left the room. Desiree let out a long exhale to help control her anxiety. Although sleepiness was written all over her face, she wondered how long it would take for her to actually fall asleep, especially knowing she was being watched by strangers as if she were the main attraction in an animal exhibit at the zoo. She also felt constricted with her movements from all of the wires attached, which she feared would interfere with her ability to fall asleep.

She scoped out the darkened room, focusing on the pulsating red dot affixed on top of the camera in the corner. She imagined that if she stared at the blinking dot long enough, it would eventually lull her to sleep.

After staring at the camera for a lengthy amount of time, her pulse slowed and her eyelids eventually closed.

*****

Desiree looked around as a familiar hallway came into view, yet the surroundings were different. She noticed her feet were covered with white ankle socks and planted on a stretch of grass extending the length of the hallway. She took a few steps and immediately looked at the door to her right. The number 107 displayed on the plaque above the door. She reached for the rose-colored, crystal doorknob and, as expected, the door didn't open.

She peered down the hallway to the next door on her left. She walked, stopping in front of the door, but didn't see a plaque on top. She turned the jade-colored knob and opened it, revealing her mother's bedroom.

Her room was completely furnished, as she remembered it. The cherry wood sleigh bed, matching nightstands, dresser, and armoire took up most of the space in the room. Towering, red velvet curtains covered the windows. A sweet cedar smell instantly hit Desiree as she entered.

After scanning the room, she observed the silhouette of someone looming in the corner by the desk. She pivoted in that direction, and with each step she took, the figure faded until it completely disappeared. She arrived in front of the desk, noting the cedar smell at its strongest in the corner, which indicated to Desiree that this figure had to represent her mother.

Desiree noted a sheet of paper resting on the desk with a red marker off to the side. She reached, flipping the sheet over to see both Jayden's and Maya's names crossed out with a sizable red X.

She dropped the note, feverishly looking around the room. She ran to the bedroom door and back out into the hallway. She twisted her head to the right and observed what appeared to be another door at the far end of the hallway. She immediately sprinted down the hallway and stopped running once she'd made it to door number 108.

Chapter 43

Desiree gripped the jade-colored knob and opened door number 108. An image of Jayden and Maya appeared, walking to a parking garage. They ascended two flights of stairs to the next level, arriving at Jayden's car. Jayden attempted to open the car door and snatched his hand back. Afterward, they both grabbed the door handles, using their shirts, before entering the car. Jayden backed out of the parking space and drove down to the parking gate. There was a brief struggle as he tried to exit the parking garage before the gate arm finally lifted.

He had his cell phone resting in the front cup holder and a bottle of water occupying the second cup holder. Maya sat in the front passenger seat with her bookbag resting on the floor. They continued to talk in the car, but Desiree couldn't hear what was being said.

Jayden parked in front of a fire hydrant, directly by the corner of Maya's bus stop. They continued to talk in the car before Jayden reached for his phone in the cup holder. The home screen on Jayden's phone showed a date of October 8th. After spending additional time in the car, Maya grabbed her bag and reached out to Jayden for a fist-bump. She left the car and stood on the corner.

Jayden waited in the car and eventually rolled down his window, talking to Maya. She attempted to get in the car, but pulled her hand back from the door. Jayden opened the door from the inside.

Maya's facial expression changed before she entered the car. They talked for a few minutes before Jayden pulled off. He drove through the streets, switching lanes to get around other vehicles. Maya continued to sit with her bookbag resting between her legs, but she kept quiet.

Jayden swerved around a city bus before stopping at a light as he participated in what seemed like a serious discussion with Maya. The light turned green, and Jayden approached the ramp to the highway.

Desiree noted the image of Jayden and Maya fade out for a quick second, and the strong smell of cedar returned briefly before the image of the car came back into focus. Jayden picked up speed on the ramp before merging onto the highway. He switched into the middle lane and continued to maneuver around a few trucks moving at a slower pace. He moved into the far right lane and looked down at his phone in the cup holder after seeing a text come through. He reached to touch his phone, losing sight of the road, and hadn't noticed a dump truck merging into the lane. He jerked his head up and snatched the steering wheel to the right to avoid hitting the truck. His car veered onto the shoulder of the road and continued to drift to the side as he tried to regain control.

Maya put her hands on the dashboard, bracing herself as the car ran off the highway and onto the grassy area alongside the road. The rear tires fishtailed to the right, losing contact with the ground, and the car flipped over several times as it tumbled down a twenty-foot embankment. Desiree could hear the crunch of metal and the screams from both Jayden and Maya as the disaster unfolded in slow motion. She let out a gut-wrenching scream.

Desiree felt a tug on her arm while in the middle of screaming. She looked around, observing that she was sitting up in bed with her hands reaching out in front of her, and Dr. Grayson was holding her right arm. She continued to yell with tears streaming down her face.

"Ms. Campbell? You were just having a dream. Everything is okay," Dr. Grayson said.

Desiree slowly lowered her arms and fought to suck in enough air while focusing on her surroundings. She spotted a young female staff member on the other side of the bed.

With unsteady eyes, Desiree looked at Dr. Grayson. "What's today?"

"It's Wednesday."

"No. I mean, what's today's date?"

"It's October 8th."

Desiree's eyes widened in horror. "What time is it?"

"It's five in the morning."

Desiree studied the various wires connected to her body. "I need to go home now," she said, frantically looking at Dr. Grayson.

"I'm sorry, Ms. Campbell, but we can't release you right now. The sleep study session hasn't been completed yet."

"It's over as far as I'm concerned."

Dr. Grayson patted Desiree on the leg. "Everything's going to be fine. It was only a dream. We could tell you were dreaming based on the data output we were collecting."

"I don't care about your damn data. I need you to unhook me from all of these wires so I can go home."

"We can do that after the sleep study is officially over."

Desiree's nostrils flared. "I told you it's over, and I'm asking you nicely to let me leave."

Desiree caught Dr. Grayson nodding to the staff member, who left the room.

"I can tell you're a little agitated right now, Ms. Campbell, and I'm not trying to make this difficult for you, but we can't let you leave right now."

Desiree reached up, ripping the two sensors affixed around her cheekbones.

"Can you please not do this? You're jeopardizing the successful completion of your sleep study."

Desiree took in a deep breath and exhaled. "If you're not going to let me leave, can I at least have my cell phone?"

"I'm sorry, Ms. Campbell, but we need to wait until your sleep study is completed, and then we can give you all of your belongings."

Desiree spotted a male staff member entering the room along with the female staff member who had previously left. She ignored the additional staff reinforcements and reached toward her collarbone, ripping two more sensors from her body.

"Ms. Campbell!" Dr. Grayson said with an urgent tone.

Desiree continued stripping the sensors from her arms and legs until she was completely free from any more wires.

The male staff member looked over at Dr. Grayson, apparently waiting for her to provide direction. She shook her head and stepped aside as Desiree swung her feet to the floor.

"Ms. Campbell, can you please get back in the bed?"

Desiree remained quiet and marched over to the wardrobe closet. She tugged on the handle, but it was locked. "Where's the key?" she asked Dr. Grayson.

"I'm sorry, but I can't give that to you now," Dr. Grayson said.

Desiree's focus shifted to the door as a security guard appeared.

She ignored him and tugged on the wardrobe handle again. "You don't understand. My family is in danger."

Dr. Grayson motioned for the security guard to step in and close the door. "Ms. Campbell, you do realize what you had was only a dream, right?"

"Yes, but it wasn't a normal dream. I don't have time to explain anything to you now. Trust and believe me when I say this is an emergency, and I need to warn my family," Desiree said as she aggressively banged on the wardrobe.

"Can you please relax before you cause damage to the wardrobe?" Dr. Grayson said.

"If you don't give me the damn key right now, I'm going to need you all to step aside so I can walk out of here."

"We can't let you do that for safety reasons. You're our responsibility now. We can't have anything happen to you under our watch," Dr. Grayson said.

Desiree lowered her head, and without warning, she charged at the security officer with her hands extended, attempting to push him out of the way. Her attempt was far from successful, based on the extreme weight difference between the two. The bulky guard outweighed Desiree by well over one hundred pounds, and he had no problems standing his ground as she attempted to push him away from the door. She started banging on his chest, which prompted him to grab her arms to prevent any further assault attempts.

"Get your fucking hands off of me!" she screamed.

The guard did not say a word and pushed her back toward the bed.

Dr. Grayson stepped to the side, shaking her head. "You're only making this more difficult for yourself, so please stop resisting."

"Please let me go. My baby is in trouble, and I need to leave," Desiree said as her angry tone morphed into more of a desperate plea.

She continued to resist, trying to shake loose from the guard. She flinched after feeling a prick on the back of her right shoulder. She couldn't tell what had happened, but her peripheral vision indicated the male staff member, who had been positioned behind her on the other side of the bed, might have injected her with something.

She persisted with her efforts to be free from the guard's grip, but her energy levels had quickly dissipated. She couldn't tell if this was from physical exertion or if the prick had anything to do with her downturn in energy.

"What the hell did you do to me?" Desiree asked.

"Sorry, Ms. Campbell, but we had to do something to calm you down before someone got hurt."

Tears trickled down Desiree's cheeks. "You can't do this. I need to—"

Her vision faded into complete darkness.

Chapter 44

Jayden reached over to shut off the alarm on his phone. He rotated his head to the left, wincing from some stiffness that had set in overnight around his neck. Although the sofa wasn't the most comfortable place to sleep, he preferred this over Desiree's bedroom. He hadn't had any more dreams about Grandma Isy, but he wanted to continue to play it safe and avoid sleeping anywhere near the rocking chair.

He opened his phone, noticing a voicemail message had been left. He reviewed his recent phone log to see that a call had come in from the sleep study center. He didn't bother to replay the message and called the number. He briefly talked with a receptionist before being transferred.

"Good Morning, Jayden. This is Dr. Grayson speaking. Thanks for returning my call. I had you down as the emergency contact and wanted to provide you with an update on Ms. Campbell. I don't know if you listened to my voicemail, but we had a little incident with her at the facility."

"What happened?"

"Let me start by letting you know she's okay. She's not hurt in any way. But she had an emotional breakdown this morning after she woke up."

"Oh. Did you catch her sleepwalking?"

"She didn't actually get out of bed, but we did catch her sitting up and screaming after an apparent dream. She woke up, saying she needed to leave and became very aggressive with our staff. She pulled all the sensors from her body and tried to leave the facility without our consent. We tried our best to calm her down, but after she assaulted our security guard, we had no choice but to sedate her."

Jayden quickly sat up on the sofa. "Is the guard all right?"

"Yes. No one was hurt during the incident, and she's sleeping now. But after we put her to sleep, her nose started to bleed. We were able to stop the bleeding without any issues, but I didn't know if that was normal for her."

"It happened recently, but I'm not aware of this being a recurring problem." Jayden looked at the time. "I have one thing I need to take care of this morning, and then I can come to the facility to check in on her."

He hung up the phone, attempting to figure out what had Desiree in such a frenzy. Thanks to the medication, her sleepwalking episodes had subsided over the past few weeks, and she also hadn't experienced any weird dreams recently. Jayden had to also consider that she'd been told not to take the medication for twenty-four hours before the sleep study, so it wasn't out of the realm of possibility that the sleepwalking or dreams could have potentially come back.

*****

Later in the morning, Jayden sat at the kitchen table, eating a bowl of cereal. He expected Maya to walk in shortly since there wasn't much time left before they had to leave for the bus stop. As the thought crossed his mind, Maya appeared.

"I was about to knock on the bathroom door to make sure you didn't fall asleep in there."

"I'm fine. If you know me, I'm never in a rush to get ready for school."

She opened a cabinet to the right of the refrigerator and pulled out a granola bar. "This won't take me long to eat." She joined Jayden at the table. "What time are you supposed to pick up my mom?"

Jayden contemplated if he should even tell Maya about the incident with Desiree. Maya had been studying for an exam, and he didn't want her worrying about her mother.

"Based on what they told us yesterday, everything should be done by eight. We can walk to my car after we leave here, and I'll drop you off at the bus stop. Then I'll drive over to the facility to get her."

Maya took a bite of her granola bar. "Do you think the sleep study is going to help her?"

Jayden shrugged. "We'll see. This is only the first part of trying to figure out what's happening with her brain while she's sleeping. I'm guessing once they have the information, they may prescribe a different medication. But, I think the medication she's been on now is working fine."

Maya smiled. "I'm sure she'll be okay. My mom is the strongest person I know."

*****

They departed the apartment lobby and headed toward the garage where Jayden's car was parked. As Jayden walked, he periodically glanced behind to confirm Maya was still with him since she struggled to keep up with his steps.

They eventually entered the garage, ascending two flights of stairs to the second level. Jayden pressed the fob to disarm the alarm and unlock the doors. He reached for the door handle but snatched his arm back after receiving a sizable shock. "Whoa. That was a serious jolt," he said, shaking his fingers. "Be careful opening the door."

Maya wrapped her fingers around the bottom of her shirt and tugged on the handle to open the passenger side door.

"Good idea," Jayden said as he followed her lead, using the bottom of his shirt to protect his fingers as he grabbed the handle.

Jayden placed his phone in the cup holder. He spotted a bottle of water that he'd forgotten to take from the car in the second cup holder. After buckling up, he reversed out of the parking spot and drove down to the first level. He stopped in front of the gate arm by the exit, inserted his ticket, which prompted him to pay the parking fee. He inserted his credit card, and after a few seconds, the screen indicated there was an issue reading his card. He waited for the message to clear and tried again. After a brief pause, his card was accepted, and the gate arm lifted.

"It feels funny driving to my bus stop instead of walking," Maya said.

"I bet it does. But, at least you get the benefit of getting some exercise when you walk to the bus stop."

"It's not too bad walking now, but when it starts getting colder, I'm not going to be happy about it, unless my mom decides to buy a car."

"I wouldn't hold your breath. Especially now that you're living in the middle of the city and can get to places using public transportation."

Jayden neared the bus stop corner and pulled into the only available space on the street, in front of a fire hydrant. "This is your stop."

"That was quick. It's probably going to be another ten minutes before my bus shows up."

"I was planning to wait here in the car until you get on the bus."

Maya gestured with a thumbs-up. "Good. I didn't know if you were planning to kick me out and leave me."

Jayden grinned. "Now, why would I do that? I need to make sure you get on the bus before I go anywhere. I want to make sure no one snatches you up."

Maya let out an exasperated sigh. "You sound just like my mother. I'm old enough now. I can handle myself."

"Glad to see you're feeling independent."

Maya shook her head. "I can't wait until I get older. Is it bad that I'm already tired of middle school and wish I could be in college?"

"No. I wouldn't say it's bad. At least you're thinking about going to college, and that's a good thing."

"I just want to be older and have the freedom to do what I want."

"Sounds good as long as you're making smart decisions when you're older."

"I have no choice. Even though I'll be older, I'm sure my mom would still kill me if I did something stupid."

Jayden laughed. "Can't say I disagree with you."

His phone vibrated in the cup holder, as he was on high alert for any additional calls that might come in from Dr. Grayson. He lifted his phone, and then quickly set it back in the cup holder after realizing the vibration had been coming from a daily challenge notification from his fitness app.

He peered up the street, looking for the bus. "I'm assuming your bus will be here shortly. You don't want it zooming by if you're not out there, since you're the only pickup at this stop. It may be a good idea for you to stand on the corner."

She grabbed her bookbag strap and offered Jayden a fist-bump with her free hand. "Thanks for the ride. And, hopefully, everything goes well with you picking up my mom."

Maya left the car and waited on the corner with her bookbag slung over her shoulders. Jayden looked at his phone once again, making sure he hadn't missed a call or text from the sleep study center.

*****

It had passed 8 a.m. with no bus in sight. Jayden rolled down his window to get Maya's attention. She stepped to the car.

"What time does your bus normally get here?" he asked.

"It's usually here before eight."

"Has your bus ever been this late?"

"No, but I'm good if it doesn't come. That means I can stay home and do my work online."

"No, that's not what it means. I guess you forgot I'm sitting in my car and can drive you to school."

Maya grimaced. "Oh yeah."

"I say we wait another five minutes, and if the bus isn't here, you can hop in and I can drive you to school."

Maya displayed a thumbs-down. "Boo!"

*****

Minutes later, Jayden peeked at his phone. "Okay, time's up. Hop in, and I'll be your bus ride this morning."

"Ugh. Are you sure I can't stay home and do my assignments online?"

"What do you think your mother would say?"

"She would probably want me to go to school." Maya paused momentarily. "You did say she would be ready by eight this morning, right?"

"Yes. Why?"

"Well, since it's now after eight, maybe we can call her and ask?"

"Um … I wouldn't want to disturb her now. We both know your mother, and I'm sure she would want you to physically be at school."

"That wasn't the answer I wanted to hear."

"Sorry to disappoint you."

Maya neared the passenger side of the car. Upon reaching for the door handle, she snatched her hand back. "Ouch!"

"What happened?"

"I got shocked."

Jayden shook his head. "I don't know what's going on with my car and these shocks." He reached for the door handle inside the car and opened it for her.

She did not immediately move and stood with her eyes fluttering for a moment.

"Come on, Maya; get in the car so I can take you to school. Don't want you to be late."

After a few seconds of remaining still, she eventually complied and sat in the passenger seat.

Jayden immediately noticed her demeanor had quickly shifted. He focused on her neck and was surprised to see the necklace was missing. He hadn't been paying as much attention to the presence of her necklace over the past few weeks since her behavior had stabilized, and she hadn't foreshadowed any events recently that he was aware of. He wasn't sure if she'd left the necklace back at the apartment on purpose, but he wasn't about to remind her about it. He'd hoped her sudden silence stemmed from her being annoyed at him for volunteering to drive her to school instead of letting her stay home.

"Are you good?" Jayden asked.

Maya shrugged but didn't say anything.

"That doesn't seem too convincing. Are you mad at me because I'm driving you to school?"

"No. It's not that."

"So, what is it?"

Maya shook her head. "It's nothing."

Jayden typed the school address into the GPS, which indicated a twenty-five-minute ride. He knew he'd be cutting it close attempting to get Maya to school on time.

He drove along the streets at a quickened pace, hoping he wouldn't catch too many lights on the journey. He peeked over at Maya, who continued to remain quiet with no discernible expression on her face while she held on to the straps of her bookbag.

Jayden maneuvered around a city bus and then pulled into the right lane as he approached a red light, coming to a stop. The GPS route showed him taking the highway, less than a quarter mile up ahead.

Maya continued sitting with her eyes now closed and tightly gripping her bookbag straps. She opened her eyes. "We should go back home," she said in a whisper while looking straight ahead.

Jayden hadn't heard what she'd said and did not acknowledge her.

"We should go back," she said again, with more volume.

"Go back where?"

"Back home."

"Why do you want to go back home?"

"I … I'm really not sure," she said, rubbing her forehead. "I know I'm probably not making any sense."

"I'm confused. What's changed between us leaving your bus stop and now?"

"I just have a feeling."

Jayden observed her neck to make sure he hadn't missed the necklace hiding under her shirt, but he clearly did not see it. This was the first time Jayden had experienced Maya making a statement like this without the necklace present, and he was unsure of how to interpret the moment.

"Sorry, Maya, but we need to keep going. After I drop you off at school, I need to make my way to the sleep center to get your mother and then get back to the apartment to log in for work."

Maya did not respond and closed her eyes again while continuing to hold on to the bookbag straps.

The light turned green, and Jayden pressed his foot on the accelerator. He put on his signal and shifted into the turning lane to merge onto the highway.

Chapter 45

Maya kept her eyes closed and continued to clutch the straps of her bookbag, with the clicking sound from the turn signal reverberating in her ears. She opened her eyes, looking straight ahead at the approaching highway ramp. "Stop the car," she said in a low tone.

Jayden couldn't completely understand what she had said and continued driving.

"Please, stop the car, Mr. Jayden," she said, but with a little more volume and a quiver in her voice.

"Unless you're feeling sick, we need to keep going," he said as they neared the on-ramp.

Maya puffed out her cheeks and exhaled as she reached up with her arms and placed both hands on the dashboard. "Stop the car!" she screamed at the top of her lungs, banging her fists on the dashboard.

Jayden flinched at her ear-piercing yell, causing his hands to involuntarily twitch on the steering wheel, which prompted the car to sway wildly in the lane. He regained control and steadied the car.

He yanked his head in Maya's direction. "What's wrong with you, Maya! You almost made me lose control of the car." But before he continued, he noticed tears streaming down Maya's cheeks. He abruptly pulled the car onto the shoulder of the road, only twenty feet away from entering the highway ramp. An SUV trailing behind swerved to avoid rear-ending his car and greeted Jayden with a blaring horn as it drove by.

Jayden clung to the steering wheel with both hands while feeling the vibration of his heartbeat pounding in his chest. He couldn't help but feel a sense of anger directed at Maya for distracting him while driving with her unexpected outburst. However, he didn't want to rattle Maya any further, as he could see she was an emotional wreck for unknown reasons.

"It's okay. Just relax," he said.

Jayden reached into the center console, grabbed a small package of tissues, and gave them to Maya. As she wiped the tears from her cheeks, he observed her hands shaking. Even if he wanted to continue the drive, he could tell she was in no condition to be dropped off at school.

She finished wiping the tears from her cheeks and said, "Thank you."

Any anger Jayden had felt quickly dissipated after looking at Maya's sad state. Confusion followed as he pondered what could have been consuming Maya's mind that had caused her to react with this sudden explosion of emotion.

"Is there something going on at school that's bothering you? Maybe something me and your mom need to know about?"

She shook her head, continuing to dab her eyes. "No, it's nothing with school."

"Do you feel like telling me what it is?"

Maya let out a massive exhale as she continued to calm down from her emotional outburst. "I … I really can't explain what happened. It was like someone else had control of my body."

Jayden struggled to make sense of what Maya was telling him. "How do you feel now?"

"Okay, I guess." She pulled down the visor, looking in the mirror at her red-tinted eyes. She jumped and twisted her body, focusing on the back seat.

Jayden followed suit, snatching his head around to get a glimpse of the back seat. "What?"

"I thought I saw somebody."

Jayden scanned the back seat but didn't see anyone.

Maya lifted her nose and sniffed. "Do you smell that?"

Before Jayden could respond, a familiar sweet cedar scent filtered through his nostrils. His heartbeat sped up, and his palms grew sweaty. He reluctantly looked in the rearview mirror, thinking he might see something different in the reflection. He was overcome with relief when he didn't see anyone. He proceeded to inhale once again, but the cedar scent had quickly faded away.

Maya glanced back in the mirror of the visor, confirming that whatever she had seen in the reflection had disappeared. They both stared at one another but didn't say a word.

Jayden calmly reached for his GPS and changed the destination from Maya's school to the sleep study center. He looked in the side view mirror to confirm there was no oncoming traffic, then pulled back onto the road, making a U-turn to head toward the new destination.

Chapter 46

Jayden entered the lobby of the sleep study center with Maya beside him. Throughout the half-hour ride to the facility, the car cabin had remained quiet, as neither Jayden nor Maya had a word to say.

Jayden had trouble processing what had happened and wasn't sure how he could even explain it to anyone. As far as he was concerned, what he and Maya had experienced went far beyond reality and was something he felt could only be understood if you were present in that moment.

Jayden's mind had been so focused on what had transpired in the car that he hadn't thought much about Desiree. He hadn't received any additional phone calls from Dr. Grayson, which led him to believe no news was good news. He also remembered that Maya had no clue about what had happened with Desiree, but she was about to find out.

He came up to the receptionist. "I'm here to see Desiree Campbell."

The receptionist made a phone call, and then instructed Jayden and Maya to wait in the lobby.

Minutes later, a middle-aged woman arrived in a white lab coat. "Hi, Jayden. I'm Dr. Grayson," she said while waving at Maya.

"How's Desiree doing?"

"Looks like she's starting to wake up, but it may take her a while before she's fully alert."

Maya stepped forward. "Did something happen to her?"

Dr. Grayson looked at Jayden, who nodded for her to move forward with speaking.

"Are you Ms. Campbell's daughter?"

"Yes."

"Your mom woke up confused this morning and tried to leave the facility before her testing was done. In order to keep her calm, we had to give her medicine, which made her sleepy. So, we want to make sure she's fully awake and okay before we release her."

Before Maya could respond, a young man opened the door from behind Dr. Grayson, tapping her on the shoulder. "We need you in the back. Our patient in room 151 is getting anxious again."

Dr. Grayson motioned for both Jayden and Maya to follow her.

They walked down a long corridor, passing several other rooms, until they neared room 151. Even before they arrived, Jayden could hear Desiree mumbling, but he couldn't make out what she was saying. Dr. Grayson motioned for them to wait outside as she entered the room.

"Are you feeling better now, Ms. Campbell?" Dr. Grayson asked.

Jayden listened intently from outside.

"No. I need to find out if my daughter and boyfriend are okay."

Jayden noticed that Desiree's voice sounded weak and sluggish.

Dr. Grayson stepped back into the hallway and called for them to enter.

Immediately upon seeing Jayden and Maya, Desiree's eyes watered. She put her hands up in prayer. "Thank you, God!" She reached out with both arms as Jayden let Maya proceed with hugging her first. She wrapped her arms around Maya and sobbed, holding her tightly. "I thought I lost you," Desiree whispered.

Dr. Grayson placed a tissue box on the bed. "I'm going to give you all some privacy. I'll be back." She left, closing the door.

Desiree eventually let go of Maya as Jayden approached. She offered him a loose hug, then quickly let go. He was puzzled by her less-than-enthusiastic greeting.

He backed away. "How come you don't seem that excited to see me?"

Desiree glared at Jayden. "I keep telling you to stop looking at your phone while you're driving."

"What are you talking about?"

"I had a dream you and Maya got into a serious car accident on the highway on your way to dropping her off at school. And it was all your fault because you were looking at your phone and not paying attention to the road."

Jayden peered over at Maya, then looked at Desiree. He shivered from a chill that flooded his body. He wondered if Desiree's dream symbolized what their fate might have been if he had taken the highway to drop Maya off at school. He was also hit with the realization that

Maya's foreshadowing ability had most likely saved their lives.

"I don't know what to say," he said before pausing. "I guess I'll start by saying I'm sorry?"

Desiree continued to fix her eyes on Jayden with a level stare.

"I'm curious, but what else did you see in your dream?" Jayden asked, hoping to break her death stare at him.

Her face finally softened as she proceeded to explain in detail about what she had seen in the dream, which was exactly how Jayden remembered everything playing out, except for the accident at the end.

Even though he'd previously discussed his theories with Desiree, this event reinforced his confirmation that both Desiree and Maya had been gifted in different ways with these psychic abilities. His eyes volleyed between them while being overcome with a sense of anxiety, now truly knowing he'd become part of a family that operated on a level above any scientific explanation. And he was even more convinced Grandma Isy's spirit had temporarily hitched a ride with him and Maya, playing a part in helping them avoid the car accident.

Jayden shifted his attention back to Desiree, aware of the extended silence. "You'll have to excuse me now, but I'm a little speechless. The way you described your dream was exactly how things happened with me and Maya, except for the accident at the end."

"That's pretty amazing, Mom, that you were able to see the future in your dream," Maya chimed in.

Desiree's face grew pensive. "It's all a little freaky to me. Is this going to continue for the rest of my life?" She rubbed her temples, still trying to clear her head completely. She eventually looked up. "So, tell me what happened? How did you avoid getting into the accident?"

Jayden patted Maya on the back. "Thanks to your daughter, she had a feeling something wasn't right, and she wanted me to stop driving. I didn't listen at first, but she literally had an emotional breakdown in the car right before we got on the highway. I finally stopped the car and … here we are."

A smile tugged at the corners of Desiree's lips as she opened her arms and reached out for another hug from Maya. "You did good," Desiree said while embracing Maya with a tight squeeze. She leaned back and pointed to Maya's neck. "And you did all of this, and I don't even see you wearing your necklace. Where is it, by the way? I haven't seen your neck bare like this in a while."

"It broke again yesterday, so I put it in my school bag and left it there." She unzipped the front pocket of her bag and reached in, pulling out the necklace.

Desiree reached for it, and Maya dropped it in her hand. Desiree stroked the pendant before kissing it.

Jayden reflected on Maya sitting in the car earlier. Everything started to click as to why Maya had been gripping the bookbag straps so tightly. It apparently didn't matter if the necklace was around her neck or somewhere close for her to display this foreshadowing ability. Jayden cringed at the thought of what could have happened if they had convinced Maya to stop wearing the necklace and she had left it at the apartment. They most likely could have been seriously hurt or not even around at this moment.

Jayden looked at Desiree, thinking whether he should even mention the incident with whom he believed to be Grandma Isy, paying him and Maya a visit in the back seat of the car. But he decided to keep quiet and not overwhelm Desiree with any more head-scratching stories.

"And in case you all want to know, I found out what the number 108 represents," Desiree said.

"What?" Jayden asked.

"It's today's date, October 8th."

Jayden stared with his mouth partly open. "I kept thinking it had something to do with the time. It never occurred to me that this could have been referencing a date."

Jayden noted a change in Desiree's facial expression; her eyes narrowed as she looked at him.

"What?" he asked.

"After what could have happened today, you need to do something about being distracted by that damn phone in your car."

Jayden put his hands up like he was surrendering. "Fair enough. I get the point. I'm convinced I shouldn't be doing that anymore."

A knock at the door interrupted the conversation and Dr. Grayson entered. "Are you all good now, or do you need me to come back later?" she asked.

"We're fine. You can come in," Desiree said.

Dr. Grayson neared the bed with a clipboard. "How are you feeling?"

"Much better now that my family is here," Desiree said, wincing when she made eye contact with Dr. Grayson. "I'm so sorry for the way I acted this morning. Please give my apologies to the security guard."

"Don't worry. Everything worked out fine, except for us officially finishing your sleep study."

"Does this mean I need to come back?"

"Not sure yet. We need to confirm there were no discrepancies introduced into the data once you removed the sensors. I'll be in touch with you within the next few days to confirm. In the meantime, if you're feeling fine and not experiencing any side effects from the sedation, I can provide you with your discharge paperwork, and then you're free to go."

Chapter 47

Three weeks later, Jayden lounged on the sofa, flipping through various channels on the TV. Desiree was snuggled up beside him, giving her opinions on what shows could be of interest. Another weekend was upon them, and they had finished eating a homemade dish of chicken alfredo that Desiree had prepared.

Maya had departed to her room after dinner to jump into reading a new fantasy book. Her behavior had returned to normal, and she hadn't displayed any foreshadowing abilities in recent weeks, even though she resumed wearing the necklace.

Desiree had heard back from Dr. Grayson a few days after her sleep study and was informed that a follow-up session would not be necessary. The results of the study did not yield any conclusive results. She'd been advised that some cases of sleepwalking could be linked to other sleeping disorders, such as sleep apnea or restless leg syndrome, both of which she did not have.

The only other factor that might have influenced her sleepwalking involved her family history, and Desiree was unaware whether her mother had ever participated in unconscious nightly strolls during her lifetime. Desiree had also realized that if there were any supernatural connections to her sleepwalking behavior, they would not have been identified through standard scientific studies. She had to accept the fact that Jayden's theory was correct and her mother had been much more than just an ordinary tarot card reader.

As much as Desiree wanted to initially deny it, she one-hundred percent recognized that both she and Maya had inherited some of her mother's mysterious psychic abilities, and those abilities were most likely here to stay.

She was provided a new medication to take as needed to help control the sleepwalking episodes, but she'd decided to hold off from taking the medication to see if her strolls from bed would stop on their own. She'd now been approaching week number four, and there had been no known instances of her sleepwalking. This had also given her a lift from an energy perspective, as she was no longer chronically tired during the day. And to Jayden's delight, she had even scaled back on her coffee consumption.

Jayden's apprehension about staying overnight at Desiree's apartment had all but disappeared since her sleepwalking episodes seemed to have temporarily stopped. They had also stopped using the nanny cam and had disabled the alarm to wake Desiree in the event she started sleepwalking. He even went back to sleeping in her bedroom, but he had one condition. Although he hadn't experienced any additional nightmares about Grandma Isy coming to strangle him, he had requested that Desiree move the rocking chair out into the living room at night before they went to sleep.

*****

Later in the evening, Jayden scrolled through his phone while sitting up in bed. Desiree was fast asleep next to him. He scrolled through his various social media feeds, which was a guilty pleasure on the weekends. He'd often become jealous after seeing his friends' posts of pictures from exotic vacation destinations. It had been a few years since he'd taken a true vacation, traveling to San Juan to soak in some sun and relax on the sandy white beaches.

Every once in a while, he'd mention going on a cruise with Desiree, but her last boat ride had ended with her getting seasick. This meant his dream of cruising in the Caribbean would most likely not happen if he planned to have Desiree by his side.

As the midnight hour arrived, Jayden put the phone away to get some sleep. He looked in the corner of the room, which seemed so empty without the rocking chair taking up space, but he'd have it no other way. Evicting the rocking chair from the bedroom was the only way he'd be able to sleep in peace. He gazed at Desiree, whose heavy breathing indicated she was in a deep sleep. He smiled, happy to see her experiencing a more consistently sound sleep each night.

*****

Jayden awoke after hearing a sound. He squinted and observed the empty corner where the rocking chair had once been. A glow from the city lights outside filtered in through the blinds, providing him with limited visibility. He listened as he lay on his side, but didn't hear anything further.

He closed his eyes, and that was when he heard the creaking sound. He opened his eyes, feeling more alert. He was happy to know this creaking wasn't coming from the rocking chair.

He kept still while listening out and hearing the creaking noise repeating itself every few seconds. He rotated on his back and moved his arm to the right to feel for Desiree. He kept stretching his arm out until he discovered she wasn't in the bed.

He pushed up on his elbows and squinted toward the sound of the noise, which seemed to be originating from the bedroom entrance. Upon further inspection, he spotted a figure standing by the door.

"Oh shit. Not this again," he whispered.

The figure continued to gently rock by the doorway as the creaking noise continued in unison with the movement.

He grabbed his cell phone and was about to flick on the flashlight, but stopped after hearing the toilet flush. He quickly realized that if Desiree was in the bathroom, then there was only one other person left in the household.

"You gotta be kidding me," he mumbled.

He flicked on the flashlight and spotted Maya with her head down by the doorway.

Desiree opened the bathroom door. "What are you doing with the flashlight on?"

Before Jayden could answer, she turned and followed the light, cupping her hands around her mouth and letting out a muffled scream.

Jayden jumped up from the bed. "Hold on. Not so loud. You might scare her awake and cause her to fall."

Desiree backpedaled her way toward Jayden. "Is she sleepwalking?"

"Looks like it," Jayden whispered.

"How can this be? I've never found her sleepwalking before," Desiree said.

Jayden shook his head. "I don't know if this is something that can start out of the blue."

"So, what do we do?"

"Same thing I did when I found you sleepwalking. I'll see if shining the flashlight in her face can gently wake her up."

Jayden closed in on Maya as she eerily mimicked the same motion Desiree had displayed when he'd first found her sleepwalking. Her eyes were open and angled toward the floor. He placed his hands in front of her eyes, waving them back and forth, but she didn't react. He aimed the flashlight in front of her face, causing her to flinch. He quickly positioned his hands near her body in case she collapsed to the floor. Her knees buckled, and he grabbed her by the arms to hold her up.

Her body jerked as she blinked several times. She looked up at Jayden, who continued to hold her before she steadied herself.

"Why are you in my room, Mr. Jayden?"

"I'm not in your room."

She looked around and saw Desiree behind Jayden. "What's happening? How did I get here?"

Jayden didn't want to startle her by mentioning she'd been sleepwalking. "I'm not sure, but let's get you back in your bed."

Jayden placed his arm around her waist. "Come on. Can you take a step?"

She nodded and followed Jayden's direction. They slowly walked back into her room, and he guided her to the bed. Desiree followed behind, making sure she arrived back in bed safely.

Maya lay down as Jayden moved aside and Desiree tucked her under the covers.

Desiree looked by the foot of the bed and spotted one of Maya's books spread open, but facedown. Her heart rate ticked up a few notches when she also found a red marker resting on the sheets, alongside the book. She grabbed the marker, turned over the book, and gasped.

"What?" Jayden asked.

She gave him the book, and written in bold marker was a sequence of numbers.

117

Desiree's eyes widened. "What's today's date?"

"November 4th."

"So, now what do we do?" Desiree asked.

Jayden reached for Desiree, embracing her in a tight hug. "We hope and pray she remembers her dreams."

Chapter 48

Thirty Minutes Earlier...

Maya shifted in bed, in and out of consciousness, before she fell back to sleep. She found herself in a strange-looking hallway with doors flanking both sides in the distance. She glanced down at the ground and could not see her feet since they were covered in a thick mist.

She took a few steps and made her way to the first door on her right. She grabbed at the rose-colored crystal knob and turned, but the door wouldn't open. She analyzed the door and spotted a plaque engraved with the number 115.

She turned her attention to the next door on her left. This door resembled the previous one and had the same rose-colored crystal knob. She tried turning it and had no luck opening the door. She saw the number 116 sitting in the middle of the plaque above the door.

She continued her march down the hallway, and with each step, the mist by her feet faded. Looking down, she realized she was barefoot and standing on a wooden floor. She took a step, which prompted the floor to creak under the weight of her foot.

She continued her walk until she arrived at the next door, which looked completely different from the first two.

This door stood a couple of feet taller with a dark cherry wood finish and a silver doorknob. Above the door was a silver-plated sign that read, "*Madam Isy.*"

She turned the knob, and the door nudged open before abruptly stopping. She leaned against the door and pushed with more force, prompting the heavy door to open wider. She was immediately greeted with the combination of cinnamon, vanilla, and a sweet cedar scent.

She looked up at a chandelier with various beads and crystals dangling, along with eight dimly lit electric candles, struggling to illuminate the room. On top of several wooden high tables to the right were various plants with vines and leaves hanging over the tabletops. A towering bookshelf stood against the wall on the left with an assortment of books populating most of the shelves. The burgundy carpet and red velvet curtains blended in seamlessly with the rest of the dark décor.

A round table covered with a black tablecloth was positioned in the middle of the room, surrounded by three wooden chairs. A large grouping of cards containing various imagery, symbols, and colors was spread out across the table. Maya approached the table and reached out, touching several of the cards.

Her eyes were drawn to a curtain in the back of the room that had moved. She walked around the table and stood in front of the curtain before extending her arm to part it. The space behind the curtain resembled a large walk-in closet, and the only piece of furniture populating the area was a desk pushed up against the back wall.

On top of the table, a brass lamp illuminated two jewelry boxes. Maya stepped further into the space, standing over the desk. The first box was empty, but Maya could see the imprint of the necklace that had once been there. She immediately cast her eyes down to see that she was wearing the silver necklace with the heart-shaped pendant.

She turned her attention over to the next jewelry box and spotted another silver necklace with a heart-shaped pendant. She lifted it from the box and turned it around in several directions, noting that it looked exactly like the one she wore.

She heard a knock at the front door and placed the second necklace back where she'd found it.

She left the room, walking to the front door. She opened it but didn't see anyone, although another door down the hallway caught her attention. She made her way down the hallway with the creaking noises continuing as she stepped.

She stopped in front of a door with the number 117 at the top. A rose-colored doorknob protruded from the door. She gripped the doorknob, felt a warm sensation in the palm of her hand, and immediately noted the color had changed on the knob from rose to jade green.

She twisted the knob, pushing the door open. Her mother's bedroom came into view, with Mr. Jayden sitting on the bed. Initially, she didn't notice her mother until she walked out of the bathroom and stood in front of Mr. Jayden. Her mother was holding a small white stick and showed it to Mr. Jayden. He jumped up as they hugged, and then he backed away, gently rubbing her mother's belly. The image gradually faded until it became completely dark.

Chapter 49

Later in the morning, Maya woke up and furrowed her eyebrows, attempting to recall the events that had transpired in a weird dream she had experienced overnight. She propped her pillows up, and something by the nightstand caught her attention. She remembered moving the two books she had resting on her nightstand to her dresser before she went to sleep. But one of the books had made its way back on her nightstand.

As she reached over to grab the book teetering over the edge, a red marker fell to the floor. She immediately looked down at her book to see a red line drawn along the edges.

She opened the book, fearing it might have been damaged further with the marker. She flipped through a couple of pages at the beginning and set eyes on the number 117. Thoughts of her mom crossed her mind, wondering if she had experienced another sleepwalking episode and had unknowingly marched into her room to write down this new set of mysterious numbers. But then something clicked, and her head jerked up as the events that unfolded in her dream rushed to the forefront of her mind.

She recalled seeing the number 117 over one of the doors in the hallway of her dream. She also recalled the short scene appearing after she'd opened the door with her mother holding a white stick and hugging Mr. Jayden in the bedroom. She might not have initially known what the white stick represented, but after Mr. Jayden rubbed her mother's belly, she could almost guarantee that this indicated her mother was pregnant.

A wide smile developed on her face, thinking about this possibility. But just as quickly as the smile crossed her face, it quickly faded away as confusion set in, wondering if she had, in fact, been the one to write these numbers in her book. And if she was the responsible party, did this mean she had experienced another sleepwalking episode?

She'd never mentioned anything to her mother, but she had woken up on at least two occasions in different rooms in the apartment—once in the hallway and another time in the kitchen. Her mother hadn't caught her since she'd been able to make her way back to her bed before sunrise. She couldn't imagine what would have happened if they had both run into each other while sleepwalking on the same night. Thankfully, this hadn't happened as far as she was aware.

She'd decided not to tell her mother about her sleepwalking instances since she already had a lot going on and didn't want to add any more worries to her plate. She also struggled to remember if she had any other dreams that might have coincided with her recent sleepwalking sessions. Because of this, she couldn't one hundred percent guarantee that she wasn't the one who had written the numbers on the wall in the hallway. Even if it turned out she was the guilty party, there was no way she would give her mother the slightest inkling that she did it to avoid her wrath. She'd done a great job sowing doubt in her mother's mind when she'd initially confronted her, and she wanted to keep it that way.

A smile returned to Maya's face, thinking about whether she was now following in her mother's footsteps with the ability to tell the future through her dreams. She thought about how fantastic it would be if she obtained this ability.

She continued smiling, thinking about the rest of her dream. She'd finally had the opportunity to see Grandma Isy's tarot card shop. She didn't know how accurate her dream was in manifesting the tarot card store setting, but it seemed similar to how she'd always imagined it would look. However, she was disappointed that Grandma Isy hadn't made an appearance in her dream. She would have loved to have met her and gotten a glimpse of what she looked like, outside of the few pictures she had seen.

Although Maya had never had the privilege of seeing her in a dream, she always had a sense that Grandma Isy was trying to connect with her on a spiritual level at certain points in her young life. But her experience in the car with Mr. Jayden had left no doubt that this was much more than a simple theory. She couldn't deny that Grandma Isy's spirit had entered her body for those few seconds while in the car, which had been one of the most incredible experiences.

She reached down and grabbed her necklace. She had to admit that wearing it made her feel different. It was almost as if her mind was stripped of any worries, and she was able to see things more clearly. Although she had been puzzled as to why her mother and Mr. Jayden kept accusing her of saying things she didn't remember saying, and wanted to take the necklace from her. This bothered her a great deal, which she could confess led to her not-so-friendly attitude change. Despite this frustration, she was determined to keep wearing the necklace. Grandma Isy had given it to her to wear for a reason, and she wasn't about to go against her wishes.

Maya's thoughts pivoted to the second necklace she had seen in her dream. She wasn't entirely sure about who the new owner of this necklace would be, but if her newfound ability to tell the future was accurate, she could almost guarantee that her new baby brother or sister would eventually be the rightful owner.

Maya's thoughts were interrupted by a knock on her door. She quickly jumped down from bed to grab the marker on the floor and put it back on the nightstand, along with her book. She flattened the pillow back on the bed and lay down, pulling the covers over her. A second knock followed, and before she could respond, the door cracked open, prompting her to close her eyes.

With her eyes still closed, she felt a nudge and spotted her mother standing by the bed with Mr. Jayden in the background.

"Are you feeling okay?" her mother asked.

Maya nodded, attempting to put on an award-winning performance as if she'd just woken up.

Her mother stroked the side of her head and said, "We were worried because you're normally up by now."

Maya blinked in succession, as if she were opening her eyes for the first time while hoping her mother didn't pick up on her act.

She sat up in bed. "I'm fine. Just a little tired, I guess."

"How did you sleep?" Mr. Jayden asked.

"Okay, I think. But I did have some weird dreams."

Her mother glanced at Mr. Jayden. "We're curious if you remember any of your dreams."

Maya pondered for another few seconds. "I remember having a dream I was walking around in the apartment and was standing at your bedroom door."

Her mother and Mr. Jayden continued to stare at her with wide-open eyes.

"Is that all you can remember?" Mr. Jayden asked.

"I also remember both of you helping me back to bed."

"Was there anything else that happened?" her mother asked.

Maya reached up to her necklace and stroked the pendant. She struggled to hold in a smirk. She moved her eyes back and forth between her mother and Mr. Jayden. "No. That's about all I can remember."

Acknowledgements

Writing a book is rarely a solitary endeavor, and I owe a deep debt of gratitude to the people who supported me throughout this journey.

First and foremost, I want to thank God for granting me with the ability, creativity, patience, and fortitude needed to write my third novel. I'm always humbled and grateful for your blessings.

To my wife, thank you for your unwavering support of my writing career. You are my biggest cheerleader as I navigate through this author journey. Also, thank you once again for acting as my beta reader. Your insights and feedback have been invaluable.

Thanks to my son and daughter for being active participants in my social media campaigns by reacting and sharing my posts to help bring more awareness to my books.

Thanks to my editor and graphic designer for polishing the novel and providing an eye-popping cover. You helped shape this book into something far better than I could have imagined on my own.

And finally, thanks to the readers for taking the time to journey through these pages. I hope the story resonates with you long after you finish reading.